OGRES AND MOM

OGRES AND MOM

CASE FILES OF AN URBAN WITCH™ BOOK SIX

MARTHA CARR

MICHAEL ANDERLE

DISRUPTIVE IMAGINATION

LMBPN Publishing
PMB 196, 2540 South Maryland Pkwy
Las Vegas, NV 89109

Version 1.00, July, 2021
ebook ISBN: 978-1-64971-898-3
Print ISBN: 978-1-64971-899-0

THE OGRES AND MOMTEAM

Thanks to the JIT Readers

Dave Hicks
James P. Dyer
Diane L. Smith
Misty Roa
Jackey Hankard-Brodie

If we've missed anyone, please let us know!

Editor
Skyhunter Editing Team

From Martha

To everyone who still believes in magic and all the possibilities that holds.

To all the readers who make this entire ride so much fun.

To Louie, Jackie, and so many wonderful friends who remind me all the time of what really matters and how wonderful life can be in any given moment.

From Michael

*To Family, Friends and
Those Who Love
To Read.
May We All Enjoy Grace
To Live The Life We Are
Called.*

CHAPTER ONE

Lucy Heron raced across the hillside of Elysian Park, wand in hand. Around her, elemental crickets were leaping back and forth, carving magical trails through the early evening air. Some left arcs of water that fell like miniature rainbows. Others left trails of earth that pattered down, lost in the dirt. The fire crickets were the most spectacular, seeming to fly past on trails of flame, but the air crickets were the hardest to catch, propelled by the winds they summoned with each twitch of their legs.

"Inretio," she chanted, waving her wand. A net of magic shot out, spreading across the crickets in front of her. The fire and air crickets shot clear, but she at least caught some of the water and earth ones within the fine glowing strands and left them pinned to the ground by the spell.

Jackie Kowal appeared around a bend in the path. Like Lucy, she was wearing her running gear and waving her wand back and forth, trying to contain the crickets. She used freezing blasts to bring them down, turning the trails of the water crickets into gleaming ice, like curved icicles, only for those trails to melt in the summer heat.

"How did they even get here?" Lucy paused next to Jackie while the two of them caught their breath.

"No idea," Jackie said. "Maybe someone left a portal to Oriceran open?"

"Maybe they escaped from some magical's private pet collection?"

"Or an experiment by an alchemist?"

"I'm just glad we were here to find them. Imagine if our running club hadn't come here this evening, and these things had spread all over L.A.!"

"At least then we wouldn't have to deal with that."

Jackie nodded down the hill to where a dozen women in leggings and t-shirts sat under the trees, looking decidedly dazed. Sarah Smith, also holding her wand, waved at Lucy and Jackie, then got back to checking on the runners. As she wasn't a Silver Griffin and so wasn't trained or responsible for containing rogue magic, it had made sense for her to play nanny while the others caught the crickets. Still, Lucy wished that all three could have been on the case. More wands would have meant more crickets caught more quickly.

"I suppose we're still getting our run," she joked and set off across the hillside again, after another clutch of crickets.

The problem with catching big batches of magical creatures was that the stupider, less agile, and less powerful tended to get corralled first. That meant although they'd captured ninety percent of the crickets already, the remaining ones were the difficult ten percent. They had some magical sense because they moved a fraction of a second before each spell burst from Lucy's wand, hopping out of the way, leaving their elemental trails behind them. The nets fell across the ground, glowing beautifully but doing nothing to contain the magical mess.

She watched in frustration as the crickets kept hopping away from her, spreading out in every direction. At least they were larger than Earth crickets, making it easier to spot them. If they had been the size of mundane insects, there would have been no hope.

As quickly as she could, Lucy started firing off freeze spells. Jackie was clearly onto something because the crickets weren't able to dodge those as easily as the nets, but still, half of them would jump clear before the spells hit and land beside the patch of frozen ground as if taunting her.

Inspired by the sight of that frozen ground, an idea crossed Lucy's mind.

"Agglutino!" she chanted, waving her wand in a wide arc.

Normally, she used the spell to create a concentrated ball of glue to stick an opponent's foot in place. This time, with a tweak to her magic and a broader sweep of her arm, she made the glue spread wide in front of her. It fell across the road, the dirt, even the trees and bushes, forming a thin, glistening layer.

The crickets leapt as the magic flew from Lucy. By the time they landed, the glue was already on the ground. Its stickiness diluted when spread out like this, but her targets were also weaker than normal. The crickets didn't have the strength that magical criminals or wild monsters did, and as they hit the ground, they became trapped. Try as they might to kick off again, they failed.

Lucy smiled at her ingenuity, summoned a magical bag, and set off across the hillside. Her feet squelched as she stepped on the thin layer of glue to pick up elemental crickets and put them in her bag.

"Hey, Heron!"

Lucy turned to see Jackie glaring at her. The other woman was glistening like the ground and the trees, dripping with a thin, watery coating of glue.

"Was this you?"

Lucy laughed. "It worked, didn't it? Look, they can't get away any more."

Jackie narrowed her eyes. "Sure, they might not be able to get away, but I..." She pointed at her hair, which lay plastered to her head. "I have a date later. What if this won't wash out?"

"Then you can dispel it." Lucy waved her wand, and a few sparks of unshaped magic fell. "You're a witch, remember? Don't tell me you've never used magic to fix your appearance because I've seen how you do your makeup when you're in a rush."

"Fine, but if this won't come out of my t-shirt, I'm bringing my laundry around to your place, and you can fix it with your magical mom touch."

"That's fair."

They gathered up the rest of the crickets, carefully collecting them in magical bags, then added the ones trapped under Lucy's nets. By the time they finished and got back down to the running group, some of them looked more alert as they emerged from the "Never was, never will be" spell Lucy had used to befuddle the minds of the mundane runners when the magical creatures showed up.

"How do we explain this one away?" Jackie asked.

"I figure we all took a break to catch our breath. If anyone notices that the run took an extra half-hour, they can convince themselves that they had a particularly long run and feel virtuous for making the extra effort today."

"And how do we explain me looking like an extra from Ghostbusters?"

"We don't." Lucy handed her friend the bags full of magical crickets. "Someone has to take these back to HQ, so you might as well go. We'll tell them you got a call and had to go to work. It's practically true."

"I suppose that makes sense. It's not like I've cut the exercise short after running all over this hillside." Jackie pulled her phone from the pack on her waist and dialed the Silver Griffins' HQ. "Transport room, please... Hi, it's Agent 782, Kowal. Can you get a portal to this location? Only needs to be big enough for one... No, not in twenty minutes. We have a 'never was' running out here, and I need to get the magical influence out... Yes, fine, I can hold while you cast the spell..."

Jackie rolled her eyes. A moment later, there was a golden glow in the air, and a dark space appeared like a gap in the universe. She hung up the phone.

"Enjoy your date," Lucy said.

"Enjoy herding that bunch of confused cats."

Jackie stepped through the portal, which promptly vanished.

Lucy and Sarah tucked their wands away and approached the rest of the running group. The women were rubbing their eyes and looking at each other in confusion, not yet aware that they had all suffered a memory loss. Now was the time to step in and provide something for their imaginations to fill the gap.

"I'm glad we stopped to catch our breath," Lucy said, facing Sarah but talking loud enough so the others would all hear. "I was starting to get dizzy."

"Me too, I think," said someone else.

"We all have days like that." Angela, the leader of the running club, shook her head. "Now, if everyone has their breath back, we should get going again."

Sarah grinned so wide that Lucy was afraid she would burst out laughing. It was easy to forget that despite dating a Silver Griffin and being friends with several others, Sarah didn't often get to see the effect of such spells in action. She wasn't used to the rapid pace at which mundane humans could rearrange their view of the world to make weird events fit their expectations.

The group set off again, running toward Elysian Heights. As they jogged, they reached a series of walls on which graffiti artists had been at work, creating images of animals and plants, each in their distinct style.

"Look at that one!" someone said, pointing at the most spectacular piece, a jungle scene full of lush leaves in bright and varied greens. "The plants look like they're swaying."

"I wonder how they do that," someone else said. "It's amazing."

Other runners exclaimed in admiration as they passed, but Lucy kept quiet. She could tell exactly how the trick worked because it wasn't an optical illusion: it was magic, and it shouldn't be out here where ordinary people could see it.

"You keep going," she said quietly to Sarah. "I'll see you later."

Lucy stopped and leaned over, hands on her knees as if to catch her breath. She waited like that until the others were out of sight, then straightened and looked around. When she was sure no one could see her, she pulled her wand from its hiding place up the back of her t-shirt.

The art on the wall really was lovely, with bold, cartoonish animals in striking colors prowling between the imaginary trees. The magic added to its sense of life and drama, making the piece seem complete. She would have loved to have left it as it was, but anyone stopping to look at it for more than a minute would see that there was something odd, and it was her job to keep the magical world out of sight of the mundane. Sadly, she waved her wand and de-spelled the power from the painting. The images froze in place, turning into an ordinary mural.

Lucy put her wand away, stretched her legs, and set off after the running group. If she sprinted, she might even catch up with them.

Behind her, a graffiti tiger stood frozen amid the painted trees, its eye gleaming almost like it was alive.

CHAPTER TWO

Lucy arrived home later than expected, thanks to the interruption to her run. In some ways, she didn't mind. It was satisfying to do her job, even in unexpected circumstances, and she had enjoyed seeing the street art in the moments before she took its magic away. That was one of the great advantages of being a Silver Griffin, getting to see the wonders of the magical world.

The downside of being a Griffin was the interruptions to home life, like arriving back sweaty and breathless as dinner was about to be served. She came in through the front door to excited yapping from Buddy the dachshund, who was always pleased on principle to see anyone come in, even when the house was already full of the mouth-watering smell of Charlie's five bean chili. Lucy patted the dog on the head, then followed him into the kitchen, where Charlie was taking a pot off the stove.

"Do I have time for a shower?" Lucy asked.

Charlie looked her up and down, taking in the sweaty

clothes and the loose strands of hair that had gotten plastered to her forehead. "I'll put this back on for a few more minutes. But be quick, Eddie's been asking for cookies for an hour now, and the promise of dinner is the only thing keeping his hand out of the jar."

"Great. Love you." Lucy kissed her husband on the cheek, then dashed through to the bathroom. Ten minutes later, she emerged clean and refreshed, dressed in jeans and a Wonder Woman t-shirt. She didn't often use magic for appearance's sake, but there wasn't time to sort out her damp hair properly, so instead, she waved her wand to dry it out instantly and tie it neatly back.

By the time she emerged, the kids were already sitting at the dining table.

"Hi, Mom." Twelve-year-old Dylan barely looked up from a history book. "How was your run?"

"Fun. It's always good to get out with the ladies. Jackie and Sarah said to say hi."

"Hi Jackie and Sarah," the kids chorused in response as if their mom's best friends could hear them.

"You took twenty-three minutes longer than usual," pointed out eight-year-old Ashley. "Did you twist your ankle? I read that ankles can be a problem with running."

"No, sweetheart." Lucy kissed her daughter on the top of her head. "I had to deal with an outbreak of magical beasties up around the Heights. What are you working on here?"

Spread around Ashley was a collection of intricate chains made with small interconnected elements of white metal. Ashley tapped one of them with a tool that was half-screwdriver, half-remote control, and the chain split in half, one part curling up while the other went to join a different chain.

"It's for my string robots," Ashley said. "The mechanics are working fine, but I'm having trouble mastering the distributed intelligence. I tried to ask the advice of some people at the university, but they stopped taking me seriously when they found out how young I was." She frowned. "Sometimes grownups can be so dumb."

"All of us?"

Ashley wrapped an arm around her mother. "There are exceptions."

There was a *thudding* sound as Eddie, the youngest Heron, bounced up and down in his chair at the end of the table. Waiting for other people to finish talking wasn't easy for a three-year-old, especially when he was excited about something, and Lucy was proud of him for waiting while she finished talking with Ashley. She and Charlie had raised a good batch of kids, even if she said so herself.

"Yes, sweetheart, what is it?" She smiled at him.

"What animal?" Eddie asked.

"Excuse me?"

"Beast! What beast!"

"He's asking about the magical creature you had to stop," Dylan said.

"Oh, of course!" Lucy laughed. "I'm afraid it wasn't anything very exciting, just a bunch of elemental crickets."

The air shimmered around Eddie, and his body changed shape, turning from a small boy into an enormous cricket with its legs tapping on the tabletop.

"Eddie," Charlie warned as he came in from the kitchen, carrying a huge pot of chili. "You know the rules."

The cricket hopped down from its seat, grabbed a piece of paper off the sideboard, and managed to mark an "X" on it with a felt-tip pen before dropping it into a jar labeled "MAGIC." Then it turned back into a boy, who took his place at the table.

Lucy sat too and eyed the extravaganza Charlie had created. Chili with fresh coriander scattered across the top, the bright green a pleasing contrast to the deep red. Bowls of guacamole, jalapeños, sour cream, and grated cheese were neatly presented in a ring around the pot. Even the tortillas were neatly folded and fanned out in a semicircle across a large serving plate.

"You've really made everything look nice this evening." Lucy smiled at her husband. "Thank you so much."

"My pleasure." He kissed her, then pulled off his apron and took his seat. "I was in the mood to make an extra effort. Besides, you know what they say. The first bite is with the eye."

"Bite with eye?" The idea clearly caught Eddie's imagination.

"No, wait, don't!" Lucy said as the air started to shimmer around him.

It was already too late. In the small boy's place sat an enamel-eyed tree frog, a creature from Oriceran that Eddie had seen in his picture books. Its purple webbed feet splayed wide as they pressed against the table and it lowered its face to the food. Its upper pair of eyes was perfectly conventional, but when the lids peeled back on the lower pair, they revealed rows of tiny teeth, with which the frog took a bite of chili.

"Eddie Heron," Lucy said sternly, "you know full well that magic is not allowed at the dinner table. Turn back this instant and put a slip in the magic jar."

The frog blinked at her with both sets of eyes. A drop of chili fell from the lower pair.

"I mean it."

The air shimmered again, and Eddie reluctantly changed back to his human form. Chili dripping from his chin, he went to the sideboard, made his mark on a piece of paper, and added it to the magic jar.

Ashley had cleared away her robot strings, and Dylan had set aside his history book, leaving the table clear for them to eat. Everyone loaded up their plates with enthusiasm, piling up chili next to heaps of fluffy white rice or running it down the middle of tortillas and folding them in like a bread version of origami.

"How's everyone's day been?" Lucy asked once she had taken the edge off her hunger with a couple of bites.

"Drew a dinosaur," Eddie said as he carefully arranged lines of grated cheese down the length of his tortilla.

"Just the one?" Lucy asked, knowing her son's enthusiasm for anything involving impressive animals.

Eddie shook his head. "Hundred." He held up ten fingers.

"More like five or six," Charlie said, "but they were great dinosaurs. The lady at the nursery was very impressed."

"We read comics at school," Dylan said.

"Cool. Did Sofia bring in the new Miss Marvel for you to read at lunch?"

"No, this was in class. We're doing a project about sequential art." Dylan took his time over "sequential," carefully pronouncing a new and unfamiliar word. "It's an art and English thing, where we're going to write stories and draw pictures together. We looked at Egyptian hieroglyphs and Aztec carvings, then some modern comics, and next we're going to make our own."

"Wow, we never got to do anything that cool when I was at school!" Lucy let her jealousy show.

"You went to school in England. Things can't be as cool in England."

"The Beatles were from England."

"There are cooler things than the Beatles."

Lucy couldn't argue with absurd logic like that, so she turned her attention to Ashley. "How about you, sweetheart? What have you been up to today?"

There was no point asking Ashley about school. She sat patiently through the lessons, though most of them were far too simple for her because she understood that it was important to be around other children and participate in society. But the things she thought about during that time weren't the content of the lessons. They were the projects she would work on when she got home.

"The string robot prototype holds some promise," Ashley said. "And we had Mini Griffin patrol. Mia saw a troll playing with trash near her house, and she caught it for the Silver Griffins."

"Wow, that's really impressive for someone Mia's age!"

Ashley shrugged. "It's what we do."

She took a bite of her tortilla and stared down at the table as though her mind had already moved on to other challenges.

"All right then." Charlie rubbed his hands together. "Whose turn is it to quiz us tonight?"

"Mom!" the kids answered in unison. If there was an opportunity to tell their parents what to do, they weren't going to miss it.

Lucy racked her brain. She had forgotten that it was her turn to provide the mealtime entertainment, and even if she had remembered, it had been a hectic day. She didn't want to let them down, but what could she muster up an instant quiz about?

Her gaze drifted through the doorway to the living room, where Eddie's dinosaur pictures lay scattered across the carpet. Of course, she could go for the topic she had studied most enthusiastically when she was younger and one she had been enjoying practicing again recently, one that had left decades of facts scattered through her memory.

"Tonight's quiz will be on art," she announced. "First question, which artist painted a famous portrait of the Mona Lisa?"

"That's Leonardo da Vinci," Dylan said.

"He was also an inventor," Ashley pointed out.

"That one was too easy," Dylan added.

"All right then, something more challenging. Which other famous Italian artist did da Vinci compete with to decorate the Great Council Hall in Florence?"

"Dinosaur!" Eddie said, holding up a shape he'd made from a piece of tortilla.

"I'll give you a point for ingenious artistic expression," Lucy said. "But would anybody care to guess the real answer?"

And so, between mouthfuls of delicious chili, the battle of wits began.

CHAPTER THREE

The sun was rising over Echo Park as VX made her way across Elysian Heights. This was the best time of day for her to work—when there was enough natural light to create by, but no one was around to see her. It was part of why she hated winter when the nights were so long, as well as cold, and her only option was to work by artificial light. She shifted the clanking bag of spray cans on her back and the stepladder over her shoulder as she made her way down the hillside, looking for an appropriate patch of wall.

VX had two reasons to want to go unseen. First, there was her nature. As a gnome living on Earth, she had two choices, stay out of sight or find a way to look human. She knew that if she set her mind to it, she could have used her skills to craft a suitable disguise and make herself seem like something she wasn't, whether through magic or simple trickery. However, art wasn't supposed to be about concealing the truth. It was supposed to expose it, to bring the hidden into the light. Using her gifts to spin a lie, especially one about who she was, went against what VX stood for. Hiding from half the world was one thing. Pretending to be someone else was taking it too far.

The other reason was more important. It would have gotten her up before dawn even in a world where magicals were allowed to show themselves because this was the thing that drove her. It inspired her, let her shape the world she lived in, and it was an activity that ran up against the stupidity of the law. VX was a street artist.

Her route took her downhill, past a piece she had created a few days before. It was a jungle scene designed to remind city dwellers of what they were missing, trapped in their concrete cages and moving steel boxes. It was also a commentary on the things that society was losing and the savagery that hid in any environment.

The viewer would have to stand and watch the painting for several minutes to get the full effect, as beasts moved between the trees and plants shifted in an imagined wind, those effects achieved by mixing magic with the paint she sprayed. Art needed to be accessible to grab the imagination, but that didn't mean it shouldn't reward patience and contemplation.

Except that when she reached the wall, she found that the magic was gone. Someone had de-spelled her enchantments, leaving an immobile image in paint. She sighed. It wasn't unexpected. After all, there were authorities in the city whose whole purpose was to make the world a little less amazing by ensuring that magic stayed hidden away. She understood that impulse, even if she didn't agree with it, but still, she had hoped that her picture might last as it was for a few days longer.

She kept on down the hill and passed another wall that

she had recently worked on. This was a precursor to the other jungle scene, the animals more stylized, the plants more blocky. She had been pleased with it but not pleased enough to infuse it with magic. It seemed like a piece that would work best when standing on its own merits.

Except that some jerk had ruined it. Some ignorant tagger, someone with all the artistic skills of a mule, had scrawled their ugly, angular signature across her picture. Street art wasn't supposed to last forever. It was good to see space repainted and reinvented, but this wasn't art. It was only letters painted in haste, the paint dribbling from the upper parts, someone marking territory like a dog peeing on a lamppost. And they'd done it all over her beautiful picture.

VX cursed. She understood the impulse to tag, knew plenty of people who had started that way before they learned how to make real use of spray cans, but doing it on art like this was a total waste, pointless vandalism. She considered wiping it away with magic, but doing a proper job would take time, as would repainting over the damage. Besides, she'd finished with this piece. That was part of the point of her work, to create and release, never to go back over the same material, the same sights.

She dragged her gaze away from the mess of her mural and stomped away, looking for somewhere new to work. Today, she had something special in mind, and she wanted to find the perfect spot for it. Except that doing something special felt like a waste now, when someone could so easily destroy it. What if she put her heart and soul and all her great new ideas into this picture, and some idiot came along the next night and sprayed over it with ugly black letters?

Well, this work would be a magical one, so maybe she could use that to put them off. Maybe, with a few tweaks, she could make sure that no one would want to mess with her work ever again.

The end of a row of shops came into sight, a bare brick wall with no signs or windows and that no one seemed to be taking care of. The perfect spot. VX set her bag down and paused for a moment in front of her chosen canvas. She closed her eyes and imagined the image she had been planning, then opened them again and surveyed the wall, working out how she should adjust her plan to fit its size, shape, and texture. Months of planning, inspiration, and predecessor pieces had gone into preparing for this moment so the adjustments came easily to her. She could picture it all, and if she could do that, she could make it happen.

She pulled a mask over her mouth and drew her hood up over her head, and with those small rituals felt her mental state shift from planning to creation, from idle wanderer to outlaw artist. Then she took out the spray cans and set to work.

First came the background, broad swathes of green and gray. Shapes were there, not just presences but absences, those crude blocks giving the first hint of reality to her work. But the edges were hazy, undefined, waiting for later layers to bring clarity and definition. She worked her way up the wall, the stepladder letting her reach above elven head height, turning the entire span of bricks from soot-stained industrial entropy to the groundwork for a piece of art.

Next came different greens and grays, bolder colors, the large foreground shapes. Trees on the left and tower blocks on the right, stylized so that the two seemed uncannily similar, even at this stage. At the top and bottom, the two blended, outstretched leaves turning from lozenges to diamonds to the oblongs of office windows, while green and gray mingled. Roots and roads tangled with one another, disrupted each other, connected each other. There was meaning in every single stroke.

As she painted, she let the magic flow through her. In the same way that a witch might cast spells through her wand, VX cast through her spray cans. Magic mingled with the droplets of paint, infusing the shapes, creating a subtle sense of depth and movement, something that would stir the emotions of people who saw the painting but that most would be able to explain away as an optical illusion. That was the key, she realized now. Use magic subtly and maybe the Silver Griffins would leave it alone, or at least not notice until people had seen the work. Although there was one part where she planned to be far less subtle.

She switched cans and moved in toward the center. Orange and black on one side, white and blue on the other, tiger stripes giving way to the crisply cut suit and tie of an investment banker. The proud hunter of the jungle blurred into the robber baron of Wall Street, the two halves sharing a predatory grin. The strokes of paint were subtle, but the meaning was direct: beware the beast.

Anger flowed through her as she focused on the details. So many people she knew had lost houses or jobs to people like this, and she had seen so many others hurting on the news. This picture was for them. It was a reminder of what they were up against.

Anger came all the more easily as she remembered what happened to her other painting. That anger was less intense, but it was more immediate, and she would accept any feeling as fuel. That was art, an engine powered by emotions, burning through raw feelings to create something more refined, something that people could share. As long as some idiot with a cheap spray can didn't ruin it.

She took the last few cans from her bag and added outlines, recesses, highlights. These smaller, more focused points of paint sharpened edges and picked out features, and still the magic flowed through her, setting the seal on her spell. Two magics for the price of one. The magic that would make the image captivating, and the one to keep it that way. One that would draw the attention of art lovers and one that would punish anyone who harmed her work. Sure, that wasn't how art magic usually worked, but why shouldn't she protect what she had created, just like the tiger protected its territory, just like these high-flying financiers protected the wealth they thought was theirs.

A final tiny white streak added a glint to each image's eyes, one in the tiger half of its face, the other on the banker. Then VX crouched by the bottom right corner of the painting and, with a flourish, made her mark.

She stepped back, lowered the mask and hood, and looked up at her work with the eyes of a connoisseur, not a creator. Was it perfect? Of course not. Art was only perfect in the artist's mind. Was it something she could be proud of? Undoubtedly, yes.

The sun was fully up now, and the city was stirring into life. The first few cars were rolling past, and pedestrians strolled by at a nearby junction. Hurriedly, VX returned her paint cans to her bag, slung the strap over her shoulder, folded up the ladder, and set off up the hill.

Behind her, a guy with a to-go coffee cup stopped to stare at the painting.

"Wow," he said out loud. "That's so cool."

VX smiled. She'd finished her work here.

CHAPTER FOUR

Lucy sat in a coffee shop on Sunset Boulevard, drinking a cup of tea. It was perfectly adequate, as these things went, but it didn't taste like the beverage she remembered from back home in Britain. After more than a decade in the States, she still couldn't find tea regularly that did taste that way.

Maybe it was the effect of nostalgia, and it hadn't really tasted all that different before. Perhaps it was her changing tastes. Either way, some part of her had never let go of the idea that Americans couldn't make tea correctly. They probably did it on purpose, a quiet continuation of the Boston Tea Party, still protesting her ancestors centuries later.

Heather Fields walked into the coffee shop and came to loom over Lucy's table. She wore a flannel shirt, loose jeans, and heavy boots, a far more grounded look than most of the hip young things enjoying their morning brew. If she cared about the disdain with which some of them glanced at her, she didn't show it.

"Hey, Lu."

"Hi, Heather." Lucy gestured to the seat across from her. "You want to sit and get a coffee?"

Heather hesitated for a moment, running her hand through her short dark hair, then shook her head.

"I'd rather get this over and done with."

"You understand that this is an opportunity, not a punishment, right?"

"Maybe," Heather said. "I'm still waiting to be convinced."

Leaving her cuppa behind, Lucy led Heather past the counter to the back room of the coffee shop. The barista winked at them as they passed, and there was a flash of magic in his eye. The back room was empty, and Lucy sensed the presence of subtle magic, something that persuaded mundane people that they didn't want to sit in here, that the seats would be more comfortable out front, the lighting better, the air fresher.

She walked to a corner and tapped her wand against a picture hanging from the wall. There was a brief pulse of magic, and a doorway opened, leading onto a flight of stairs.

"It's a version of the magic we use to access the magical subways," Lucy said. "Just on a smaller scale."

They walked up the stairs and the wall reformed behind them, turning the back room into an ordinary part of a typical coffee shop. At the top, the stairs emerged into a spacious area with a high ceiling, wide windows, and skylights. The whole place was bright and airy. Polished floorboards and bare brick walls created an atmosphere of post-industrial refinement, a perfect setting for the paintings hanging from the walls and the sculptures standing on plinths down the center of the room.

"Lucy!" An elf hurried over. He wore skin-tight jeans, a white shirt, and a vest. Two small gold studs glittered in one of his ears. "It's so lovely to see you." He leaned in to kiss her on the cheek, then turned his attention to Heather. "Who is this darling young woman?"

"Seriously?" Heather raised an eyebrow.

"Penley, this is Heather Fields, the chief of the Tolderai," Lucy said. "Heather, this is Penley ap Gawain, and this is his gallery."

"Hm." Heather held out her hand. "Pleased to meet you, I suppose."

"And you, my dear."

Penley shook her hand, then darted in to kiss her on the cheek. Lucy stifled a laugh as Heather flinched away from the greeting.

"So." Penley beamed at Heather. "You're the woman taking care of these fine pieces I've heard so much about."

"What have you been telling him?" Heather asked.

"Nothing, I swear." Lucy held up her hands. "Penley approached me, not the other way around. Penley, why don't you show Heather around first? Show her what the place is about before you get down to business."

"Of course, how rude of me. But if we're going to do this, let's do it in style." Penley clicked his fingers, and a silver tray appeared in the air next to him, holding three slender glasses of sparkling wine. "Champagne?"

"I'm not into champagne," Heather said. "Or day drinking."

"Don't be such a sour puss." Penley handed them each a

glass. "It's important to enjoy the finer things in life. That's what my gallery is all about."

Sipping from his glass, he led them down the room, gesturing to artworks as he went.

"As you can see, my collection here is small but refined, eclectic yet elegant, a sampling of works from across the world that were created by and for magical communities. In many cases, they incorporate magic into the work." He stopped in front of an oil painting, on which abstract shapes in black and red shifted across the canvas like angry storm clouds. The rippling texture of the paint, its rising and falling ridges, added to the sense of tangible menace. "This, for example, comes from the dwarven community in Berlin and reflects the anxieties that city went through in the middle of the twentieth century. You can feel the horror in each swirl of the brush, the grief staining each strand of the spell."

It wasn't the first time that Lucy had been to the gallery, but with her busy schedule, it was a rare treat. She attentively listened as Penley talked about the works on display, from a levitating marble statue of young trolls at play to a dynamic charcoal sketch of an Arpak in flight. Heather seemed far less interested, her champagne largely untouched, and Lucy worried that Penley was losing both her attention and her goodwill. She was about to find a way to cut him off when he stopped of his own accord in front of an empty pedestal.

"What do you think?" he asked.

"I think it looks empty," Heather said.

"Exactly! This is the space I have set aside to display an item from your recently retrieved Tolderai grave goods. I hear that there is a particularly fine sacrificial bowl, and this would be the perfect place to display it."

"You've built a display stand before you even got my agreement to this?"

"I wanted to show you that I'm serious about—"

"How did you hear about what we found?" Heather turned her glare on Lucy. "Has your kid been blabbing about the dig?"

"I assure you, no children have been blabbing anything." Penley sighed dramatically. "If you must know, I heard about it through one of your people, a young woman with an artistic bent who I got to know through online art communities and whose drawings are frankly—"

"Carol told you." Heather ran a hand over her face. "I should have known this would happen. Centuries of secrecy, hiding from the world, and the minute we let the mask slip a little, everyone gets sloppy." She put her glass down on the pedestal and turned to walk away. "This was a mistake. I'm going."

"Please, wait!" Penley hurried after her. "Think about the opportunity you're missing here. The chance to share your people's culture with a wider audience, to celebrate the beautiful things you have created."

"We don't want to share our culture. Secrecy is safety."

"Think about the money, then. I have access to some very wealthy benefactors, not to mention a hoard or two. I would generously recompense you and your people for permitting me to display one or two of the wonderful pieces in your possession. This is a historic moment, the first time Tolderai art will go on display in the modern world. I am begging you, let me be part of that."

"We don't need your money. We don't want your attention."

"Perhaps you don't, but what about others? What about poor Carol, who is trying to raise interest in her work?"

"What part of 'no' do you not get?"

Penley turned to Lucy, his hands pressed together as if in prayer. "You understand what this represents. Can you talk some sense into her?"

"Heather has plenty of sense of her own," Lucy said. "But why don't you give us a few minutes to talk."

"Of course, of course! I'll go get a latte."

Penley hurried off down the stairs, leaving the two witches alone.

"I'm sorry about all that," Lucy said. "Penley can be pretty full-on."

"It's like being attacked by a chihuahua, all noise and annoyance."

"He means well, and he's right. This is a good opportunity for you and the Tolderai. Rumors are spreading about your return, and people are interested to learn more. An art exhibit would be the perfect opportunity to present yourselves in a positive light."

"I don't want to present us in any light. I want to be left alone."

"I know, but sadly that's not an option. The Silver Griffins have been fairly discreet since they found out about you, but there's only so much secrecy achievable around a powerful tribe of nature witches and wizards. This is the information age, and news travels fast. Wouldn't you like to turn those dark rumors into something more positive?"

"Those dark rumors have kept us safe."

"They could also turn people against you and mean you have no friends when trouble comes. Is that what you want?" Lucy took in the stubborn look on Heather's face. "All right, is it what the other Tolderai want?"

Heather sagged. "Probably not. At least not all of them."

"Then you need to find a chance to shape your image, and art could be it."

"I don't know. This Penley guy seems a mess. If we're going to put one of our artifacts on display, and that's a big if, I need to make sure that we keep control of that artifact and of how he presents it."

"But you're open to the possibility?"

"Perhaps, if it's on our terms."

"Then let's go tell Penley that. Just be ready for the fact that he might get overexcited, especially now that he's had coffee."

"He wasn't overexcited before?"

Lucy laughed. "Just wait until you see him in full flow."

Heather gritted her teeth, but she still followed Lucy down the stairs. "I'm already regretting this."

CHAPTER FIVE

Ellis Ellis sat in the swaying subway car as it shot along the track. This was the secret system within the secret system, the line of the magical underground network set up specifically to reach the Silver Griffins' L.A. headquarters. He'd used it more times in the past few months than in the whole of his career before then, a job that had lasted over a decade working within the magical community, bringing bad guys to justice all across the world. A career that had been bringing him to L.A. more and more, as he started picking his assignments so he could come back to the city. That pattern had become a sign. It was time to make a change.

Across the carriage from him sat a wizard in his early twenties, wearing a lab coat and a look of great weariness.

"Say, you're Jenkins' assistant, ain't you?" Ellis asked.

"That's right." The wizard nodded without enthusiasm. "My name's Nigel."

"Not a fan of your work, Nigel?"

Nigel's hesitation told Ellis that this wasn't a straight-forward question.

"I like working with all those devices," Nigel said. "Testing out wands, making new machines, trying artifacts to see what they do. I just wish I didn't keep ending up as the test subject. I mean, someone's got to do it, but…"

"But you'd like to turn the tables on Jenkins once in a while?"

Nigel gave a small yet urgent nod. "It's like today. We're testing a teleportation matrix. That's fine. Someone has to get teleported, but this is the sixth time I've had to find my way back from some random spot around the city, and it's only midday." He pointed at his pants, which were soaking wet almost to the knees. "This time I ended up in a fountain. If he were just a little more careful, I'd be walking around in dry shoes, but no, it's squelch, squelch, squelch, all the way home."

They reached the station, the doors *hissed* open, and sure enough, Nigel squelched out, leaving a trail of wet footprints as he made his way across the platform and down the corridor beyond.

Ellis grabbed his suitcase and followed at a slower pace, taking his time to appreciate the simple elegance of the station and to greet the gnome who ran it.

"Howdy, Normandy. How's it going?"

"Very well, thank you, Agent Ellis." Normandy held up a small square painted in a soothing mix of blues and greens. "We've been designing tiles in my pottery class. What do you think?"

"Very nice. Maybe I'll come to you next time I have an apartment to decorate."

"Thank you, Agent Ellis, but I don't think I'll be going into mass production. That's more like work for dwarves."

Ellis followed the wet footprints down the corridor, up a spiral staircase, and out through a secret door into the Griffith Observatory. The place was bustling with visitors —he supposed that he still counted as one of them—and it took a little while to negotiate his way around the school groups and international tourists, past the pendulum and down the exhibition hall, to another secret door. He checked that no one was looking, then opened it with a tap of his wand.

Two Arpaks and a dwarf were waiting in the reception area of Silver Griffins HQ. They looked up hopefully when the door opened, then returned to distracting themselves by playing on their phones.

"Wand, please." The receptionist pointed at a box on his desk.

"I figured you'd know my face by now." Ellis pressed his wand against the box. A green light on one end lit up.

"I do, Agent Ellis, but everyone has to keep going through this, no matter how familiar they are. I wouldn't let my mother in without checking that she's not a doppelgänger."

"That's very diligent of you."

"Thank you. You can go in now. Have a nice day."

Ellis walked into the office as two pigeons flew out, carrying mission instructions strapped to their legs. He ducked to avoid having his head clipped as they shot past. Then he headed down the main floor of the office, past desks where agents were answering their emails, writing up reports, and whittling away at the eighty percent of their job that was boredom and bureaucracy. As every one of them knew, it was worth living through that for the other twenty percent.

"Hi, Ellis." Lucy waved at him as he approached. "Good to see you."

"What are you doing here?" Jackie asked.

"The usual. Hunting monsters, stalking criminals, keeping the world safe from wild magic." He set his suit-case down. "Can I leave this here with you while I go talk to your boss? I haven't had a chance to check in at my hotel yet."

"We're not a left luggage office."

"What Jackie means is that will be fine. We'll take care of it. Right, Jackie?"

"I suppose." Jackie rolled her eyes. "Remember, you only get this treatment because Sarah likes you so much. Break her heart, and I will crush you, fancy suit and all."

Ellis flushed, his cheeks almost matching his sneakers and tie. Then he hurried over to the desk outside the regional manager's office.

"I have an appointment with Mister Applegate," he said.

"That's fine." Sam, Applegate's PA, nodded at the door of the glass-walled office. "You can go on in."

Roger Applegate was sitting behind his desk with papers spread out in front of him. In Ellis's experience, Applegate always had papers spread across his desk, even when the things he was working on were all on his computer. Maybe it was a comfort behavior, bringing up soothing memories of an earlier era. Maybe it was a way to make sure he looked busy so no one questioned him when he passed off tasks onto his subordinates. Either way, it made Ellis smile, and for a moment, he felt more relaxed.

Then he remembered why he was there and how much it meant to him. His guts tightened like a spring winding up.

"Agent Ellis, splendid to see you." Applegate gestured at the seat across from him. "Please, make yourself comfortable. I assume you're here with a new case? Or perhaps to connect with my team on an existing one?"

"Actually, sir, it's about a different matter, though still a work one."

"Really?" Applegate's eyebrows rose. "Color me intrigued."

Ellis settled into the chair and stretched his legs out in front of him, then thought better of it and brought them back in. He was talking to a senior manager, someone who held his future in their hands. Best to stay more decorous and show the maximum possible respect.

"As you know, I've been coming to L.A. a lot lately," Ellis said.

"We've been very grateful for it. You were a huge help in dealing with the Knights of the Hinterland, not to mention that Mr. No case."

"Thank you kindly. I do my best."

"Something tells me that you're not here fishing for compliments. Do you need a reference, perhaps? Looking to climb your way up the greasy pole? The view's not bad from up here." Applegate chuckled and leaned back in his seat, hands folded across the front of his three-piece suit.

"Not exactly, though it is about changing jobs." Ellis licked his lips. "Fact of the thing is, I've been very impressed with how things run in this office. L.A. keeps you busy, but you never get overwhelmed. The folks here are very professional. The work's first-rate, and it's a branch of the Griffins anyone would be proud to associate with.

"As you know, I've been on a roaming brief for a long time now, attached to the security directorate. The work's interesting and all, I've got no complaints, but it ain't giving me a normal perspective on our work. I've been thinking it might be time to settle down in one place for a bit, get myself some stability, take part in some normal policing of magic. And I can't see anywhere better to do that than here."

"So you're asking if you can join this office?"

"Yes sir, if you have space, and if you don't mind an outsider bringing in their strange ways. I'm willing to adapt, of course, to learn how things work around here."

Applegate chuckled. "I'm sure you are, and I don't think you'll have the least trouble fitting in. Director Sunder's methods may be unorthodox at times, but her department still turns out fine agents. I'd be honored to add you to our staff, as long as the director is willing to let such a valuable asset go."

"She already gave me her blessing, sir."

"Well, then, it's a done deal." Applegate stood and held out his hand. "Welcome to the Los Angeles branch of the Order of the Silver Griffins, Agent Ellis. It's a pleasure to have you."

"Thank you kindly, sir." Ellis shook Applegate's hand.

"Now that's settled, tell me, is any of that waffle about your career true?"

"Excuse me, sir?" Ellis blinked, taken aback by the directness of the manager's approach.

"I mean, do you really think that this place will be good for your career, or is it all about that young lady doctor that Agents Heron and Kowal are friends with?"

"I, um…" Ellis didn't know Applegate well enough to judge his reactions, and he really didn't want to piss off his new boss on the first day, but he was giving up a prime job to take this one. Griffins from all over the world competed to get the traveling position he was about to leave behind. "Sure, Sarah's the main reason I'm doing this. I figure we need to at least be in the same town to make our relationship work. But I am looking forward to working here too. You've got some mighty fine agents who I like to think I can call friends, and L.A. seems to be where the action is. It might not be the smartest career move I could ever make, but I reckon I can make it work."

"Thank you for your honesty, Agent Ellis. Now, why don't you go tell your colleagues the news, and I'll get the paperwork started. The sooner you're on the books here, the sooner we can get you a desk of your own."

"Actually, sir, could we keep this between ourselves? There's someone else I need to tell first."

"Of course. For now, you're here on assignment." Applegate winked. "Give me the nod when you're willing to go public."

CHAPTER SIX

Lucy sat in the back yard, a sketchpad on her knees and a pencil in her hand. It had been a long, tiring day, but at last she had some time to herself, and she was determined to make the most of it.

She closed her eyes and drew a deep breath, trying to clear her mind as her yoga instructor always encouraged her to do. It was quite hard to find a clear space after a day tackling magic. Memories whirled around her brain, from the flying bicycles she and Jackie had stopped over Dodger Stadium to her Oriceran rainbow prairie dogs they had flushed out of tunnels under Chinatown. How was she supposed to focus on the rhythm of her breath when her mind was full of madness and magic?

Maybe those memories would provide some good inspiration instead. She opened her eyes and started sketching one of the prairie dogs, beginning with an oval for its body and a smaller one for its head. Legs and paws emerged in a few lines, then its big eyes, jutting teeth, and long whiskers.

Without the creature in front of her, it was hard to judge the proportions, and something about the picture didn't come out right. Was the body too small, the whiskers too long, the eyes the wrong shape? She couldn't put her finger on it, so she turned the page and started again. After all, this was part of the process, trying different versions until you got to one you liked.

By the time she turned the page from the third malformed prairie dog, she felt a little frustrated and a lot in need of a change. Maybe drawing something from life would work better. Across the garden, a finch sat in a tree with its round chest puffed out and its head tilted to one side. She held up her hand and whispered a spell, quiet enough not to disturb the bird, and something like a magnifying lens appeared floating in front of her, a disk of pure magic. She shifted it slightly so that the finch appeared in the middle of the lens, large enough for her to see details clearly, and she quickly started sketching before it flew away.

She was halfway through and feeling pleased with her efforts when the back door burst open, and Eddie tottered out, carrying two fistfuls of silver string. He saw Lucy sitting at the edge of the lawn and came over to see what she was doing. The finch, alarmed by the sudden noise and movement, fluttered away.

"What you doing?" Eddie looked down at the sketch pad.

"I'm drawing, sweetheart."

"Dinosaurs?"

"No, but their descendants."

Eddie gave her a puzzled look.

"I was drawing a bird."

"Oh." Eddie dropped the fistfuls of silver string, which wriggled on the grass, and picked up Lucy's spare sketchbook, along with one of her other pencils.

"I draw dinosaurs for mommy."

"That's very kind of you. I can't wait to see how they come out." She prodded with her pencil at the wriggling pile of silver string. "Are these your sister's robots?"

The door opened again, and Ashley ran out. "Eddie, did you take some of the strings?"

Eddie didn't respond. His mind had moved on to drawing dinosaurs. Stringy robots were yesterday's fun.

"They're here, sweetheart." Lucy pointed at the pile in front of her. "I'm sure your brother wanted me to see what great work you're doing."

Ashley came over with a plastic bucket, scooped up the robot strings, and dropped them into the bucket before slapping a lid onto the top. She glared at Eddie.

"I told him not to touch them."

"I know, but he's only three. Remember what you were like at that age? You wanted to touch everything, to see how it worked and what you could do with it."

Ashley sucked on the tip of her finger as she considered what her mother had said.

"I suppose so. But I wish he didn't do that to my things."

"I know, and I appreciate how patient you are with him."

"Dinosaur!" Eddie exclaimed, holding up his picture. "T-Rex."

"That's brilliant." Lucy tried to work out which of the scribbled lines was the head. "Is there anything you can do to make it even better?"

"Colors!"

Eddie got to his feet and headed indoors.

Ashley was looking down at the other sketch pad resting in her mother's lap.

"It looks so real," she said. "I can't make my pictures do that. Can you show me how?"

Lucy was constantly surprised by her daughter's intelligence and imagination, the way she could come out with insights that were beyond most adults she knew. This was the first time it was something the girl couldn't do that surprised her, though the calm, considered tone of the request was less surprising. Ashley was bright enough to understand that everyone had limits and mature enough to want to stretch hers, rather than getting frustrated to discover that they were there.

"I'll do my best," Lucy said, "although I'm no teacher."

She turned the page on both sketch pads and handed one to Ashley, along with a pencil.

"Let's pick something that's still here to draw, so you can practice doing it from life. How about the lemon tree?"

While Ashley watched, Lucy sketched out the first few lines of her drawing, explaining as she went how she had judged what to draw, showing how to use a pencil to measure relative lengths and get the proportions right. Then Ashley set her pencil to paper to have a go.

Eddie tottered out again, carrying two fistfuls of wax crayons.

"Dinosaur?" He looked around for the pad he'd been working on.

"I'll go fetch some more paper."

Lucy headed into the house to the art supplies box in the corner of the living room. A trail of dropped crayons ran from the box across the room and out through the kitchen, where Eddie's ambition had outstretched his carrying capacity. She pulled out a bundle of paper, then thought better of it. This was the sort of situation that could easily escalate, so she might as well be prepared. She picked up the whole box.

"What are you doing?" Dylan looked up from where he was sitting on the couch, watching TV.

"We're drawing in the back yard. Do you want to join us?"

"Sure." He switched off the TV and followed her out.

The scene in the back yard was so idyllic that it drew an involuntary sigh of contentment from deep inside Lucy. Eddie and Ashley sat next to each other on the grass, sketch pads in front of them, happily drawing together. Ashley had moved beyond the first few lines that Lucy had shown her, and her tree was taking shape. Eddie had decided that trees might be as fun as dinosaurs although he drew his in green and brown crayon instead of plain pencil. Dylan picked out some paper and pencils, then went to join them.

Lucy picked out a pencil and paper of her own, then sat against the back wall of the house. Now she had a subject for her art that really inspired her. Instead of drawing a bird or a tree or some magical creature that she'd been chasing earlier in the day, she started drawing her children sitting peacefully in their back yard, drawing together. She sketched Dylan's tall, thin frame, legs crossed beneath him, his dark hair a wavy mess on the top of his head. Then came Ashley with her hair neatly tied back and her back ramrod straight, the side of her face visible as she turned to examine what her brothers were doing, learning from them. In between was Eddie, bottom sticking in the air as he knelt over his paper, leaning way down as he scribbled in color between the outlines of his tree.

Buddy waddled out of the back door and over to them. He sniffed the pages, rolled a pencil across the lawn, then looked up, hoping someone would throw this painted stick for him.

Lucy suggested, "How about an art game?"

"Yay!" the kids cried in unison.

"What are the rules?" Ashley asked.

"We all have sixty seconds to draw Buddy. Then we're going to show him the pictures and see what he thinks. Are you up for it?" They all nodded. "All right, I'm setting a timer on my phone. Three, two, one, go!"

For a minute, the only sound was the frantic scratching of pencils across paper as they all focused on their drawings. Then Lucy's phone *bleeped,* and she set her pencil aside.

"All right, let's show him what we have."

One by one, they displayed their works to the bemused dog, and in the process to each other. Eddie's was a mass of brown scribbling, with two black eyes and a mouth on one end.

"You've really captured his energy," Lucy said. "Who's next?"

Ashley held out her pencil drawing, a set of loose shapes that were clearly Eddie's proportions. The details weren't there yet, but Lucy had the sneaking suspicion that, with a little time and attention, Ashley would quickly surpass her in art, as in almost everything else.

"Great work, sweetheart," she praised. "You're learning fast."

"I cheated," Dylan said, then held his out for them to see. He'd written the word "BUDDY" in big capital letters, then added a tail at one end and two floppy ears at the other. "Turns out I'm better with words than with pictures."

"Not cheating, experimenting with style." Lucy smiled. "It was a very clever approach. Well done."

"What about you, Mom?"

Lucy held up her pad for them to see. She had added Buddy to her previous drawing so that he wandered in front of the kids, the pencil in his mouth matching the ones in their hands.

"It's so lovely seeing you all together. I couldn't resist adding him."

"That's me!" Eddie exclaimed, looking at the picture. "And Dylan, and Ashley."

"That's right."

"I draw me."

He picked up a pink crayon, a determined look in his eyes.

The back door swung wide one more time, and Charlie appeared, wearing a button-down shirt and dress trousers, straight from work.

"What's going on out here?" he asked.

"Art club," Lucy replied. "We need a new life model. No need to strip, but please don't move until I tell you to. New game, everyone, sixty seconds to draw your dad. Ready? Three, two, one, go!"

Now she could get the whole family into her picture.

CHAPTER SEVEN

"Am I going to start coming home to art club every evening?" Charlie asked as they were washing up the dishes that evening. "Or was this just to keep the kids quiet for a couple of hours?"

"It would be nice to do things like that more often, don't you think?" Lucy said. "Encouraging them to be creative."

"I don't think our kids have any shortage of creativity." Charlie grinned. "Remember that Lego tower they built to make Buddy extra tall after he stopped being a bloodhound?"

"I remember poor Buddy standing on top of it, looking very confused. Wish I'd had a chance to draw that too."

"I'm sure they'd be willing to recreate it, even if he wasn't. But in answer to your question, yes, I think it would be nice to do more things like that. We've been talking about spending time together as a family, going places to make some memories, so why not throw art into the mix? I'll even encourage the kids by showing them that they can all draw better than me."

Lucy wrapped her arms around her husband. "You're the best. You know that?"

"Is there a prize for being best?"

"Maybe." She kissed him. "But only after we've finished the dishes."

Charlie flourished his dishcloth. "Then I am all over this."

The doorbell rang.

"Are you expecting anyone?" Lucy asked, heading for the door.

"Oh, I totally forgot!" Charlie slapped himself on the forehead. "We have a business meeting tonight."

Lucy opened the door to see Ringo Fuller, level three bounty hunter and occasional pain in her neck, standing on the doorstep. Max Petrie, the husband of her work rival Kelly, was striding up the driveway behind him.

"Hey there, 485," Ringo said, greeting Lucy by her badge number. "Is your husband in?"

"Good evening, Level Three." Lucy held the door wide. "He's in the kitchen."

Ringo took off his wraparound shades and stepped inside. A moment later, Max reached the doorway.

"Hi, Lucy. Sorry to intrude upon your evening."

"Not a problem, Max. It's always good to see you."

Lucy still couldn't get over that Max, so friendly and considerate, was married to the scheming and self-serving Kelly. They might seem well matched on the surface, a pair of smartly dressed and ambitious magical professionals, but there was a gulf in attitude that made them seem like they should never have been together. She understood all sorts of magic, but not the kind that held that marriage together.

She closed the door and followed the others to the kitchen.

"Sorry about this, guys," Charlie said. "I just need to finish the washing up. Then we can get down to business."

"I'll deal with this." Lucy took the cloth out of his hands and waved them all away. "You go have your meeting."

"Are you sure?"

"Positive. Now go."

Charlie grabbed cold beers from the fridge for the three of them, then led the others into the dining room. That space often acted as an impromptu headquarters for their side business, converting the cars of magical drivers to make them more environmentally friendly through a mixture of magic and technology.

While she did the dishes, Lucy half-listened to the start of their meeting. It seemed that business was going well, with the first few customers very satisfied and news of their work spreading by word of mouth. Lucy smiled proudly. It was great to hear that her husband and his friends were making the world a cleaner place.

"We've reached the point where we should start thinking seriously about branding," Max said. He didn't work on the cars like the other two, but as a high-powered lawyer, he understood the way businesses worked better than either of them and often took the lead on these topics.

"I hate the word branding." Charlie made a face. "It makes us sound like cattle."

"You can hate it all you want, but it's vital to any

modern business. We have to make sure that we're clearly recognizable so customers know to come to us."

"Customers are coming to us already."

"True, but word of mouth will only get us so far. If we want to reach customers all across L.A., if we want to maximize both our earnings and our environmental impact, then we need to create a strong identity that will help word spread."

"You sound like the managers at work."

Max laughed. "There's a reason for that. Well, all right, there are two reasons, and one of them is people trying to make themselves sound important. The other reason is that this stuff works."

"If we're getting branding, do we need a logo?" Ringo asked.

"That's a part of it, yes, and probably a good starting place. Then we can pick fonts and a color scheme to match. There's other work to be done around how we present ourselves through words, but we can work on that while someone else is coming up with our visuals."

Max opened his laptop to reveal a spreadsheet listing graphic designers he had found.

"I've shortlisted some promising local designers who fit our budget, but before we approach any of them, we need to put a briefing pack together."

"A briefing pack?"

"What we want our logo to say, what we want to include in it, anything we want to avoid. We might pick out examples of other logos we like to give the designer an idea of our style."

Charlie and Ringo looked at each other.

"Do we even have a style?" Charlie asked.

"I do." Ringo smoothed a wrinkle from his tight t-shirt. "But I don't think that's the same thing."

"Try answering this," Max said. "What objects could represent the work we do?"

That launched them into a thoughtful silence as the three men sipped their beers and contemplated the possibilities. Charlie had sometimes heard managers say that there were no bad ideas, but ten minutes later they were usually calling someone an idiot. If he was going to come out with a suggestion, he wanted it to be a good one.

"How about a wand?" he said. "We're using magic so we could use that as a symbol."

"Or a rune," Ringo said. "Same reason."

Max scribbled those ideas down on a piece of paper. "What else?"

"Some sparkles, like someone cast magic?" Ringo looked dubious as he said it.

"A wrench to show the other side of our work."

"Or a screwdriver."

"Or a drill."

"How about a car? That's what we work on."

Max tapped his pen against the paper.

"Those ideas capture the how of our work, but not the why," he said. "What could represent the green side?"

"Coloring it green." Ringo looked at the others. "Or is that too obvious?"

"It's worth considering, but what about when we're printing in black and white?"

"We could use a globe," Charlie said. "Lots of organizations use that to show that they're looking after the world."

"Or a tree or a leaf, the nature side of things," Ringo said. "How about a flower?"

"Seriously, you want me to drive around in a van with a flower on the side?"

"You drive around in a van with an eagle on the side."

"Exactly."

They all stared at their list. There were a lot of ideas on there, but not a lot of connections between them.

"So, maybe we put two of these things together?" Charlie suggested. "Like, a wand that's got a leaf growing out of the top?"

"We need to include the mechanical part," Ringo said. "After all, we're working with machines. How about a wand and a wrench crossing each other, like swords on a pirate flag?"

"You know someone used that before, right?" Max said.

Ringo shook his head. "Who? Maybe they don't need it anymore."

"It was a symbol for the magical Communist movement, back in the fifties and sixties. It's a take on the old Soviet hammer and sickle design."

"I don't want a commie symbol on the side of my van." Ringo shook his head vigorously. "Not even in green."

"How about a wand going around the world?" Charlie said. "That's magic and environmentalism in one place, right?"

"Too vague. That could be for anything magical."

They all sat staring at the list.

"Something with a car, then?" Max asked.

"But what?" Charlie asked. "A car with a wand, or a

wrench, or a leaf? Do we try to fit them all in? That sounds kind of crowded."

Having put the last plate away in the cupboard, Lucy made herself a cup of tea and went to join them.

"Can I make a suggestion?" she said.

They all nodded or said something in the affirmative.

"You're going to hire a professional designer, right?"

Again, they nodded.

"Then don't worry so much about the content of your design. That's what you're hiring them to do. Instead, focus on what you want it to say." She picked up a pencil. "What were the themes you picked out again?"

"Magic," Charlie said.

"Mechanical stuff," Ringo added.

"The environment," Charlie said.

"Great." Lucy scribbled those down on a piece of paper. "Was there anything else?"

"Cars, or vehicles." Charlie scratched his head. "That's the big one, isn't it, if we want people to see our logo and remember what we do. It should include a car."

"Not necessarily," Lucy said. "Even if you want a reminder that cars are involved, you could show a wheel, or a road, or all sorts of other things. What matters is to tell the designer what your business is about and what sorts of things you want to be associated with. If you pick the right person, they can take it from there."

"If we tell them our business, that limits our options," Max pointed out. "We can't tell a mundane designer that we're a magical car company."

"That's okay. There are plenty of artists and designers

in the magical community. I can introduce you to some of them if you like."

"Magical, mechanical, green, and cars." Max typed the words into his spreadsheet. "That's our brief, isn't it?"

"Seems that way." Charlie smiled. "Now let's go find a designer and get them to do the design work because we sure don't know how."

CHAPTER EIGHT

Lucy turned the steering wheel, propelling the Rivian SUV off the main street and up a side road. Behind them, the traffic continued its sluggish progress as people headed for work or to drop the kids off at school. L.A. roared in the voice of a million engines while the electric Rivian offered a softer, more soothing purr.

In the passenger seat, Jackie wasn't so calm.

"We could have gotten a portal there," she said. "Would have been a lot quicker."

"It's rush hour," Lucy pointed out. "We can't teleport around the city now. Too much risk of being seen."

"As opposed to the certainty that someone is seeing rogue magic right now?"

"We were already nearby. It made more sense to go this way."

"Not the way you're driving. It's like being chauffeured by a little old lady."

"This thing is faster than it feels. It's the engine noise that tricks you."

"The engine noise and the speedometer. Come on, put your foot down. There's work to do."

Lucy took them along a couple of back streets, avoiding the busy roads, then back toward a junction where cars were crawling by as thick as ants across a picnic basket. This street was quieter, which was lucky for the pedestrians who had gathered near the junction, pointing and staring at a brightly painted wall.

Lucy pulled up a few feet away from the small crowd. She and Jackie got out, wands concealed but accessible, and approached.

"What's happening to him?" one of the spectators said, gazing open-mouthed at the wall. "How is it even doing that?"

The wall in question was the blank end of a row of shops, without a single window or door breaking up its flat surface. Across the brickwork, someone had spray-painted a mural of bold colors and dynamic shapes. It showed jungle on one side, lush in its greens and yellows, reminiscent of the scene they had spotted on their run. On the other side was a cityscape, tower blocks grasping greedily at the air. Between them loomed a strange figure, man on one side and tiger on the other, his split persona united by a predatory grin and an avaricious gleam in his eyes.

"That's impressive." Lucy looked up at the image. "I love how the artist has made the forest and the city blur into each other, blending the grays and greens, turning leaves into windows."

"I'm sure it's a masterpiece of graffiti," Jackie said. "But we're not here for the art appreciation, and neither is this crowd."

Around twenty people had gathered around. Some of them had phones out, leaning around each other to take photos and videos of what they saw. Peering over their shoulders, Lucy could see why they were so interested.

The figure in the center of the painting had escaped from his two dimensions into the third. One of his hands— the one that was furred and clawed like a tiger—was reaching out of the painting. Wide fingers had wrapped around a man standing in front of the image, and the claws pressed against his chest, threatening to pierce his baggy t-shirt and the flesh beneath. He squirmed and shouted for help as the tiger fist lifted him off the pavement.

"Excuse us," Lucy shoved through the crowd. "Police coming through."

"You don't look much like police," one of the people said.

"Since when do they hire Scottish police in L.A.?" another asked.

"Actually, I'm English, and I have my ID right here." Lucy held up her wand. "Never was, never will be."

A wave of magic swept across the crowd and their expressions went slack. Arms hung limply by their sides, and they stared straight ahead, lost to the world.

"That's bought us a few minutes," Lucy said. "But now what?"

The tiger man still held his victim and waved him through the air, like a cat toying with a mouse before the kill. The artist could make a cat twelve feet tall and half-dressed in a suit, but there was still something inescapable about feline instincts, something playfully cruel. Or perhaps that was how the artist saw them, and that view had seeped into the work through their magic. Either way, it had to be stopped.

"Can we dispel this?" Jackie pointed her wand at the wall.

"While it's throwing that lad about?" Lucy asked. "He'll fall straight onto the pavement, could get badly hurt."

"So rescue first?"

"I think so."

"Great." Jackie shoved her wand through her waistband. "Cover me."

She tensed, then leapt as the arm swung by and caught hold of it. As the arm kept moving, she swung as wildly as the poor victim in its grip, her legs flailing. That didn't last long. On a backswing, Jackie used her momentum to bring her legs up and hook a foot around the gigantic arm, then pull herself on top of it. She crossed her ankles underneath, gripped tight, and wriggled down the arm toward the hand.

On the flat expanse of the wall, the tiger man tipped his head on one side and looked at Jackie with curiosity. His mouth shifted, and there was a purr so low and bassy that Lucy felt the rumble in her chest. His other arm, gigantically human and wrapped in a fitted business suit, reached out of the painting.

"Oh no, you don't." Lucy pointed her wand. "Agglutino."

A thick ball of glue shot from her wand, hit the suit arm, and slapped it back against the wall. The tiger man stared and strained, but he couldn't break free. His hand and arm remained stuck against the brickwork.

"Do you need any help?" Lucy asked.

"No, I've got this." Jackie had reached the tiger's paw

and taken hold of one thumb-like claw. She pulled it back toward her, and the creature loosened its grip on its captive. "Get ready to catch him."

Lucy raised her wand. Jackie looked at the sway of the arm back and forth, judged her moment, then kicked one of the other claws.

The tiger man yelped and let go of his victim.

"Subvolo." Lucy's spell caught the man as he was released and levitated him gently to the ground.

The tiger man turned his angry gaze on Jackie.

"Sorry, man," she said. "It's just not your day." She let go of the paw and dropped to the sidewalk. "Now!"

"Renuo!" Countermagic flew from Lucy's wand. It hit the painting, and the air rippled as magic and anti-magic met, obliterating each other. The arm that had reached out of the picture retreated into it. The image became still, the gleam in the tiger man's eyes purely an artistry effect rather than living magic.

Lucy took a step back and almost fell as a spray can rolled out from under her foot. She picked it up. The sharp smell of solvents was fresh, and the paint wet around its nozzle.

"What do you think?" Jackie looked down at the tiger man's victim, who lay slumped on the sidewalk under the influence of the "never was" spell. "Did he get caught by his magic?"

Lucy looked again at the mural. It looked too complete to have been interrupted mid-painting, and though that didn't rule out Jackie's theory, it still seemed unlikely. The paint in the can was a brilliant blue, which didn't feature in the image, except for a single, misplaced streak near the bottom felt-hand corner.

She unzipped the pack strapped to the guy's back and looked inside. There were a few cans of paint, but nothing like the varied and carefully chosen colors that had made this image.

"He's a tagger," she said. "Probably saw the picture and decided to mark it himself."

"Like putting his signature on and claiming it as his own?"

"More like a dog peeing on a lamppost to blot out another dog's smell. Except that this time, he was peeing on a work of art."

"It is pretty good," Jackie said. "Weird style, though I can't quite work out what's bothering me."

Lucy smiled. "I could go full art critic if you like, give you some idea of the techniques involved and what you might be responding to."

Jackie shook her head. "No thanks. It's too early for any of that. I need more caffeine before I try any deep thoughts. Besides, we have a bunch of phones to deal with."

They went around the crowd of slack-jawed onlookers, hastily taking phones from their hands and removing any pictures or videos of the mural in action. If social media apps were open, they checked those too, in case the onlookers shared anything already.

"The older Griffins in my family, they all hate the cameras on phones," Jackie said. "Uncle Harold reckons they're one of the biggest risks ever to threaten the magical world, that it's only a matter of time before an image gets out that we can't cover up."

"We might have reached that time already." Lucy held out one of the phones. "This woman shared a short video of the tiger swinging that guy around, and it's already had a load of likes and shares."

They watched the video, one eye on the screen, the other on the people around them. The spell would wear off soon, and they had to finish by then.

"That's not too bad," Jackie said. "It's rushed and blurry. Even if it's been screen capped and reshared, I think we can explain it away."

"How?"

"A guerrilla advertising stunt for an upcoming film. Some sort of holographic tech used to sell the next big hit."

"How do we get that story out?"

"I have a bunch of social media accounts I set up, fake PR companies, things like that. They're great for a cover-up."

Lucy put the phone back in its owner's hand. The crowd was starting to stir, people shaking their heads and looking around.

"Wow, it was almost like that thing moved, huh?" Lucy said, loud enough for them all to hear.

"I wonder how they did that." Jackie ran a hand across the wall. "Ah well, we should get to work."

They headed for the car. Behind them, the tagger picked himself up off the pavement, saw the crowd around him, and made a hurried exit. The bystanders looked at each other in confusion, then up at the mural. A few half-heartedly took pictures while others tried to remember what they had been doing, how they had ended up here. Soon, they would have found a way to fill the gaps, a story that fitted the evidence they had and the people they thought they were. For now, they simply started to drift away.

"Another good morning's work," Jackie said as they climbed into the car. "Now, how about we grab a coffee and you explain some art to me?"

CHAPTER NINE

Amid the tunnels beneath L.A., Heather Fields stood at the front of a concrete chamber fitted out as a schoolroom, a pen in her hand and the teacher's desk behind her. Her students sat facing her from rows of mismatched desks and chairs, the misfit magical teenagers of the Underfoot Brigade. This eclectic mix included elves, dwarves, gnomes, witches, wizards, a diminutive Willen, and an Arpak with a crippled wing.

They weren't what she had expected from life, but she felt pride and affection as she looked at them. It was like the camaraderie she felt toward the rest of the Tolderai, but softer and somehow more relaxing, despite the hard work that teaching involved.

Today, some of that work would be off her shoulders.

"Who remembers what we're due to study in today's lesson?" she asked.

In the front row, a gnome in a glittery top shot her hand into the air.

"Yes, Kix?"

"Art, Miss."

"That's right, art." Heather didn't smile often, but Kix's unmistakable enthusiasm almost lifted the corners of her mouth. "I'm not much of an artist, so I've brought someone in to help. Everyone say hello to Miss Winters."

In the corner of the room, Carol Winters stood and waved to the class.

"Hi," she said. "You can call me Carol."

"Hi, Carol," the kids responded.

"Carol is another of the Tolderai," Heather said. "She's also a professional artist, and she's agreed to do me a favor by teaching you some of her skills."

That part about doing a favor was only half the story. After hearing that Carol had let slip about the Tolderai artifacts, Heather had gotten straight onto the phone to the younger witch to forcefully point out the dangers of giving away information about the tribe. Carol had been wretchedly apologetic when she realized how her enthusiasm had gotten the better of her and had begged for a chance to make it up. While there wasn't much she could do for the tribe right now, Heather wasn't going to miss the opportunity.

"Today we're going to learn all about perspective," Carol said. "And about how you can use it to improve your drawings. Everybody, please get a pencil and some paper from the ones I've put out at the side, and we'll get started."

The Underfoots rushed to grab the shiny new art pencils and the thick, creamy sheets of paper that sat with them. Carol's guilt had stretched to supplying some new classroom materials as well as her time.

"I love your skirt, Miss," Kix said as she returned to her seat. "The velvet looks beautiful in this light."

"Oh, thank you." Carol smiled and swirled her skirt. As she did so, her dark hair drifted across the shoulders of her blouse. Even for Heather, who had seen her in action, it was easy to forget that Carol could be as ruthless a fighter and as fearsome a magic user as anyone in the Tolderai tribe. Her gentle demeanor was enough to put almost anyone off the scent.

Once the Underfoots were all back at their desks, Carol approached the whiteboard, pen in hand, and started the lesson. She talked about vanishing points and perspective lines, using examples from great works of art to show the teenagers how it all worked. Then, starting with simple boxes, she made the beginnings of a picture.

"Now you all try that too," she said. "Draw the horizon line and vanishing points first, then some shapes around them."

While Carol roamed the room, helping the students with their work, Heather stepped outside. The class was behaving themselves, and she had other business to deal with.

She pulled out her phone, which she'd magically enhanced to get a signal down here in the depths, and called another of the Tolderai.

"Mackam, how's it going?"

"As awful as ever," a gruff voice replied. "Did you know that the government is experimenting with putting microchips in all of us? That's why they put them in dogs and cats, to pave the way, you see. First animals, so you can keep them safe. Then kids, for the same reason. Then they grow up, and they start using them for ID, and suddenly we all need microchips to prove who we are. But I'm not going to let them get away with it."

Heather sighed and squeezed her eyes shut. She had once tried talking to Mackam about seeing a psychiatrist. That conversation hadn't ended well.

"Just keep wearing the tinfoil vest," she said. "That should keep out the signals from the chips."

"Good thinking. I might make a hat too."

"Sure, why not. Now, what have you found out about this elf, Penley ap Gawain?"

"Old elf from an old family, but he works hard on hiding the years. Oriceran money behind him, and lots of it, but he has backers on this side too. He has a magical gallery and a mundane one, so he has lots of contacts in the art world. The elf has influence."

"Any connections to old opponents of ours?"

"Not that I've found yet. Not many deals with criminals either, which is unusual once you get that far up the artistic food chain."

"Really?"

"Oh, yes. It doesn't matter if they're drug barons or white-collar Wall Street bandits. All the worst people invest in art. It's a high-value commodity that's easy to move around and keeps its value."

"Good to know. But this guy's relatively clean?"

"Yes. If we're going to deal with anyone, it might as well be him."

"That's a big 'if' though, isn't it?"

"It's your 'if' to deal with, chief." Mackam cackled, and

the crumpling of foil crackled like static down the line. "I'm just a lowly lunatic in the woods."

"Well, good work. I'll get back to you if I need anything else."

Heather headed back into the classroom. The Underfoots were all hard at work, turning their initial perspective drawings into street scenes, transforming simple box shapes into buildings, then mixing them with sketches of people and cars.

"Look, I've drawn Chinatown," Siltor the elf said, showing his picture to Leontine the Arpak. "There are restaurants, and that's us, poking our heads out of a utility hole to look around. I can practically smell the dim sum."

"It's good." Leontine looked up from this picture as Heather passed. "Miss Fields, I have a question."

"Then you should ask Carol," Heather said. "I'm here as a spectator today."

Leontine turned his attention to the artist. "Carol, did you help plant the underground forests?"

Carol blinked in surprise, then glanced at Heather, who hesitated for a moment before giving a small nod.

"Yes, I helped," Carol said. "All the Tolderai did. It takes a lot of magic to carve out caves like that and to fill them with growing plants."

"How do you keep them alive?" asked Twylan, one of the brightest of the kids, a teenage witch with wild magic flashing from her eyes. "I mean, most plants rely on sunlight and rain, so I was wondering how you replace them and how much effort it takes to keep it going."

"Well, um…"

Carol paused. After getting into trouble for talking

openly about the artifacts the tribe had recovered, she was even warier of talking about their secret project to grow hidden forests beneath the streets of L.A. Clearly, Heather had told her students something about it, but how much, and what was she allowed to say?

"Let's focus on the lesson for now, shall we?" She looked at Twylan's picture. "Is that the Griffith Observatory?"

"I go there sometimes, to the Silver Griffins' base," Twylan said. "Some of the agents are showing me how it works, so I can join them when I'm old enough."

"That's fantastic. Maybe you'll be able to use your artistic skills there, become the magical equivalent of a police sketch artist."

Twylan shook her head. "I'm going to be a field agent. Besides, I'm not as good at this as Kix."

The lesson continued for a few minutes longer, pencils scratching quietly across paper while some of the kids held whispered conversations. Then Leontine held up his hand.

"Could we use these same perspective tricks to draw plants as well as buildings?" he asked.

"Yes, of course, though it's more complicated," Carol said. "We're starting with buildings because they have straight lines and regular shapes, which map neatly onto the lines we're using. But with more practice, you can use this for almost anything you want to draw."

"Could you take us somewhere we can draw plants next time?"

"I suppose so if it's all right with Heather, I mean Miss Fields." Carol looked awkwardly across the students. She didn't know how to raise the topic of their physical appearance, of how difficult it would be to take an Arpak with a crippled wing, a witch with glowing eyes, and their other friends to a park to draw the trees. "Although I'm not sure where the best place for that might be, given, um..."

Heather shook her head. She could see where this was going, even if Carol couldn't.

"How about one of the underground forests?" Twylan asked. "No one else would see us there."

"Oh." Carol looked at Heather. "Well, I..."

"Fine," Heather said. "You lot aren't going to be satisfied until we take a trip to one of the caves, are you?" Her students turned their attention to her, some with guilty looks, some defiantly, but most just excited at the prospect. "I'll take you there for a lesson or two, okay? You can see what we've been making and how it works. We'll study some biology and ecology, as well as the magic."

"I'd be happy to do another art lesson, too," Carol said. "Drawing plants is very relaxing."

"There we go. Happy now?"

The students cheered their agreement.

"Fine. But that lesson's not happening yet. For now, I want you to concentrate on this one. Think of the field trip as a reward, and you only get it if you focus on your other work."

The room went silent as a whole class full of teenagers turned back to their art with renewed determination. They were going to earn their trip to the magical forest.

CHAPTER TEN

Gruffbar sat at the back of the bar, at a quiet table with enough shadows to hide him from view. With his neatly trimmed beard, he could pass as a particularly short human, which let him hang out in places like this, but it was still good to avoid drawing attention. The last thing a dwarf wanted to deal with was a bunch of drunks making *Lord of the Rings* jokes.

It was early afternoon, and the place was only doing a little business. The lunchtime crowd had passed, and there weren't the steady mob of daytime drinkers that would fill the weekend, only a few people having a quiet beer, enjoying a place with an old-fashioned woodwork and bare bricks aesthetic, and with a good selection of craft beers to choose from. One more reason to stay out of the way: places like this drew hipsters like gold drew dragons.

Technically, Gruffbar was supposed to be meeting a client here, someone who preferred a relaxed chat over a drink to the formality of a lawyer's office. But that meeting had been due half an hour ago, and the client was still a no-show. Gruffbar hung on, partly because he enjoyed his beer, but mostly because he needed the business. Rent was due, and the cash wasn't coming in half as fast as he would have liked. It was worth waiting a bit longer for the client, just in case they showed up.

He gulped his beer and watched as a man walked into the bar. He looked like a mundane human, but there was an air of magic about him that made the hairs on the back of Gruffbar's hands stand on end. The guy ordered a drink, then turned to face the room.

"Who's feeling strong?" he called. When no one responded, he drew a bunch of bills from his pocket and slapped them down on the bar. "My name's Johnny Townsend, that's a hundred bucks, and it'll go to anyone who can beat me in an arm-wrestling contest."

The other drinkers laughed. The guy was skinny as a rake, his arms like sticks. When he flexed them, a fresh tattoo poked out from under the sleeve of his t-shirt, the skin still raw where the needle had done its work.

"I'm serious," Johnny said. "Come on, one of you challenge me."

"I'll do it." The barman set his elbow on the counter and thrust out his hand. "Tips are short today. I could use the extra cash."

The barman was clearly the kind of guy who took care of himself, with a smart, on-trend haircut and the sort of toned body that came from regular trips to the gym. It was no wonder that he was feeling confident, but Gruffbar wasn't convinced. There was more going on here than a trial of strength.

Johnny rested his elbow on the bar. The two competitors locked hands and locked eyes. Across the room, someone shouted, "Go!"

The barman grinned, then flexed his arm but didn't move. He grimaced, strained, and pressed against his opponent's hand, but it wouldn't budge. In mounting frustration, he pushed with all his might.

Johnny grinned, then slammed the barman's hand into the top of the bar so hard that something splintered. One of the watching drinkers laughed. Another gasped. The barman clutched his knuckles and reached for some ice.

"How the hell did you do that?" the barman said. "Got to be a trick."

"I'm stronger than I look," Johnny said. "Anyone else want to give it a go?"

As someone else stepped up to take a turn, Gruffbar knocked back more of his drink. He could tell when a situation was going to escalate, and this was one of those moments. The barman looked annoyed, and it was only a matter of time before someone decided that cheating was involved or Johnny got carried away with whatever magic he was using.

As he reached for his briefcase and got ready to go, Gruffbar had a change of heart. Why should he let some showoff ruin his relaxed drink? There was another way to deal with this. He pulled out his phone and dialed a number he never expected to use.

"Hello, Silver Griffins," a voice said at the other end.

"I'm at Clayton's Public House, down by Skid Row," Gruffbar said quietly. "There's a guy in here. I think he has a magical tattoo, and he's using it to show off. You might want to get someone down here."

Then he hung up.

While he had been talking, Johnny had wrestled another guy. This one was clutching his wrist and standing at the end of the bar, staring in amazement at Johnny and his wide, confident grin.

"Nobody else?" Johnny asked. "Then let's make this more interesting." He counted more bills out onto the bar. "Two hundred, three hundred, four, five. Half a grand to anyone who can beat me." He flexed his tattooed arm. "One of you must be up to it. I mean look, I'm no challenge."

"I have a challenger for you," one of the other customers said while putting her phone away. "If you can wait a few minutes."

"Sure, why not?" Johnny took a bill off the top of the heap and tossed it to the barman. "Gimme a beer while you're about it."

"What sort of beer?"

"You know, beer beer," Johnny said, ignoring the row of taps in front of him. "A Bud."

Everyone stared at Johnny as if he'd taken a dump on the floor, but none of them said anything. Up until now, Gruffbar had been annoyed at the guy for being a noisy showoff. Now he realized that he was a barbarian, coming into a place like this and ordering beer like that. He half hoped that things did get out of hand and that Johnny faced the consequences.

The barman slid a glass across the bar, shaking his head.

Then the door opened, and a woman stepped in. She was tall, with long dark hair and broad shoulders. When she took off her leather jacket, she revealed biceps almost as wide as Gruffbar's waistline.

"Alice here was a runner-up for world's strongest woman," said the woman who had phoned a friend. "But that shouldn't be a problem for you, right Johnny?"

For a moment, Johnny looked genuinely worried, but then he looked at his new tattoo, and his cocky grin returned.

"No problem." He sat at a table and planted his elbow on the polished wood, hand up and ready. "Let's do this."

The chair creaked under Alice as she sat, and customers gathered around to watch, blocking Gruffbar's view. He sat back and sipped his beer. There was a grunt, a *thud*, and a gasp from the spectators.

"You cheated," growled a woman, her voice low and menacing. Presumably, that was Alice, though Gruffbar couldn't see her.

"Sore loser, much?" Johnny replied.

"How'd you cheat?"

"I'm stronger than I look. Turns out maybe all those gym trips were a waste of time."

"Bullshit."

There was a *whap* of flesh hitting flesh.

"You shouldn't have done that," Johnny said.

Alice appeared, flying into the air above the assembled spectators. She slammed into the ceiling, then crashed back down, reducing the table to splinters. The others backed off, staring at Johnny.

"What?" He got out of his seat. "No more challengers?" He turned to one of them. "How about you?" The guy shook his head and pressed himself back against the wall. "What about you, or you? Someone must be willing to take me on." Johnny grabbed the end of the bar, and it splintered between his fingers. "Who's weak now, huh?"

"I think you should leave," the barman said, his voice trembling.

"Or what, you gonna throw me out?" Johnny grabbed the barman's arm and flung him across the room. He hit the wall close to Gruffbar and slid to the floor. Johnny's eyes fell on Gruffbar. "How about you, Bilbo Baggins? Want to show me that hobbit strength?"

Gruffbar shook his head. He would've fought many people over a comment like that, but he wasn't going to take this guy on. "I just came here for the beer."

"And I came here for the challenge, so where is it?"

"Over here." Everybody turned to look at the entrance, where Lucy Heron stood, hands on her hips. Gruffbar saw the handle of her wand sticking out of one pocket and the palm of her hand resting on it.

"You want a fight, little lady?" Johnny's expression had grown ferocious, his eyes wide and wild. He bared his teeth like an attack dog.

"A fight? I thought you were arm-wrestling."

"Well, now I want a fight." Johnny grabbed the end of the bar in both hands and heaved. There was a string of splintering and *popping* sounds, then the whole top of the bar came away. Johnny flung it across the room and through the window, scattering broken glass across passersby.

"Then I'd better give you one," Lucy said. "Renuo."

Everyone else's attention was on her, so only Gruffbar saw the rippling of light across Johnny's tattoo. Of course, most of them wouldn't have known what a counterspell was even if they saw it. Gruffbar grinned.

"What did you say, Scottish lady?" Johnny asked.

"Actually, I'm English." Lucy raised her fists. "I said bring it on."

Johnny charged across the pub, screaming at the top of his lungs. He swung his fist, and everyone gasped as Lucy caught it effortlessly in her hand.

"What?" She looked around at them. "Couldn't you deal with this scrawny bugger?"

Johnny swung his other fist. Lucy ducked under the blow, then brought her knee up between his legs. Johnny crumpled over with a hideous moan. Around the room, every other man winced.

"But how…" asked Alice's friend, staring down at the man lying curled up on the floor.

"Me or him?" Lucy asked. "He was clearly on steroids. You can tell by that weird look in his eye, you know?"

People nodded as if to say that yes, of course, they were also streetwise folks who could identify steroid abuse.

"How did you…"

"Timing," Lucy said. "That's the problem with drugs. When the high wears off, you're an even bigger mess than at the start." She hauled Johnny to his feet, then looked over at Gruffbar. "Could you give me a hand taking him to the hospital?"

"Sure." Gruffbar downed the last of his beer, then went to stand on the other side of Johnny. Together, they led him out of the pub.

"Steroids, huh?" said one of the other customers behind them. "That shit gets worse every year."

They headed down the street toward where Lucy had parked her SUV.

"Were you the one who called this in?" she asked. "I didn't think you'd be the lad to help uphold the law."

"I'm a lawyer. I'm always upholding the law. It's just that sometimes it's not the laws you like."

"Riiiight." Lucy shook her head. "This might sound like an odd question, but do you know anything about the law around art?"

"Sure, I've dabbled. A sales contract here, an authentication there. You'd be amazed at how many of my clients are into that stuff."

"I'm not sure I would. Still, I might have some business for you if you're interested. A friend who needs legal advice around an art show."

Gruffbar hesitated. He didn't want any more attention from a Silver Griffin than he could avoid, but he also needed the work.

"All right," he reluctantly agreed as he helped bundle Johnny into the back seat of Lucy's car. "Give me a call. We can set up an appointment."

CHAPTER ELEVEN

Lucy glanced at the clock on the dashboard as she headed northwest out of Skid Row. She was supposed to be heading for Ashley's school for a meeting, and now she was going to be late, no way for a responsible member of the PTA to behave. She wondered if she could leave Johnny the tattoo guy in the back of her car to sleep off the after-effects of his magical adventure, but that didn't feel like a very responsible way to behave either. Instead, she used the voice control on her phone to make a call to Jackie.

"Are you busy?" Lucy asked.

"When you ask like that, I wish I could say yes," Jackie replied. "What is it?"

"I have a prisoner who needs taking in for questioning, but I'm already late for a PTA meeting. Is there any chance we can meet up so you can deal with him?"

"Seriously, you're slacking off work for the sake of the PTA? I'm pretty sure they can arrange a bake sale without you."

"I have cookies…"

"Tempting, but I have work to do."

"Kelly's on the PTA, and if I'm late, she'll get everything her way."

"Why didn't you start with that? I'm on the subway already, will hop off at the next station. You can meet me at the Starbucks on South Vermont."

"Thanks, Jackie. You're a lifesaver."

A few minutes later, Lucy pulled up outside the Starbucks. In the back of the car, Johnny was sitting up straight, staring around in a dazed way.

"What are you doing?" he asked. "You can't just take me to...to wherever you're taking me."

"Actually, I can, ever since you got that tattoo." Lucy pointed her wand at him, and sparks flew around the end. "Now, do you want to come quietly, or do you want to see how much more I can do to you?"

Johnny instinctively clutched his tender crotch. "I'll come quietly."

"Good. Then in we go."

Lucy grabbed her Batman travel mug and headed into the Starbucks, Johnny trailing after her. While they waited for Jackie, she joined the short queue, and a minute later was at the front.

"Tea, please," she said.

"And for him?" The barista nodded at Johnny.

Lucy looked at the poor man, trying hard not to clutch his aching groin in public.

"Iced coffee, I think," she said. "Something good and numbing. And can we have a triple shot cappuccino for my other friend?"

Jackie appeared from the back of the coffee shop, a

backpack slung over her shoulder.

"You're lucky I was in the area," she said.

"You're an absolute star." Lucy beamed. "This lad got a magical tattoo and trashed a bar. He can tell you all about it, including where he got the tattoo, can't you mate?"

Johnny nodded. "Yes, ma'am."

"Good lad." Lucy grabbed her mug of tea off the counter and swiped her card to make a payment. "I've got to dash, but your drinks are on the way."

"Hold on there. You said there were cookies," Jackie said.

"Oh, yes, of course." Lucy held out a paper bag. "Sorry there aren't more, but I did bake them for the PTA."

"Those smell good," Johnny said.

"Don't push your luck."

Lucy rushed back out, got into her car, and headed north. The after-school traffic rush was underway, and it took her longer than it should have to reach Valentine Heights Elementary. Even with a cup of tea to soothe her along the way, she was fidgeting with impatience by the time she reached the school.

She parked the car and headed in, carrying her tea in one hand and a big box of oatmeal cookies in the other.

"Hi, Annie," she said, stopping at the front desk. "Do you know where the PTA is meeting today?"

"Principal's office," replied the school's receptionist and admin worker. "I suspect they've already started. Kelly arrived fifteen minutes ago, and she had her bossy face on."

"Thanks for the warning." Lucy took a couple of cookies out of the box and placed them in front of Annie. "Enjoy!"

Sure enough, when she reached Principal Reyes' office, the meeting was already underway. Nearly a dozen people crowded the room, but Lucy squeezed into a chair at one side.

"Sorry I'm late," she said. "I got delayed by a work thing."

Kelly glared daggers at her, but Reyes was far more cordial.

"I totally understand," he said. "I was almost late myself, helping the first graders plant trees in the schoolyard."

"I know it's not much compensation for your time, but I brought cookies." Lucy took the lid off the box and held it out. The rush of grabbing hands and appreciative noises reassured her that this was all the compensation anyone would need to forgive her tardiness.

"Now you're all here, we can get onto the main topic of business," Reyes said. "I want to invest in some new science equipment. It's one of the big areas where the kids could benefit from improvements in their lessons, but it's not as glamorous as sports, so we can't get sponsorship like we can for the teams. I was hoping that you ladies and gentlemen could come up with some fundraising ideas."

"I suggest a cocktail evening," Kelly said. "A chance for parents to dress up nicely and mingle. We can have cocktails themed around different subjects, served by the staff and PTA. I'd be happy to play hostess and keep things moving."

"Interesting." Reyes made a note. "Do you think many of our parents would go for that? It sounds a bit formal."

"That's part of the appeal. Who doesn't want a chance to do something different, to dress up like you're living the high life? We normally see each other dressed down to pick up the kids, so this would be extra special."

Kelly's outfit of a creaseless suit and high heels that matched her makeup was nowhere near what Lucy considered dressing down, but that didn't mean the idea was inherently bad. Still, she wondered if something else might suit parents like her.

"How about a sponsored run?" she suggested. "I've seen other schools do it. Lots of people go running these days, and even the ones that don't can join in. We could have a part with the kids and let them get the better of us."

That got a few chuckles as parents and teachers imagined racing against the smaller children.

"Like you said, other schools have done it already," Kelly said. "Lots of them. Do we want to do something that's the same as everyone else?"

"If it raises funds, I'm okay with that." Reyes made another note. "This is about the science, not the publicity."

"It can be both. If we do something that stands out, we can get some interest in the local press. That way, we might even get some sponsorship money for science after all, as well as what we raise ourselves."

Reyes tipped his head back and looked at the ceiling. "Good point. All right, what else could we try?"

Lucy looked around. No one else seemed to have any suggestions, and Kelly had a determined look that said she was set on making her cocktail night happen. Perhaps she thought it was the sort of high society idea that would impress the other wives at Max's law firm.

"Why not something for the kids?" Lucy said. "Like a read-a-thon. We could sponsor them based on the number of pages they read in a week, and it would be good publicity because it's helping with literacy as well as making money."

"I like the literacy angle," Reyes said. "That might help us with reports on the school as well."

"Hm." Kelly tapped a pen against her notebook. "Do we really want to put the pressure of fundraising onto the kids? I mean, we're supposed to be providing for them, not making them pay their way."

"I don't think that's what it's about," Lucy said.

"But it might be how it looks."

Reyes tipped his head back and gazed upward again. "I'm not great at understanding the press, but I worry you might be right." He leaned forward and made another note. "Let's call that Plan B. Any other options?"

"An art class?" Lucy asked. She'd tried for options she thought might be popular, so why not go for one she would enjoy? "We could get one of the teachers to lead it and display some of the pictures at the end, so the kids see that education is for adults too."

"Really, you think we'll raise money by setting home-work for everyone?" Kelly shook her head. "Come on, Lucy, this is supposed to be fun."

Lucy glared at Kelly. The other woman seemed set on shooting down every idea she had. She might as well not be here for all the good her presence was doing.

Mary Holmes, Ashley's teacher and the staff representa-tive on the PTA, raised her hand.

"You have an idea, Mary?" Reyes asked.

"Not one of my own," Mary said. "But how about if we mix two of the ideas we've heard already. If we combine the art class with the cocktail evening, we could run one of those paint and sip sessions, where people make art while drinking and chatting. If we make dressing up optional, it could appeal to parents who want a more relaxed evening, as well as those who want to make a special effort. The art would give everyone something in common to talk about."

"I like it," Reyes said. "Those classes are getting popular, so we might even get money out of people who aren't parents here. And a school providing adult education for the parents makes for good publicity, even if that education comes with a martini on the side." He grinned. "What do the rest of you think?"

Relieved of the pressure to come up with more ideas, the others all nodded enthusiastically except for Kelly, who sat glaring at Lucy. She couldn't complain that she hadn't gotten the evening out she was after, but she clearly felt that her high-class cocktail night was going to be ruined by all the art.

Let her take that attitude, Lucy thought. This would be a fun evening for everyone, and with any luck, a great source of new science equipment.

She turned her sweetest, most cooperative smile toward Reyes. "What would you like us to do?"

CHAPTER TWELVE

After the meeting, Lucy went to the room where Ashley was waiting, along with several other kids with parents on the PTA. The school had arranged for a teacher to supervise them, to make it easier for parents to attend.

"Has she behaved herself?" Lucy asked with a wink and a smile. Ashley had never yet got into trouble for bad behavior.

"It was absolute carnage." The teacher grinned and shook his head. "She was racing around the place, kicking other kids' toys over, and threatening to bite the head off the class hamster. Honestly, I don't know how you tolerate her."

"I didn't do any of that!" Ashley said indignantly.

"Really?" Lucy asked. "Well, you can tell me what you did do on the way home."

They headed out to the SUV and down the road to Eddie's nursery. Along the way, Ashley talked about the lessons she'd had that day and what she had learned while the rest of the class studied topics she already knew.

"Would you like it more if we sent you to another school?" Lucy asked. "One with smarter kids and more challenging lessons?"

Ashley contemplated this for a moment, sucking on the tip of her finger as she watched the world go by outside the car window. Then she shook her head.

"I can challenge myself wherever I am. This way, I get to stay with my friends and learn about what interests me, in between the things they're talking about."

Lucy laughed. "I can't argue with that."

Eddie was on the steps of his nursery when they arrived, a member of staff waiting with him. He tottered over with a fistful of drawings and hugged Lucy around her legs.

"I drawed dinosaurs," he announced.

"A lot of dinosaurs," the staff member added. "I've never seen so many, and all really good."

"That's fantastic," Lucy said. "Why don't you get into the car and show them to Ashley?"

Enthusiastic talk about dinosaurs, robots, and colors filled the rest of the journey home, those being Eddie's current main obsessions. Lucy missed the superhero phase but had to admit that was mostly because it was also her interest, and it was important for her son to grow beyond her tastes. Maybe he would get back into Superman someday soon.

They pulled into the driveway, and everybody climbed out, Eddie scattering dinosaur pictures behind him like a trail of brightly colored leaves. Buddy met them at the front door, yapping and bouncing up and down at the sight of so many of his humans.

"Who's a good boy?" Lucy patted him on the head.

"Buddy a good boy." Eddie hugged the dog, who then followed him into the living room. Eddie spread his pictures across the floor and started explaining them to anyone who would listen while Ashley pulled her silvery robot strings out of her bag and started on her latest experiment.

Lucy headed into the kitchen to make herself a cup of tea and contemplate the possibilities for dinner. As she rummaged through the cupboards, she realized that they were out of bread, which they would need for sandwiches the next day. She wouldn't have a chance to get to the shops now, but maybe she could bake some of her own. Then, as she opened the fridge, she noticed the note she had left there for herself: "Al's cake."

Suddenly there was a lot more than dinner to cook and only so much time to do it. Maybe she should call in reinforcements.

"Kids," she called. "Would anyone like to do some baking?"

Eddie and Ashley both appeared in the doorway with excited looks on their faces.

"Cookies?" Eddie asked.

"Not cookies. I want to make a birthday cake for Al next door and some bread."

They looked at her uncertainly.

"Baking bread is lovely and soothing. I think you'll enjoy it." They still looked dubious. "And you can lick the spoons once I finish making the cake."

That did it. Both kids grabbed aprons from their hooks on the back of the door and hurried to wash their hands.

Lucy gathered the ingredients from the cupboards and set the oven to preheat, then set two bowls down on the folding table where the kids would work. When their hands were clean and dry, they took their places at the table, eager to begin.

"Here." Lucy tipped an appropriate amount of flour into each of their bowls, then handed Ashley a teaspoon. "One teaspoon each of sugar, salt, and yeast into both of your bowls, then mix it into the flour. Can you do that?"

"Yes." Ashley dipped the spoon into the sugar bag and began the serious business of measuring.

While the kids dealt with their dry ingredients, Lucy got to work on the cake. Al, their next-door neighbor, was such a kind, helpful guy. She didn't want to miss the chance to mark his birthday. She quickly beat together butter and sugar, then whisked the eggs in one at a time.

"How's it going?" she asked.

"All done," Ashley announced.

Eddie held up his hands. "Flour!"

"That's great." Lucy added a little oil to each of their bowls, then placed a jug of warm water between them. "Now, I want you to add water to your flour, a little at a time, mixing it in as you go. You won't need all the water. Just keep adding little bits until everything sticks together, okay?"

"Yes, Mom."

Ashley poured a little water into both bowls, then she and Eddie started mixing again. Lucy kept half an eye on them while she added lemon zest, vanilla, flour, and milk to her bowl and mixed it all thoroughly. By the time she poured her cake mix into a pair of tins, there was no more dry flour in either of the kids' bowls.

"You can stop now," she said. "Let me put these in the oven, then I'll show you the next part."

While the cake started to bake, Lucy examined her children's efforts. Ashley had, through a careful, measured approach, achieved a dough that was just damp enough to hold together. Eddie, inevitably, had gotten carried away and ended up with a mix that was a lot more sticky, verging on runny.

"Brilliantly done, guys." Lucy kissed each of them on the top of their head. "Now it's time to knead the dough. Do you know what that means?"

"It means that we massage and squeeze the dough until it achieves the correct consistency," Ashley said.

"That's right, sweetheart. Why don't I show you on Eddie's?" Lucy reached into Eddie's bowl and started working the dough. It was just solid enough to stand up to the initial kneading, and with a bit of work, it clung together better, though it also clung to her hands. Despite the challenge of the sticky dough, something was soothing about the process, and Lucy relaxed into it, working the bread smoothly and steadily.

"Me, me, me." Eddie reached into the bowl.

"Okay, my little baker. I'll let you two get to work."

Lucy left them to their kneading while she made the buttercream filling and the icing to go on Al's cake. To her surprise, a quiet fell across the kitchen. Even Eddie didn't say a word, caught up in the hypnotic process of rolling the dough back and forth, pressing and squeezing, feeling it strengthen beneath his hands.

Lucy fetched a couple of loaf tins out of the cupboard and set them down on the counter. The bread dough looked almost ready, but she didn't want to disturb the peace of the moment. Instead, she took a wooden skewer and tested her cake, which had cooked through. She took both halves out of the oven and turned them out onto a wire rack to cool.

"I think we've finished with the kneading." She placed the loaf tins on the kids' table. "Can you put it in those, please?"

"Cook now?" Eddie asked as he deposited his dough in a tin.

"Not yet. First, we need to leave it in a warm place to rise. Can you think of anywhere?"

"Cooker?"

"That might be a bit too warm. Remember, we're not cooking yet."

"In the window?" Ashley suggested. "The sunlight will become heat as it comes through and hits the bread."

"Great idea."

Using a chair to reach up, the kids placed their loaves on the counter just inside the window, close to the sink. Lucy draped a towel across them.

"Now, it's time to decorate Al's cake. What do you think it should look like?"

"Dinosaur," Eddie said.

"I'll remember that idea when it's time for your cake, but what is Al interested in?"

"Garden."

"Yes, he does like gardening."

"Fishing," Ashley said. "He goes several times a week."

"Another great idea. So how should we decorate the cake?"

"Trees," Eddie said.

"Fish," Ashley said.

"Flowers."

"Water."

"Spade."

"A rod and line."

"Those are all brilliant ideas." Lucy waved bottles of food coloring. "Why don't we use all of them?"

With the kids' help, she took lumps of icing and mixed them with different colors. Then, while Eddie made icing trees and flowers and Ashley made fish shapes and a slender rod, Lucy magically cooled the two halves of the cake. She layered them together with buttercream and covered it with icing in two colors, half green for the garden, the other blue for water.

Carefully, the kids transferred their decorations onto the cake. Some of the shapes were harder to make out than others—Eddie's trees in particular had a blobby quality—but the love and care they'd poured in were clear.

When it was all assembled, Lucy took a picture for posterity, then took off her apron. "Shall we take this 'round to Al?"

Together, they went out the front of the house and across the driveway, then knocked on Al's door. After a minute, he appeared, gray hair sticking up wildly around his head.

"Hi there, Herons," he said. "What can I do for you?"

"Ready, kids?" Lucy said. "One, two, three…"

Together, they burst into an enthusiastic chorus of "Happy Birthday" before presenting Al with his cake.

"Well, that's great." He smiled and wiped a tear from the corner of his eye. "I wasn't expecting any of this. Why don't you come in and we can all have a slice?"

As they walked in, Eddie took hold of Al's hand.

"We made bread," he said.

"Really? Why don't you tell me all about it."

"Can't yet. It's rising."

CHAPTER THIRTEEN

"This is where he has his office?" Heather stared appalled around the auto repair shop. "And you want me to do business with him?"

Lucy surveyed the busy workshop, where mechanics in stained overalls were working on half a dozen different vehicles, many of them old and battered, seemingly held together as much by wishful thinking as by engineering.

"I was expecting something a little more upmarket," she said, "but it does seem like the perfect place for a dwarf."

"I don't think we should do this." Heather folded her arms. "You told me already that he works with criminals. Now I see that he's in league with polluters as well."

"Gruffbar is many things, some of them awful, but first and foremost, he's a magical lawyer. Not only that, but he understands art and has been doing business successfully in L.A. for years. We can't do much better where lawyers are concerned."

"Then I shouldn't hire a lawyer, and I shouldn't put our art on display."

"You've come this far. Why not hear him out? You can always decide not to hire him if you don't like him."

"Fine." Heather scowled. "Let's get this over with."

Lucy approached one of the mechanics. "Excuse me, do you know where we can find Gruffbar?"

The mechanic turned to shout down the room. "Boss, there's a Scottish lady here to see the dwarf."

"Hey, I'm English, not Scottish."

"I thought Scotland was in England."

"Never, ever say that to a Scot."

"Whatever." The mechanic picked up a wrench and got back to work.

A man lumbered down the workshop toward them, wiping his hands on a rag. He was so huge and looming that Lucy thought he must have some ogre in his ancestry.

"What are you here for?" he asked.

"We have an appointment with Gruffbar. My name's Lucy Heron. This is Heather Fields."

The man looked them over. "You're not cops?"

"No."

"Griffins?"

"I am, but Gruffbar knows that, and it's not why we're here."

"Office is up there." He pointed at a set of iron stairs at the back of the room. "No snooping around anywhere else."

"Of course not." Lucy made a mental note to come back and snoop around when she had the chance to find out what the mechanics might want to hide. Watched by the mechanics, she and Heather headed up the stairs. At the top, an open door let them into an office outfitted with second-hand filing cabinets, threadbare seats, and a battered desk. The only new piece of furniture was the swivel chair in which Gruffbar sat.

"Come in," he said. "Close the door behind you. I keep it open when it's only me here, but clients get privacy."

"Don't you find all that noise distracting?" Lucy gestured toward the *clangs* and *bangs* on the shop floor.

Gruffbar shook his head. "It's soothing. Reminds me of home." He held out his hand. "I'm Gruffbar Steelstrike."

"Heather Fields." There was a swift, firm shake of hands.

"You're the chief of the Tolderai, right?"

"That's right."

"I have to admit that I wouldn't have expected to work for you. My people haven't exactly been good for the trees."

"I'm told that some dwarves appreciate nature."

"I was talking about lawyers." Gruffbar patted the fat pile of paperwork on the corner of his desk. "Why don't you both take a seat and I'll make us a coffee."

While the witches sat, Gruffbar went to the corner of the room and pressed a button on the front of a coffee machine, which started to gurgle, clunk, and whir.

"What do you want?" he asked. "It has pods to make a wide range of different coffees although the cappuccino's missing its froth."

"Those things make masses of waste." Heather scowled as he tossed an empty plastic coffee pod into the waste bin.

"They're also marvels of modern ingenuity." Gruffbar looked around. "Seriously, do you not want anything?"

"No."

"I'll have tea if you've got it."

"Tea, tea, tea..." Gruffbar looked down the controls. "No, sorry. Maybe it's not so marvelous." He switched the machine off and returned to his seat behind the desk. "So much for that. Let's get down to business. What can I do for you?"

Seeing Heather's expression, Lucy decided that it was better if she took the lead.

"An art gallery owner has asked to display some Tolderai artifacts," she said. "Grave goods that the tribe recently uncovered. Heather is considering the offer, but only if she can ensure that the Tolderai retain control over how the artifacts are displayed, that they're well protected, and that the tribe gets properly paid."

"Pay is the least important part," Heather said. "What matters is controlling the artifacts and making sure they're safe."

"I understand." Gruffbar took out a fountain pen and started scribbling notes. "Still, even if you're not bothered about the money now, it's worth planning for. You don't want to see someone else making a fortune off your people later when you're not getting a dime."

Heather nodded slowly. "That makes sense."

"So, your concerns around control. You want a contract that gives you veto powers over how the artifact is displayed?"

"We can have that?"

"Of course."

"Then yes."

"You'll probably want some clauses around publicity materials for the show as well. That's a big area for loopholes. Do you want to have active input on those materials, or just veto powers again?"

Heather shrugged. "I don't know. How do I best control how they present the artifacts?"

"Do you know anything about advertising, PR, or design work?"

"No."

"Then you do it through a veto clause and trust that the gallery owner knows what they're doing. Who is the gallery owner?"

"Some elf."

"Penley ap Gawain," Lucy said. "He has a gallery on—"

"I know Penley. Never worked for him, so there's no conflict of interest here, but I've worked with clients who worked with him."

"I thought Penley's business was all aboveboard," Lucy said.

"No need to sound so disappointed. If all my work was for evil overlords and criminal masterminds, I'd never pay the bills. Sometimes I do work for honest citizens too." He smiled at them. "Unless there's something you're not telling me about yourselves." He turned his attention to Heather. "Do you have any other concerns?"

"Should I?"

"Good question." Gruffbar sat back and drummed his fingers on the desk. "You might want to include a clause around offers to buy your work."

"The artifacts aren't for sale."

"I guessed that, but this is an opportunity for you to prepare yourself in case of future problems. If Penley has to tell you the details of any offers, you can find out who's interested in your artifacts. Then, if someone tries to steal them later, you'll know where to start looking."

The faintest hint of a smile caught the corner of Heather's mouth. "I like that."

"Of course you do. And if Penley's reward for this is a percentage on any sale, but you don't plan ever to sell, then he'll end up gathering your intelligence for free."

"Maybe I misjudged you, dwarf," Heather said. "You might not be as bad as your coffee machine."

"That might be the worst compliment I've ever received, but I'll take it." He set his pen down. "So, you know what I can do for you. I imagine you'll need time to decide if I'm the right lawyer for the job."

"We can't afford much time," Lucy said. "Penley wants to get the artifacts into his gallery yesterday."

"I've decided," Heather said. "I'll hire you."

"You haven't even heard my fees yet."

"I told you, this isn't about the money."

"Law is always about the money." Gruffbar slid a contract across the desk. "You'll find that my fees are very reasonable for the quality of service I provide. Give that a read, sign on the line, and Agent Heron can witness your signature."

They quietly sat while Heather read through the contract with Gruffbar, then handed it to Lucy for a second opinion. The sound of mechanics at work drifted up from the workshop below: banging, clanging, the occasional curse.

"What happens next?" Heather asked once she had signed the contract.

"Next, I talk to Penley and his lawyer. Penley has the

money for round-the-clock legal services, so if he wants to make this happen quickly, we might have a contract for you by tomorrow."

"That seems very fast."

"Nothing can stand between a rich magical and the things they want, not even the slow-moving cogwheels of the law." Gruffbar signed the contract, handed one copy to Heather, and put the other carefully away in a drawer. "I'm curious, these grave goods, what are they?"

"There are several things. Wands, ornaments, a scrying bowl."

"Earthenware scrying bowl?"

"I think so. It's old, quite thick clay, with a colored layer over it."

"What sort of glaze?"

Heather shrugged. "Green?"

Gruffbar shook his head. "I'm a lawyer, not a potter, but you're making me look like an expert in the art. I thought you'd know more about your ancestral artifacts."

"I know that they connect me to my ancestors, that they keep alive a tradition stretching back centuries. That is enough."

"I can appreciate that attitude. Is there any chance I could see the artifacts? Curiosity of a craftsman, you understand, even if I work with different materials."

"Perhaps you could come to the gallery opening?" Lucy suggested. "I'm sure we could persuade Penley to give you a ticket in return for your good work in negotiating this deal."

"Good thinking," Gruffbar said. "You should have been

a lawyer, Agent Heron. You're wasted on the Silver Griffins."

Lucy and Heather headed out of the office, leaving Gruffbar to call Penley and begin negotiations. As they crossed the garage floor, the big mechanic watched them warily.

"You were right," Heather said as they stepped out into the street. "That was worth doing. I think the dwarf will do well."

Lucy laughed. "I'm starting to like him too."

"Oh, I don't like him, and I certainly don't trust him. But if I'm going to have a lawyer, I want one who understands the way bad people think. It's easier to do that when you're one of them."

CHAPTER FOURTEEN

Ellis and Sarah sat at a window table in a Japanese restaurant on Sunset Boulevard, picking at the last of the pickles from a shared bowl.

"That was delicious," Sarah said. "Thank you."

"Thanks go to you for finding us another fine place to eat." Ellis looked down at the few remaining crumbs from his eggplant katsu sandwich. "You full from your salad, or can I interest you in a pastry?"

Sarah laughed. "You mean that you're interested in a pastry, but ordering for both of us will give you an excuse."

"So you don't want a chocolate croissant?"

"I'm not saying that."

"Good, because I might have ordered them already."

One of the serving staff appeared with fresh coffee and a plate of pastries. "These are for you, right?"

"Oh, yes."

Once they were alone again, Sarah took a bite of the croissant. Crisp pastry flaked away to reveal melting chocolate within.

"Mm." She licked her lips. "So good." She reached across the table to take Ellis's hand. "Almost as good as having you in L.A. again."

"How could I resist when this city has so much to offer?" He smiled at her. "I mean, who doesn't love eggplant sandwiches."

"I suppose you have to get back to work soon? There must be some magical monster out there, waiting for you to track it down."

"There always is, but I'm not in a rush today."

"Good, because I'd like to keep you to myself for a little longer." She squeezed his hand. "For a lot longer, in fact."

"Guess I'll have to let the dragons run rampant for a while." He leaned across the table and kissed her. "They need the exercise."

"So what are you in L.A. for this time?"

"I can't exactly tell you that."

"Ooh, something secret!"

"Not exactly." Ellis took a deep breath, psyching himself up to take a risk. "In fact, if you have time, there's a surprise I'd like to share."

"Really?" Sarah raised an eyebrow. "How mysterious."

Intrigued as much by Ellis's demeanor as by his words, Sarah rapidly finished off her coffee and croissant, then followed him out of the restaurant. They walked west along Sunset, through a stream of people hurrying back to work after lunch, then off into a residential area at the south end of Silver Lake.

"Walking me home won't be much of a surprise," Sarah said. "Not after the last few times." She squeezed his hand. "Not that I'm complaining."

"We're not going that far," Ellis said. "At least, not yet."

He stopped in front of one of the houses, a two-story place with a gently sloping roof and a palm tree protruding from the small, overgrown front yard. He pulled a set of keys from his pocket and led her up the driveway.

"What is this?" Sarah asked. "They're sending you to Airbnb places now instead of hotels?"

"Not exactly."

Ellis unlocked the front door and led her in.

The house was unfurnished and largely uncarpeted. Paint was peeling from dusty walls, and the floor looked like no one had cleaned it since the start of the millennium.

"Wow, you take me to all the most romantic places," Sarah said. "What next, dinner at the dump?" Then she noticed Ellis's suitcase sitting in the corner of the living room, one pristine, well-kept thing amid the grime and neglect. No, not one, two suitcases, and his hand luggage. He had come with more baggage than usual. "Wait, you are staying here? Surely they can do better. I know that budgets are tight, but this is absurd."

Ellis drew a deep breath.

"Actually, I found this place myself."

"Really?" Sarah looked around. "But why? I know the hotels they put you in are usually pretty generic, but there's a difference between finding somewhere with character and finding somewhere abandoned."

"I wanted somewhere I could stay a little while longer. Somewhere I could rent for myself instead of the Griffins putting me up. Somewhere close to you."

"Oh." Sarah looked around the house with new eyes. Now she felt bad for being so negative about it. "It's got a lot of potential. Plenty of space. I'm sure it will look lovely once you clean it up." She turned to him again, still trying to get a grip on the situation. "So you'd move your stuff into this place and come back here between missions?"

"My things are already here." He pointed at the suitcases.

"That's all you have?"

"I ain't exactly accumulated a lot of belongings down the years. They don't go well with the roaming lifestyle."

The way he talked about that lifestyle brought up swelling sadness in Sarah. She loved her life in L.A., all her friends and colleagues, the familiar places and activities. She knew that Ellis enjoyed working around the country, but she still felt like he had missed out on something, and perhaps now he realized that he'd been missing out too.

She wrapped her arms around him and hugged him tightly. His chest swelled as he drew another deep breath.

"About those missions..." He looked at her nervously. "How would you feel if I was around here all the time, working in L.A. instead of hopping here, there, and everywhere?"

"That would be amazing!"

"Glad to hear you say that because I've talked to Applegate, Lucy's boss, and he's arranging the transfer."

"You idiot!" Sarah slapped him lightly on the arm. "Why didn't you tell me you were planning all this?"

Ellis blushed and shrugged.

"Guess I wasn't sure if it would work out, so I didn't want to get your hopes up. Truth be told, I didn't know for sure how you'd react. You're used to me coming to town every once in a while, a few days of excitement, and I'm gone again. You might not have wanted me here full time."

"Of course I do." She kissed him. "I can't believe you ever doubted it."

Ellis laughed, a sound that was still as much nervousness as relief.

"I guess that, after Maria, I ain't good at believing I can judge these things right, that my dreams can come true."

"Well, this one can."

They kissed again, and for a few long, wonderful minutes, the rest of the world faded away. At last, they came up for air.

"So, are you going to show me around?" Sarah said.

"There ain't much to show yet." Ellis gestured through a doorway. "Kitchen and dining room in there. That's gonna be the very first thing I clean up."

He led her up the stairs and around the house, showing her each room in turn. The place was more than big enough for a man living on his own and all as run down as that first room.

"It ain't much." Ellis stood in the middle of the master bedroom. "I'm still excited. It's the first time I'll have a place I can call my own."

"I'm sure it's going to be lovely," Sarah said. "But won't this mean that your landlord gets a lot of work out of you for free? I mean, if you clean and decorate, then move on, he gets a pretty sweet deal."

"That's how I got the rent so low. It's a sort of package deal: I get the place decent so he doesn't have to. He's planning to sell, and as well as getting the place ready, I get first refusal on buying it further down the line."

"So this really could end up being yours?"

"If I want it, yep." He smiled at her. "If you ain't sick of having me in L.A. by then."

"I could never get sick of that."

They headed back downstairs to where Ellis's luggage was waiting. He opened one of the suitcases and took out a bottle of champagne, peeled off the foil, and popped the cork off. It bounced off the wall and landed in the corner of the room, kicking up a cloud of dust.

"I ain't got no glasses yet, but I figured we should celebrate."

"Allow me." Sarah pulled out her wand and magicked up a pair of champagne flutes. Ellis poured two glasses.

"Here's to living near you."

"To your new home."

They *clinked* glasses, sipped, and burst out laughing as they caught each other's eyes.

"I can't believe that this is real," Sarah said.

"Me neither, and I'm the one who's been planning it." Ellis walked over to the kitchen, set his glass down, and peered into one of the cupboards. "I should clean this place up if I'm gonna cook dinner later. I'm not used to doing that for myself."

"You're not planning on staying here tonight, are you?" Sarah asked, incredulous.

"Of course."

"You don't even have a bed!"

"It's the first night I've got this place. That's special. I want to mark the occasion."

"Wasn't champagne enough?"

Ellis shook his head. "This is me putting down roots for

the first time in a very long while. I've got to start like I mean to go on, treating this place like it really is home." He patted the kitchen counter. "Ain't that right, old girl?"

Sarah gave an affectionate laugh. "I have an old camping mattress and a big sleeping bag. That should keep us comfortable enough for one night."

"Us?"

"Like you said, this is a special occasion, and I want to be here to help you celebrate." She stepped close and looked up into his eyes. They sparkled with excitement that she could feel matched inside her. "I love you, Ellis."

He smiled and wrapped his arms around her. "I love you too."

CHAPTER FIFTEEN

A few streets over from the Japanese restaurant, Lucy and Jackie were sitting on a bench beside Echo Park Lake, eating sandwiches and watching the world go by.

"I can't believe you made me a packed lunch." Jackie brushed crumbs from her t-shirt.

"Don't get too used to it. I'm not your mum. I'm not going to make them every day."

"My mom never made me sandwiches. She was too busy fighting magical crime."

"I'm sure she made them sometimes."

"Nope." Jackie shook her head. "Got the nanny to make them some days, but not her."

"Oh, sweetheart!" Lucy put a hand on Jackie's shoulder. "That's so sad."

"Really?" Jackie shrugged. "Didn't seem that way to me at the time. It was how I expected a mom to be."

"That makes it even sadder."

"Well, now I've got you. I can belatedly catch up on

mom-made sandwiches, and they're great. Where did you find this bread?"

"Eddie made this batch."

"You've started use child labor in the kitchen? I approve. Kids have to be good for something."

"Just be glad it wasn't all down to him, or you'd have dinosaur-shaped sandwiches."

"I'd be cool with that." Jackie pulled the slices of bread apart and flapped them about like the two halves of a mouth. "Roar, I am breadosaurus rex. Fear my wrath!"

A pigeon fluttered down across the lake and landed on the path in front of them.

"You looking for a feed?" Jackie shook her head. "Sorry, man, normally you'd be in luck, but this Eddie bread is too delicious to share."

"I think he's brought his lunch." Lucy set her sandwich aside and held out a hand. Once the pigeon had hopped on, she untied the message strapped to its leg and unrolled the strip of paper. "Message from Dispatch, there's another magical street painting causing trouble down at the cathedral. We've got to go."

Jackie tossed away the last crusts of her sandwich. The pigeon looked at them with interest but hopped the other way as the message paper disintegrated into a heap of juicy, wriggling worms.

The witches jumped into Lucy's vehicle and drove off down the street. They turned left just after the 101 and drove down West Temple Street until they arrived in front of the Cathedral of Our Lady of the Angels.

Our Lady of the Angels was an imposing building, with

its sharp angles and towering walls of sand-colored concrete. To Lucy, raised with the medieval monuments of England, it always felt strange to see such a building given the title of cathedral. Growing up, she had wandered around the likes of York Minster, with its ancient carvings and gray stones worn to soft edges by centuries of rain and wind. Nothing in modernist concrete could match that gothic style, which she had long associated with faith and mystery.

But Our Lady of the Angels was awe-inspiring in its way. From the rows of bells hanging on the roadside wall to the angular roofs and the sleek lines of the nave, it spoke to a modern sort of faith. This was a suitable home for God in an age of digital platforms and self-driving cars, and its sheer imposing immensity could match anything the Old World offered.

To Lucy's surprise, the cathedral grounds had been closed, with priests and volunteers standing at the entrance points, blocking the way in.

"Looks like Father Christopher got here ahead of us," Jackie said.

"Father Christopher?"

"You'll see."

Jackie approached one of the priests. After a swift whispered conversation, the priest pulled a phone from his vestments, made a brief call, then gestured for Jackie and Lucy to go inside.

"I didn't think you were religious," Lucy said.

"I'm not."

"Then how do they know you?"

"Partly family connections, partly work. Somebody has to cover the holy beat, and apparently important people feel reassured when the Silver Griffin has the name of Kowal."

Lucy laughed. "You're the cathedral's pet Griffin? Doesn't that clash with...you know..."

"They don't ask about my sexuality. I don't ask about their scandals. Working with people in power is the same anywhere, from DC to the Vatican: a certain level of hypocrisy is considered polite. Besides, Christopher's a decent dude, for someone who thinks I'm going to Hell."

A short-haired man in a black cassock strode toward them from the main cathedral building.

"Agent Kowal, good of you to come so quickly."

"Just doing my job. Father Christopher, this is Agent Lucy Heron, badge number 485."

"Pleased to meet you." Christopher gestured along the front of the building. "It's this way."

He led toward an open-air shrine, and Lucy assumed that they would have to clear out a nest of trolls or other magicals that had taken up residence, but instead, Christopher pointed at the concrete wall facing the shrine.

"Bad enough that anyone would vandalize a religious building," he said, "But then there's this."

Someone had spray-painted a mural across the side of the building. In the upper left hand, it showed something like a classical vision of Heaven, but with the angels playing on synthesizers and mixing desks instead of harps and trumpets. The lower right was Hell, where the devils were forcing inmates to stare at reality shows, and social media feeds. In the middle, a priest stood between an angel and a demon. He was shaking hands with both.

It wasn't exactly subtle, but it was well-executed. Lucy

admired the boldness of the caricatures and the control in the use of paint.

"We sent a cleaning crew to try to get rid of it before the public arrived, but then…"

Christopher picked up a broom lying near the base of the wall and waved it toward the image. The moment it got close, the angel and the demon at the center of the painting sprang to life. The demon grabbed the end of the broom, which burst into flames, then the angel took hold of it and flung the fiery thing at the shrine opposite.

Lucy pulled out her wand and pointed it at the burning broom. "Partum aqua."

A spray of water doused the flames before they could do any harm.

"See?" Christopher shook his head. "Three of our janitorial staff now need medical treatment, and the good Lord only knows how we'll explain this to them. It's a good thing I was on duty, or this might have been on the TV already, with a whole mob of priests lining up to exorcise it."

"Any idea who did it?" Jackie asked. "You must have security cameras around here."

"Whoever it was, they were smart enough to circumvent our security and to keep their face hidden as long as they were on camera. We have some footage of a short, hooded figure with a stepladder, and that's the most likely suspect, but it's not exactly Fort Knox around here."

"Send us the footage when we finish here. With any luck, we can track the artist down and stop this happening again."

"This might help." Lucy leaned in closer with her

camera out to take a picture of a signature near the bottom corner of the painting. As she got close, the angel and demon loomed out of the image again. A fiery hand grabbed hold of Lucy's neck, while a halo knocked the camera from her hand.

"Jackie!" she gasped as she grabbed at the burning fingers clenched around her throat.

"Renuo!" Jackie waved her wand.

The priest in the painting held out his hand, and magic flashed around it, blocking Jackie's counterspell.

"Oh, come on!" she exclaimed. "Who gives magical powers to a spell?"

The demon had emerged fully from the picture and was rising into the air on wings of fire, its hand tightening around Lucy's throat as it lifted her above the others' heads. Unable to breathe, she struggled to muster any kind of magic, never mind a coherent spell. In desperation, she brought her legs up, then slammed her feet into the demon's belly. The force of the blow knocked the creature back and broke its grip. She fell to the concrete below, knocking the breath out of her chest, while the demon swooped around, found its bearings, and came in for a second attack.

"Partum aqua," she croaked.

Water shot from her wand, extinguishing the fire that was the demon's wings. It fell to the ground, hissing and steaming.

Jackie and Lucy both pointed their wands at the painting and called in unison.

"Renuo!"

The painted priest caught one of the counterspells, but

the other one got through. There was a rippling in the air as it hit the painting, magic and antimagic annihilating each other. Then the priest and the angel collapsed back into two dimensions, while the demon fell to the ground where it stood, reduced to nothing but a smear of red and black paint.

"Is that it?" Father Christopher asked. "Is it safe now?"

"Should be," Jackie said.

"Amazing. The miracles our Lord works through your hands."

"Pretty sure this one had nothing to do with Him, Father."

"And I am certain that you are wrong."

Jackie and Christopher looked at each other and laughed. Meanwhile, Lucy had picked up her phone again. The screen had survived its angelic battering. She took a few photos of the whole mural, now missing its demon, and wished that she had managed to get a shot when it was complete. Soon, this would be gone, and the world would be a little poorer for it. If only the artist didn't insist on painting in places where they shouldn't or wielding magic where others should never see it.

She moved in closer and took a picture of the signature at the bottom corner.

"VX," she said, reading that signature. "Does that mean anything to you?"

Jackie shook her head. "If you don't know an art thing, I'm certainly not going to. How about you, Father? Has the church pissed off any VX's recently?"

The priest shook his head. "Not that I'm aware of, but God's work is not quiet. Some people will blame the institution for the failings of its rotten parts, however hard we deal with them. Of course, there are also those who will tell us that we are misguided purely on principle."

"You're going to blame this on Lutherans?"

"Not this time, but if I see anyone nailing their theses to the cathedral doors, I'll be sure to let you know." He took out his phone. "I'd better get the cleaners in again, then go tell the other priests to put their holy water and exorcising bells away."

As he walked off, Lucy looked up at the painting one last time.

"We need to track down this VX," she said.

"You looking to commission something?" Jackie asked, seeing her friend's wistful expression.

"Sadly, no. This is one artist we need to discourage from public exhibitions at least."

CHAPTER SIXTEEN

Dylan pointed his wand down the practice room and drew a deep breath. It was always hardest to control a new spell in moments like this. Not at the very beginning, when it was fresh and fragile, the instructions recently etched across his mind, but in the time immediately afterward, when he was trying to master it, to make the movements instinctive. He had learned the magic's outline, but it was still something new and difficult, something that regularly went wrong. That was frustrating, and his instinctive response was to tackle it with brute force and ram as much power as possible through the spell and make it work.

His instincts were wrong.

"That's it," Twylan encouraged, standing next to him at the end of the practice room. "Slow. Controlled. A little at a time."

Dylan chanted the spell again, quietly, and shifted the tip of his wand an inch. A few feet from him, something appeared in the air. At first, it was only a gray blob, but as the moments passed and Dylan focused on the spell, more specific shapes emerged. Legs extended from underneath, a head at the front, two broad ears, and a trunk. Details appeared: the wrinkles of its skin, the alertness of its eyes, the small tail twitching at the rear. At last, an elephant stood in front of them, looking silently around.

"Very good," Twylan said. "You're really getting the hang of illusions. Right, Siltor?"

Siltor the elf pushed off from the wall where he had been leaning and went to examine the elephant more closely.

"It didn't burst apart this time, so that's an improvement." He peered at the animal's head. "Seriously though, this is cool work."

He touched the elephant, and his hand passed through the skin of the illusion. He stood like that for a long moment, looking at the pattern of wrinkles as his fingers broke them up.

"You've really got the texture," he continued. "Did you go to the zoo to check out the elephants?"

"I got my brother to turn into one and studied him. He doesn't need to understand the details to get his animals right. It just sort of happens."

It was the first time Dylan had ever knowingly been jealous of Eddie. Normally, his kid brother's antics and abilities ran along a spectrum from amusing to annoying, and Dylan didn't give much thought to how hard it would be to transform the way he did. Now, having spent a week trying to perfect a single animal illusion, he had a whole new appreciation for what was involved.

"That's pretty awesome too. I might come and ask your brother next time I'm working on a tricky animal." Siltor stretched his long arms, fingertips almost brushing a light on the ceiling of the underground practice room. "All right, next up is working on sound."

"I got Eddie to make some elephant noises, so I think I know what I'm aiming for."

"That's cool, but it's not what I want to start with. Before you add sounds, we need to take one away."

Dylan looked at Siltor in puzzlement. He was incredibly grateful to Twylan for bringing along a specialist in illusions to help him train and to Siltor for taking the time, but some of the things he said seemed a little odd, and this was one of them.

"How can we take a sound away when the elephant isn't making any yet?"

"Not the sound from the elephant, the sound from you." Siltor pointed at his mouth. "The sound of the spell."

"Oh!"

"For an illusion to have its full effect, you often need to cast it without making any noise. That's especially true if you're trying to convince people it's real. So, you need to cast without saying the words out loud."

"How do I do that?"

Dylan let the magic he had summoned disperse, and the elephant disappeared from the middle of the room.

"A step at a time. First, you cast the spell while speaking the vocal really quietly. Then you do it while moving your mouth as if you were speaking, but without the breath coming out. Then you pay attention to how the magic feels when your mouth is moving, and you sort of…" Siltor hesitated, waving his hands in the air. "I don't know, it's hard to describe, but you sort of learn how to make that pattern work through the power of your mind."

"That sounds difficult."

"It is, and you have to practice it for every illusion you want to perform silently. After a while, you get an idea of how it works, and it starts to become instinctive. Like anything else with magic, I guess."

"So I should try making the elephant with a whisper now?"

"The elephant, or anything else you're comfortable with. Just think about—"

"Hey, Dylan!" someone shouted down one of the tunnels. "Are you around?"

"Through here," Dylan replied. He looked sheepishly at Siltor and Twylan. "Sorry, I forgot that we were practicing when I said my friends could come over."

Lance moonwalked into the room, then stopped and raised an eyebrow. Behind him came Sofia. Both had backpacks on.

"Hi, guys," Dylan said. "Twylan and Siltor are helping me practice my magic. Is it okay if we carry on for a bit?"

"Can we watch?" Lance asked. "Because that would be awesome!" He ran back into one of the other rooms, then reappeared with a pair of beanbags. He dropped them by the wall and flung himself down on one of them. "I still can't believe you have this awesome underground lair and, like, friends who are elves and things." He stared at Twylan. "Your eyes are so cool."

"Don't be a doofus." Sofia punched Lance in the arm, then smiled in a slightly embarrassed way at Twylan. "He's been spending too much time at drama club, where everybody says whatever's on their mind."

"That's okay." Twylan made an effort to restrain the wild magic flaring from her eyes. "I don't see why you shouldn't watch if that's all right with Dylan."

"Sure." Dylan felt a little awkward. After all, Lance and Sofia weren't supposed to know that magic existed, never mind see him practicing it like this. Still, it was too late now to pretend to them that none of it was real when they'd helped him cover up magical spells and artifacts. "Though it might not be very exciting to watch."

"Are you kidding?" Lance said. "You're doing magic! That's super exciting."

"We can work on our homework while we wait." Sofia took a drawing pad and pencil from her bag.

"Homework, at a time like this?" Lance looked appalled.

"We're making comics. That's the coolest homework we've ever had. Do you think I'm going to miss out on an opportunity like that?"

Lance reluctantly took out his paper and pencil, but his attention was elsewhere in the room.

Dylan got back to his illusion. He thought about the spell's elements, the way he spoke the vocal, the way the magic felt flowing through him. He could do this.

He raised his wand and whispered the words of the spell as quietly as he could. Concentrating on that part as well, it took longer to complete the magic. The elephant emerged slowly, shifting from gray blob to full animal over two minutes, but it worked.

"That is so cool!" Lance stared open-mouthed. "Can you make other animals too?"

"It's not real."

Dylan waved his hand through the elephant, and Lance leaped up to join in. He laughed as he charged through the great gray beast.

"It doesn't matter if it's real. You made it appear. This is so cool. Can I have a go?"

Twylan shook her head. "Sorry, but if you're not a wizard you won't have the power to make magic happen."

"Aw." Lance sagged. "Wish I was a wizard."

"Maybe that could be your comic character?" Twylan said. "You, but as a wizard. If you can't make it happen in real life, you can at least tell the story of how it would be."

"Yes..." Lance sat and picked up his pencil. "And I can change other things too, like make myself taller..."

He started sketching.

"Ready for another go?" Twylan asked.

Dylan nodded and dismissed the elephant he had cast, then braced himself for another one. This time, he moved his lips without making a sound. It was strange to imagine making words without actually doing it, and something didn't work right, as the elephant emerged squashed up and covered with pink spots. Dylan blushed at the mess he had made.

"Wow," Siltor said. "I can't believe you got that close on your first try."

That made Dylan brighten up considerably. "This is good?"

"Are you kidding? It's really difficult to adapt your casting like this, and you got it almost perfect the first time." Siltor shook his head. "I don't think you need me here."

Dylan thought the older boy was probably exaggerating to encourage him, but even that felt good. He dismissed the elephant and got ready to cast again.

Siltor went to lean against the wall again, looking down at Sofia's and Lance's art.

"Hey, is that me?" he asked.

"It's an elf," Sofia said. "Inspired by you, but not you."

"I don't have a bow."

"I told you, it's inspired by you, not your life story."

"Is that Twylan?"

They all gathered around to see what Sofia was drawing. She looked up at them defensively with her pad clutched close to her chest.

"What?" she snapped. "Don't you have things to work on?"

"Could I possibly see the pictures?" Twylan asked. "Only if that's okay with you, of course."

Sofia looked at her, then around at the others. Finally, she lowered her pad so they could all see. In the middle of the page, winds whirled around the hands of a tall woman. Fantastical robes were flying around her, and lightning flashed from her eyes.

"It's going to be a fantasy story," Sofia said. "But based on you guys. If that's all right."

"All right? It's the coolest thing ever!" Siltor struck a pose. "You want me to show you some of my magic, so you can get it right?"

"Siltor, we have other things to do." Twylan took his

arm and led him back out into the training room. "We're here to help Dylan. You can show off later."

"Fine, but you have to admit, being the inspiration for comic characters is really cool."

Twylan smiled and glanced back at Sofia. "It really is."

CHAPTER SEVENTEEN

"Who would have thought that this many people would want to make art?" Charlie asked as he and Lucy took seats in the busy classroom. Out in the corridor, more parents were coming in, many of them carrying snacks and bottles of wine for the paint and sip fundraiser.

The evening had proved so popular that the school had opened several classrooms, and every teacher with any art training was supervising a group. Most of the other teachers were directing guests to their classrooms or had turned up as guests themselves, keen to join in the fun.

"I thought they would," Lucy said. "Making art is a lot of fun."

"Smart as well as beautiful." Charlie squeezed her hand. "I lucked out when I found you."

"Yes, you did." She smiled and waved as people she knew walked past. Some had dressed up for the occasion, while others had come casual, like Lucy and Charlie. Everyone seemed to be enjoying themselves, and the room was full of lively chatter.

"Mind if we join you?" Max asked, approaching their table.

"Of course not!" Charlie grinned. "It's great to see you, buddy."

Lucy fought back a frown as Max and Kelly took the remaining seats at their table. Spending time with Kelly wasn't her idea of a relaxing evening out, but she could hardly object. After all, the two were colleagues and had to maintain a civilized relationship, especially now that their husbands were friends.

"You did great work advertising this." She smiled at Kelly.

"Thank you," Kelly said. "Someone had to do the job, and fortunately, I had a little time to spare."

Before Lucy could respond, their teacher called for quiet and started the class.

"Hi, everyone. As many of you know, I'm Mary Holmes. I normally specialize in English, so this evening is going to be interesting, but I promise, I watched three whole videos on how to draw cats before coming here tonight." Everybody laughed. This wasn't going to be as smooth or as informative as a professional class, but no one expected it to be. They were here to have fun and to raise some money for the school.

Mary introduced the exercise, which was to draw a still life based on items in the middle of each table. Then she talked for a few minutes about perspective and texture, the fundamentals of the session. Several parents had their drinks open already, and the slosh of wine pouring from bottles and the chinking of glasses accompanied the lesson.

"That's enough from me for now," Mary said. "Why

don't you all get started, and I'll come around to see how I can help."

At Lucy's table, Max poured them all a glass of very good wine, the sort of thing that high-priced lawyers got a taste for, and they set to work. Paints were available, but initially, they were using pencils to sketch out the outline of their pictures.

Lucy glanced around. She didn't know what artistic skills or experience all the parents had, but she expected that she would be one of the better artists there. That was something she probably shouldn't draw attention to. It wouldn't be appropriate for a PTA member to outshine the others at an event the PTA had organized.

She started drawing the bowl of fruit they had been given, her pencil dancing across the page. With a glass of wine at hand and Charlie for company, this was going to be a lot of fun.

A flash of color caught her eye. Something was moving under a table in the corner of the room. She glanced over and saw a small, humanoid form with bright purple hair disappear into the corridor. A troll. Fortunately, everyone else was too busy chatting, drinking, and drawing to notice.

"Back in a moment," Lucy said quietly to Charlie. "A work thing just came up."

"You want a hand?"

"No, I've got it, but if you see anything odd, let Kelly know."

Lucy headed out into the corridor. It was less noisy than the crowded classroom, but with the chatter from several different classes drifting out, it wasn't anywhere near quiet enough to hear the footsteps of a single troll. With her hand on the wand in her pocket, Lucy peered up and down the hall.

There it was, a flash of movement and that bright purple hair again. The troll was heading down the corridor toward the principal's office.

The door to the office hung open, and chattering voices came from inside, high-pitched and overexcited. Now that she was out of sight of the other parents and teachers, Lucy drew her wand before peering in.

The room was in chaos—papers flung everywhere, books scattered from the shelves, and the chair tipped over next to the window. Principal Reyes lay unconscious on the floor in front of his desk. One troll used him as a trampoline while another sat on his leg eating from a bag of gummy bears. Three others were also in the room, emptying the desk, playing with the keyboard, and jumping between pieces of furniture.

Lucy needed to get control of the situation fast before someone else turned up. She stepped briskly into the room and slammed the door closed behind her, cutting off the trolls' escape route. "What are you lot doing here?"

The trolls looked at her. One of them said something, but she couldn't work out what it meant. Two others braced, then leapt straight at Lucy.

She caught the first one with a freeze spell, and it fell to the floor, encased in a layer of ice. The other one landed on her upper arm and pulled its head back, ready to take a big bite.

"Oh no, you don't, you little blighter!" Lucy hit the troll in the head with the end of her wand. Distracted and frustrated, it looked up with angry eyes, just in time for a stun spell to hit it in the face. Its grip went slack, and it fell to the floor with a *thump*.

The three remaining trolls had gathered behind Reyes's desk, using the furniture as an improvised fortification. From there, they threw anything they could find at Lucy: papers, thumbtacks, rubber bands, a Cape Canaveral souvenir coffee mug. Lucy caught the mug to stop it from breaking and let the rest bounce off her. She had faced far worse assaults, even from trolls.

"You know you shouldn't be here," she said firmly. "I don't want to make any more mess or fuss than I have to. I'm going to give you until the count of three to put your hands in the air and surrender. One, two…"

One of the trolls grabbed hold of the monitor on the desk and pulled it back, ready to fling it at Lucy.

"Stupefacio!" she snapped. The spell hit the troll right between the eyes, stunning it. The monitor slipped from its hands and fell. "Subvolo!"

The monitor stopped an inch above the floor and hung there, levitating in a bubble of magic.

Two trolls remained. One leaped from behind the desk onto the window sill and started scrambling up the blinds, heading for an open window.

"Agglutino." Another wave of Lucy's wand, another burst of magic, and that troll became glued in place. As it struggled to break free, it only got more stuck, tangled and trapped by the blinds.

The final troll stepped out from behind the desk. Its arms were held wide, and Lucy felt a sense of relief. This one was going to surrender.

Except that it wasn't. Instead, it started to grow, from a few inches tall to a foot, two feet, three, muscles expanding along with its fierce grin.

"Incarcero." Lucy waved her wand and put an extra thrust of power into her spell. It would take something strong to contain a growing troll, but fortunately, she had just the thing. A cage appeared around it, made of bars of toughened steel. The troll's head slammed against the top of the cage, and its back bent as it tried to keep growing, but soon it had to give up. It shrank back down to its starting size and stood glaring at her, tiny hands gripping the bars. It said something, but Lucy still didn't understand.

"Sorry, but maybe you can talk to someone at HQ once I get you there."

Reyes groaned and shifted. He was waking up.

Lucy shoved the cage under his desk, unglued the troll from the blinds, and stuck her uncaged captives into a filing cabinet, which she locked with a wave of her wand.

"Ut servetur." Lucy waved her wand at the chaos around her. Books flew back onto shelves, papers settled into a neat pile, and the monitor returned to its place. The desk drawer slammed shut a moment before Reyes opened his eyes.

"What happened?" he asked.

"I don't know," Lucy said, hastily hiding her wand. "I was on my way to the loo when I heard a *thud*. I came in, and you were lying here. Do you remember what happened?"

"No, but it feels like something hit me." He rubbed the top of his head.

"Maybe you fell and knocked yourself out?"

"That would make sense."

"We should find someone to take you to the emergency room, just in case."

"I'll be fine."

"Seriously, what would you say if one of the kids had been unconscious?"

Reyes chuckled. "Fair point."

She led him out into the corridor.

Admin Annie was walking past, carrying half a dozen empty bottles. "Seems to be going well." She waved the bottles, then stopped in her tracks as she saw Reyes press his hand to his head and wince. "Are you all right?"

"Do you have a car?" Lucy asked. "He needs to go to the hospital and have his head checked. "

"Of course!" Annie set the bottles down. "Come on."

Annie led Reyes out of the building while Lucy returned to the office. She summoned chains to bind the trolls, locked them back in the cabinet to be doubly secure, and locked the room behind her.

"I'll be back for you later," she said as she left them behind.

Back in the classroom, the paint and sip evening was nearly at an end. Lucy just had time to finish off her single glass of wine and sketch the outline of her fruit before their time was up.

"Is that all you managed?" Kelly asked scornfully. "Some of us actually made an effort."

She held up a watercolor painting of the same fruit bowl. It was fine, but Lucy could have done better if she'd had time.

"Very good, Kelly," Mary Holmes said as she walked past. "You should put it in for the auction."

Lucy sighed. She'd thought that her piece might end up one of the top ones in the next stage of fundraising, an auction of the art from the paint and sip, but she had barely even got started. Instead of having a chance to show off her skills, she was being out-shone by Kelly.

It had been worth it, of course, to stop the trolls running free, but sometimes she wished the magical world would stop for a while and let her enjoy the rest of her life.

"Sorry about this," she whispered to Charlie as people started to leave, "but we need to take a detour on the way home. I have five special presents to drop off at HQ."

CHAPTER EIGHTEEN

VX hurried down the hill into Chinatown. Dawn had almost arrived, and she didn't want to waste any of the daylight. Safe time to paint in public was a limited, precious resource, and she had big plans to fit within it.

She'd cast a spell around herself before setting out, one that she'd learned specially for the cathedral piece. It wouldn't hide her from people who saw her in the flesh, but it would keep her image from appearing on security cameras. That would do a lot to help conceal her identity and hopefully buy more time to get today's piece finished.

The spot she had chosen for today's work was at an intersection that would get busy during the day. She wanted to move away from the safe, comfortable spaces where she had been painting up until now. She wanted to make her work more visible.

At the foot of her chosen wall, she checked for observers, put up her ladder, and opened the bag of paints. There were few greens today. She was finished painting jungles. Today, she was going for something more unusual, something more memorable.

The cans rattled as she shook them, one in each hand, ready to get started. She needed to be quick. That, as much as accuracy or inspiration, was the street artist's gift. Up the ladder she went, hood and mask in place, and started painting.

It was never just about the paint anymore. She wasn't making pictures. She was casting spells, directing her magic through the nozzles of the cans. Power flowed through her, and she rode it, a high that helped to keep her moving, keep her painting, keep the image alive in her head.

Great arcs of blood red and fiery oranges spread across the wall, forming a body, a neck, a tail, hind and front legs with paws raised, ready to receive the claws she would add at the detailing stage. Simply a blob now, but with the shape of what it would become later, the loose silhouette of a dragon, with a black background for its cave mouth and a motley mix of yellows around its feet, ready to become the gold of a treasure hoard.

Somewhere along the line, the magic had started lifting her off the ladder and across the surface of the wall, letting her get to exactly where she needed to be, to paint faster and more accurately without straining or risking a fall. Had that happened with the previous pictures? She didn't remember. Maybe, maybe not. This blur of paint and fumes and magic had been there, this exhilarating sensation of the world whirling around her, bright and brilliant and filled with potential.

She reached for the white, and it rattled as it came out

of the bag. Except that she wasn't next to the bag. Her magic, the magic of art in motion, had reached out and snatched it up. Instead of one can or one in each hand, she was wielding three. No, four, five even, others she hadn't noticed were floating around her, that she had simply willed into action.

On some level, VX wondered if she ought to be scared. After all, this was either her magic slipping out of control or some foreign magic seizing hold of her. But she didn't care. As long as the art happened, that was all that counted, and she could complete it far faster if she did it this way. The magic was a gift, and only an idiot would turn their nose up at it.

She took a step back to look at what she had achieved so far, to see what she still needed to add or refine. Her feet settled on the top step of the ladder, and the cans floating around her landed gently on the ground.

"That's amazing," said a voice behind her.

She turned. A rat-faced Willen was standing on his hind legs in the middle of the street, looking up at VX and her painting. He had a bag over his shoulder and a skateboard in his hand.

"How long have you been watching me?" she asked.

"Long enough. What does the spell do?"

"It lets me paint faster, so I won't get caught."

"No, not that one, the one that you put into the painting."

"It protects it. Well, technically, it lets it protect itself."

"The dragon can fight back?"

"Yes. If anyone tries to wash it off or paint over it."

"Cool." He shook his bag, which rattled. "Guess I'd better keep these out of sight, then?"

"Unless you want someone to breathe fire on you, yes."

The Willen didn't seem to be a threat. He wasn't going to arrest her, didn't seem to want to attack her, and certainly wasn't stopping her from working, so she figured that she could carry on. He might even prove useful, an extra pair of eyes and ears watching out for trouble, something she clearly needed if she hadn't noticed his arrival.

She was onto the fine details already. That moment seemed to come faster and faster each time. Maybe it was practice, or the power of the magic, or both together. Her instincts were growing stronger, the paintings themselves bolder and more vivid, more full of life.

"I've seen your work elsewhere," the Willen said. "It's fantastic. You've got a really distinctive style."

"Thank you." She added pupils to the eyes, a glitter of light on the edges of the gold, a few drops of blood on the claws of one paw.

"You've used magic to make the paintings move before, right? Like in your jungle scenes?"

"That's right. I don't want my work to be passive. I want it to draw attention, to force engagement, to make people stop and think."

"Could you teach me how?"

She looked back at him. "I'm no art teacher."

"I'm not looking for a class in anatomical drawing. I want to learn the fundamentals of what you do. How to combine magic and art, you know?"

She nodded. She did know, deep down in her belly, where truth and inspiration came from. But could she explain it? Could she even show it to someone when they were paying attention?

"Your art brings the city to life," he said. "It brings your message to life. I've been out looking for you every morning because I want to be like you."

How could she say no to a request like that?

VX added the final touches to the dragon and put her paints away.

"What's your name?" she asked.

"Double-Rezz."

Good. An artist's name, not a birth name. A sign that he really was part of the community, not some outsider. And sure, he could still be a poser or a wannabe, but there was only one way for her to find that out.

"Follow me." She picked up her ladder and headed through the streets. More people were starting to emerge, but that was fine. She'd finished her real work, and what she did now, nobody was likely to see. Double-Rezz coasted along beside her, drifting along the sidewalk on his skateboard, one large blue sneaker pushing against the tarmac every few yards, hood pulled down to hide his rodent features from the mundane humans.

They arrived at an untended lot. It was a building site abandoned when the company behind it went bust. The half-built beginnings of an office block rose out of the weed-strewn ground, metal bars protruding from concrete sections like steel fingers, the rusting hand of a vast urban zombie trying to escape its economic grave.

Once they'd got through the wire fence and onto the lot, it was easy to get out of sight of the street. VX picked an area of blank concrete.

"Show me what you do," she said. "If I like it, I'll teach you."

Double-Rezz's nose twitched, and his eyes darted back and forth.

"Seriously? You want to see me in action?"

"Yes."

"I'm not that good. Nothing like you."

"I'll judge that."

"But seriously…"

"Fine, I'll go."

"No, wait…"

Double-Rezz yanked his bag open and grabbed two cans of paint. Purple and gold. Flashy. Not a brilliant start. The rattle of the cans filled the air as he shook up the paint and popped off the lids. Then he went still for a moment, standing and staring at the concrete canvas, only his whiskers twitching.

Finally, he started. His right hand moved in a wide arc, outlining a shape in purple, then filling it in. He switched cans and brought in the gold, adding the features that turned an uneven oval into an animal's face. Then he added a mane running down the back of its head, whiskers, glinting eyes. Lips curled back from glittering teeth. Dark blue added shadowy recesses, texture in the main, and a deeper menace to the eyes. Then he stood back, looking at what he had done.

"Not my best work," he said, "but there's some pressure here, you know? And obviously, it's a different style from you. I don't aim for realism but something otherworldly. I want people to look at my pictures and think, 'that's not what a lion looks like,' even while part of their brain is still screaming that yes, that's what a lion looks like because they're looking at it right now."

"Always lions?" Her question was mostly flippant, but you never knew. Some people got obsessive about specific subject matter, exploring a single form or motif for years.

"Not just lions, but that's what I've been working on lately."

He looked at her nervously, waiting for a reaction.

"I like it," she said. "It's not my thing, but it's good in its way. I think it would work with what I do." She drew a deep breath. "I've never taught anybody before, so this might not work out, but if you still want to try—"

"Hell yes!"

"All right then." She selected a new stretch of wall, picked up one of his cans, and gave it a shake, buying herself time while she thought this through. She was an artist, she specialized in images, and now she was being called upon to draw with words. "Think of your arm as like the can. Paint flows from one, magic from the other. The trick is in mixing them as they emerge…"

CHAPTER NINETEEN

The doorbell rang, and Charlie went to answer it. As expected, Ringo and Max stood on the doorstep, with Ringo's van parked down the driveway.

"I brought beers." Ringo held up a bag.

"And I brought coffee." Max held up a smaller bag. "In case you had enough to drink at the art class last night."

Charlie laughed. "I certainly had enough drawing. Turns out I'm not much of an artist."

He stepped back to let them both in, and they made their way through to the kitchen.

"Something smells amazing," Max said.

"Lucy's baking cookies. If we're lucky, we might get some of them."

Charlie got out coffee mugs and glasses for the beer. They chatted a little about TV shows and local news while they poured their drinks, then took their refreshments through to the dining room.

"I brought something else today." Max took his laptop

out of its bag and placed it on the table. "Our brand designs."

"Any good, man?" Ringo leaned back in a seat and stretched out his legs.

"I didn't look yet. It seemed like something we should do together."

"Like opening presents after the wedding," Charlie said.

"Let's not get carried away." Ringo held up his hands. "After all, we've only just started dating."

That got another laugh from everyone.

"It's funny how much setting up a business is like getting married," Max said. "Or buying a house together, for that matter. You're legally bound to the other people involved, for better or for worse, until you get your happily ever after, agree to go your separate ways, or it all descends into something really messy."

"Is there something you need to tell us about you and Kelly?" Charlie asked.

"We're fine, thank you, but I've seen enough other cases not to have too many illusions. Sadly, not all businesses make it either."

"Well, let's hope that ours does. And in that spirit, let's have a look at the presents."

Max had commissioned several designers to provide samples for how they would present the company's branding, including a logo, some sample web pages, and a couple of choices of fonts for emails and letters.

"I like this one," Ringo said, "where the car in the logo has pictures of the world for wheels. Or maybe this one, with a wand in place of the exhaust."

"The world wheels are pretty cool," Charlie agreed. "But is it too much detail? I mean, think about how that would look as a thumbnail or a profile pic on social media. It might not be clear what's going on."

"I'm not clear about this one at all." Max pointed at another of the designs. "Is that sparks of magic around the world, or are they showing that it's on fire? Either way, it doesn't feel very positive."

A *clunk* in the kitchen made them all look up. Lucy was taking cookies out of the oven. The mouth-watering smell washed over them.

"Yes, you can have some," she said, seeing their expressions. "But not yet. They need time to cool."

They forced their attention back to the designs.

"That burning world one does come with good page design," Charlie said. "And the fonts are very clear."

"But we could use different fonts with any of these, right?"

"Sure, but the designers will have a better grip of what font goes well with a logo, so it's worth considering the choices they've made."

Max brought up another of the designs. "I like that this one sent us the image in different colors. It makes it easier to see how it'll look in practice."

"I'm not sure about the image, though," Charlie said. "What is it?"

"A sort of combination of car and leaf, I think. Trying to show a greener kind of transport."

"Huh. Well, it's certainly different and directly about us."

"A plant-based car sounds like something from Oriceran," Ringo said. "Not that I've ever been, but, you know, you hear stories."

They went through all the designs, making a pro and con list for them, trying to work out which was their favorite. The problem wasn't that one of them liked one design more than the rest, it was that which one they each liked kept changing, depending on what aspect of the design they were trying to make a judgment on.

"It's tough, thinking that we might tie ourselves to the wrong choice," Charlie said. "What if we pick something and all our potential customers hate it? Then we're spending money on a design that's worse than useless."

"Or what if it's just mediocre and we keep working away on a business that never quite takes off?" Ringo let out a long breath. "This stuff is tricky."

Lucy emerged from the kitchen, carrying a plate of warm chocolate chip cookies.

"Here, these should lift your spirits. And while I'm about, can I have a look at the designs?"

"Hey, that's a good idea," Ringo said. "485 here can be our stand-in for the common magical on the street."

"Who are you calling common?"

"Figure of speech. Anyone who makes cookies this good is extraordinary."

"Well, all right then." Lucy sat in front of the laptop. "Show me what you've got."

Max had set up a slide show of the potential logos, cycling through the images one at a time. There was the world as wheels, the wand exhaust pipe, the leaf car, even the world that might or might not be on fire. Detached from the fonts and pages designs, they had to stand on their own merits, as they would do out in the world.

"The world wheels are really striking," Lucy said, "but it feels a bit weird as if it's about the weight of cars crushing the world."

"I hadn't even considered that," Max said. "We need to be careful about what other messages people might take from our logo."

"The leaf car is good too if people understand what it represents."

"That's a big if," Ringo said, "and if it fails, we're going to look like idiots. We need to make sure that anyone who sees it can work out what they're looking at."

"Let's get some more test subjects in." Lucy raised her voice. "Kids, could you come in here for a minute please?"

Dylan, Ashley, and Eddie came in from the living room, where they had been watching cartoons.

"Have a look at this," Lucy said. "Work out what you think it is, but don't say anything yet. Everybody got an idea?" They nodded. "Okay then, Eddie, what do you think?"

"Leaf car," he said.

"Ashley?"

"Like Eddie said, someone has engineered a car from a leaf. I don't think that would be very resilient in bad weather or a crash."

"Dylan?"

"What they said. I think it's pretty cool."

Lucy smiled at the men who made up the small business. "There you have it. Even children can work out what that logo is, and at least one of them likes it. Does that make it good enough for you?"

Max exchanged a look with the others, then nodded.

"I'll email the designer," he said. "We should be able to get a full set of files from her by tomorrow."

The garage was one that Ringo had already been hiring as a place to store his van and his bounty hunting equipment. It had been a natural next step to turn it into a workshop for the magical-mechanical side of their business, somewhere to assemble custom parts and store the materials they needed.

Max sat at the back of the workshop, with his computer set up on the small desk they'd managed to fit in, with a larger monitor bolted to the wall above it.

"That's the first of the web pages set up," he said. "What do you think?"

The other two looked over his shoulder at the image on the monitor. There it was, their company logo, their chosen font, their page design, though admittedly all the work of someone else with more artistic talent than them.

"It looks good," Charlie said. "I'm ready if you guys are."

Ringo slowly nodded. "Got to commit sooner or later. We might as well get it over with."

"Okay then." Max hit a button, then another to confirm his decision. "There it is. We have officially launched on the magical internet. We have a webpage, a social media feed, and most importantly a list of our prices and how to contact us. Now we wait for the business to come in."

"One more thing first." Ringo held up an airbrush.

They stepped away from the computer and gathered facing Ringo's van, looking at the eagle painted on its side.

"You've been good to me, man," Ringo said, reaching out to stroke the eagle's beak. "You made my wheels look totally badass. Got me into conversations with cool people, and more than a few crazies. Introduced me to that chick with the bird obsession out in Arkansas. And I swear, you made this old machine move faster. But now, your time is up. Farewell, my friend."

He pulled a mask on and the others stepped back, then he pressed the button on the airbrush and started covering the eagle in black paint.

While that was happening, Charlie took the giant printout they had made of their new logo and carefully cut pieces out, creating a stencil. He set it down with the bottle of green paint, ready for later.

"It feels like the end of an era," he said, watching as the last few eagle feathers disappeared beneath the black spray.

"And the beginning of another one," Max said. "We're a fully incorporated company now, with our branding, web presence, and once two layers of paint have time to dry, we'll have our corporate vehicle."

"Is it weird that I'm more excited about this than about my main job?"

Max shrugged. "I often get to help the environment in my job. If I didn't, I think I'd feel the same way. We're going to make a difference, and that's a great thing."

Ringo stepped back from the van, surveyed his work, and pulled down the mask. He sighed.

"That was tougher than I thought." Then he picked up the stencil, and a grin seized him. "Okay, maybe I won't feel so bad after all. This thing is freaking cool."

CHAPTER TWENTY

Lucy opened the heavy door of the Special Equipment and Weapons lab, bracing herself for the wave of noise and magic that usually assailed her on entering the area. This was, if not the beating heart of the L.A. Silver Griffins, then the organization's distracted imagination, a place where all manner of weirdness took place.

She stepped cautiously inside. Quiet should have been reassuring, but it somehow managed to be ominous. After all, this was Toliver Jenkins' domain. Surely quiet could only be a sign that something had gone horribly wrong. She walked down the short corridor and past the traps set to catch escaping experimental subjects. Today, there were only a selection of giant beetles, each one around the size of Lucy's hand, legs twitching as they tried to break free of a magical mesh. By Special Equipment standards, that was fairly mundane.

Around the corner, a soft buzzing emerged through the main test lab. Lucy followed it into a side room. There sat

Nigel, Jenkins' assistant, shirtless in a large, padded chair that they'd tipped back until he was nearly horizontal. A bright light shone from above. Jenkins himself stood over his assistant with a device that Lucy didn't quite recognize buzzing in his hand. Wires and tubes ran from it to a larger set of machines at the side of the room, one of which was covered in magical glowing runes and had an assortment of wands strapped onto the side.

"Please don't tell me you're doing magical dentistry now," Lucy said. Nigel's position, combined with the buzzing sound, was a little too familiar for comfort.

"Hahaha! Of course not." Jenkins looked up and grinned. "Nothing so serious. We're doing tattoos."

He pressed the device in his hand against Nigel's upper arm, who closed his eyes and gritted his teeth.

"Tattoos?" Lucy asked. "Do you know anything about how to do those?"

"I've done my research. Kept me busy for several hours yesterday afternoon."

Lucy looked down at poor Nigel, who had opened one of his eyes and was watching nervously as his boss put ink into his arm. A few hours didn't seem like long enough to learn to tattoo, never mind the artistry involved in doing them well, and for Jenkins to get his practice on Nigel seemed particularly harsh.

"Maybe this isn't such a great idea," Lucy said.

"I know what you're thinking," Jenkins said, "but don't worry, I've set up a computer with the designs. That should make sure that they come out looking good."

That hadn't been the whole of Lucy's concern, but it was a start. She wasn't even going to think about the question of how a computer could match a professional artist.

The buzzing stopped, and Jenkins took a step back.

"There you go, time to test it out."

Nigel got out of his seat.

"It's not as painful as it looks," he said. "I just wish we didn't have to do so many."

Lucy looked down Nigel's pale and scrawny torso and arms. She could only see one tattoo, a stylized eagle on his left bicep. It wasn't the best image she had ever seen, but Jenkins' computer was at least competent at copying designs from somewhere.

"Where are the others?" she asked, not entirely sure that she wanted to know.

"Magicked them off." Jenkins waved his wand. "I can't have one interfering with the other at this early stage in the experiment, and I only have one test subject. Unless, of course, you'd like—"

"Absolutely not!" Lucy exclaimed. "Er, I mean, that's kind of you, but no."

"Suit yourself. Let's go see if this one worked."

Lucy followed the two wizards into their main test hall, which usually acted as a magical firing range. Today, it was empty of both targets and weapons.

"What's this all about?" she asked.

"The guy you arrested for trashing that bar," Jenkins said. "He got his magical strength from his tattoo, but he won't tell us who did it. If I can at least replicate the procedure, that might give us a clue. Right, Nigel?"

Nigel nodded his head in a resigned way. "It does make sense."

He walked into the middle of the hall, then raised his arms out by his sides.

"Remember, Nigel, think eagle thoughts," Jenkins said. "And focus on the tattoo."

Nigel closed his eyes. Lucy could sense him mustering his power. Without a wand in his hand, it took longer to accumulate, and the result was less focused, but it was there, shining out from him like an invisible light. In particular, it seemed to come from the tattoo.

"That's it," Jenkins called. "Now lift!"

"I'm trying!"

"Try harder!"

Slowly, Nigel rose into the air until he hung a foot above the floor.

"It's working!" Jenkins exclaimed. "Now flap your arms a bit."

Nigel did as he was told, slowly, tentatively, starting with small flutters of his hands. Sure enough, he rose higher and higher. He opened his eyes and laughed out loud.

"It is! It's working! I'll try flying around."

He flapped his arms and took off down the hall, soaring through the air.

"I can do it!" he called. "I'm an eagle. I'm a hunter of the air. I'm—"

His words cut off as he lost control, veered right, and slammed into the wall. Lucy got a levitate spell off just in time to catch him as he fell and lowered him gently to the floor. She and Jenkins rushed over to check on the fallen assistant.

148

"No blood," Jenkins said. "Nothing broken. I call that a win."

"He could have a concussion," Lucy said. "Or be damaged inside."

"I'm fine." Nigel peeled himself up off the floor. "I've had enough concussions to know how they feel."

That didn't reassure Lucy half as much as he meant it to.

"How many fingers am I holding up?" she asked.

"None, that's a wand."

"Good. Now, we should get you sitting."

"Absolutely," Jenkins said. "Back to the chair, so we can remove that tattoo and put another one on. We're making real progress here."

"Another one?" Lucy stared at him. "Are you serious?"

"Of course! Progress will only come with hard work and dedication, right Nigel?"

"Yes, boss," Nigel said wearily.

Lucy shrugged. Who was she to argue with them? After all, they were the experts in magical equipment.

Using his tattooing machine to direct the magic, Jenkins removed the eagle, then put a spider in its place. They returned to the testing area, and Nigel scurried up a wall, then exclaimed in alarm as sticky threads shot out the bottom of his pants.

"No, no, no, no, no!" he shouted. "That feels so weird."

"But it could be useful for—"

"I said no!"

The spider was followed by an ant, a horse, and a bear, all with similar results. Each time, Nigel gained some benefit based on the animal Jenkins tattooed him with, whether strength or speed or endurance, but each time, he also gained some less helpful side effects. After the jellyfish gave him a powerful sting but reduced him to flopping around in the chair, Jenkins declared that it was time for a coffee break.

"I have tea too," he said, approaching a machine in the corner of the lab's break room. "Would you like one?"

"It doesn't use those plastic pods, does it?" Lucy asked.

"Certainly not. I'm not a barbarian."

The three of them sat with their steaming cups and the chocolate chip cookies Lucy had brought with her, contemplating how the experiments had gone.

"That was impressive," Lucy said, "but none of it looked like the criminal's tattoo. That was much more abstract."

"I know," Jenkins said, "but I couldn't see how they related to the ability it gave him. I thought that using a more concrete design might help us understand how the magic interacts with the tattoo. Is it about the ink, or the scars, or simply the symbol of its presence? Does the power stem from the body or from a mental conception of how the body works? I think we've answered that one at least, right, Nigel?"

Nigel looked up from removing sticky strands of spider web from around his ankle.

"It's definitely there in the body, in the tattoo," he said. "It feels different from when I cast normally. I can feel something flow through the image, like water down a funnel."

Lucy sipped her tea and contemplated what that meant. This case was sliding from evidence she didn't have into theoretical magic she didn't understand. Everyone had their limits, and it was interesting to tackle a case that pushed past hers.

"What will you do next?" she asked. "Try some different shapes?"

"Possibly." Jenkins had a distant look as if his thoughts weren't really with them. "Or we could take a break to compile the results. Nigel, your view?"

Lucy had expected Nigel to come down emphatically on the side of stopping, but instead, he looked nervously at her.

"You're friends with Agent Kowal, right?" he said.

"With Jackie? Sure."

"Does she like tattoos?"

"I don't think she has a strong opinion either way."

"Oh." Nigel looked at his upper arm. "But it can't do any harm to work hard at a thing, can it?"

"No, that's a good way to solve cases."

"Solve cases. Yep." Nigel took a bite from his cookie, then threw the last bit of it at Jenkins, who blinked and looked around in surprise.

"Sorry, miles away," Jenkins said. "Where were we?"

"Let's keep going," Nigel said. "I want to help Agent Heron get to the bottom of this mystery."

"Brilliant." Jenkins leaped to his feet. "Give me ten minutes. I have an idea for how to adjust the equipment, to control the results better." He looked down at his half-eaten cookie. "Oh, and Agent Heron, you might as well go, I don't think we'll have any answers for you today. But the theory is starting to come together. Get back to me later in the week, and we'll see if I can't tell you how our tattooist makes this work."

That was good enough for Lucy. Leaving the rest of the cookies to help fuel the research, she headed out of the lab. She had somewhere else to be, somewhere even more interesting than the Special Equipment and Weapons lab.

She had art to view.

CHAPTER TWENTY-ONE

The railway car swayed and clicked on its tracks as it carried Lucy away from Silver Griffins HQ. She'd just had time to change before leaving the office and was wearing a purple blouse, a smart black pair of pants, and boots with a short heel. She didn't know what people usually wore to L.A. gallery openings but felt like she ought to make some effort. After all, it was a special occasion.

The train stopped, and Lucy hurried out onto the platform. Winding metal stairs led her up an echoing tunnel, through a wand-operated security barrier, and into a tunnel full of magicals on the main line. This was the early evening crowd, a mixture of people who had stayed late at work and those who were already on their way out for something more fun. There were as many in suits or overalls as in casual or trendy attire.

A small queue had formed at the tunnel exit. They couldn't all rush out at once, or the Starbucks staff would wonder how they had fit twenty customers into a small back room. Instead, they departed in ones and twos, stepping through the magical wall and a haze of perception-blurring chocolate-scented magic into the mundane world. Lucy glanced at her watch and tried not to tap her foot. It wasn't anybody else's fault that she was running late, so there was no point spreading her impatience.

At last, she reached the front of the queue, waited a minute, then stepped through the wall. The Starbucks was relatively empty, and she strolled through with ease, resisting the urge to buy a cuppa on the way. Maybe a quirky artist could get away with turning up at an opening with a steaming cup of tea, but it didn't feel like the right move for someone who was only a guest.

She hurried down a couple of streets and in through the door of another coffee shop. Heather was sitting by the window, a black coffee going cold in front of her, scowling out at the world. If she had dressed for the occasion, it only extended to changing into a different flannel shirt.

"Sorry I'm late." Lucy took a seat across from Heather. "Have you been waiting long?"

"Long enough." Heather turned the cup between her hands. "I've seen a lot of people go in."

"That's good, isn't it?"

Heather shrugged. "It's not how the Tolderai live. We don't share our art with the world."

"That changed when you signed that contract."

"I know." Heather drank half the coffee in a single gulp. "I don't like change."

"Think of the good things that have come into your life in the past year, like teaching the Underfoot Brigade. Change can be good."

"Maybe." Heather downed the rest of the coffee. "Come on, let's go see how bad it is."

"That's the positive spirit I was looking for!"

"You're determined to make me enjoy this, aren't you?"

"You'll enjoy it all by yourself, I'm sure."

They walked into the back room, through the hidden magical doorway, and up the stairs to Penley's gallery. The atmosphere was completely different from their last visit. Instead of the fragile quiet of an empty gallery, filled only with its precious works, the room was full of visitors.

Dozens of magicals were scattered in small groups around the room, drinking champagne, examining the art, and making the sort of playfully impromptu conversation that was only possible thanks to years of practice and preparation. At the top of the stairs, a Kilomea bouncer ticked Lucy's and Heather's names off a list, his face crumpling as he pushed the pencil across the page, before a waiter cycled around, a welcoming smile on his face.

"Champagne, ladies?" he said, holding out his tray. "Or mineral water, perhaps?"

If he thought they seemed out of place, he didn't show it, but Lucy would have been hard-pressed to work out what qualified as in place here. The guests wore everything from black tie to torn jeans, though she assumed that the jeans were the artfully ripped sort where designer holes added two hundred bucks to their price.

"I don't see our things," Heather said, grabbing two glasses off the tray and passing one to Lucy.

"They must all be in among that crowd at the far end of the room."

"Hm." Heather frowned. "If one of them breaks our scrying bowl, I'm going to kill them."

"I'm sure they'll be careful."

Penley appeared out of the crowd, dressed in a pair of shimmering gray pants and a white shirt unbuttoned halfway down his chest. His smile glittered as brightly as the diamond studs in his ear.

"Ladies!" He kissed Lucy on the cheek, then made to do the same to Heather, who blocked him with her hand.

"Where are they?" Heather asked.

"Exactly where I said they would be." Penley gestured toward the crowd. "A point specified in your contract and approved by your lawyer, who, I have to say, was excessively thorough in his demands. Where did you find him?"

"Running errands for supervillains," Lucy said.

"Fine, don't tell. He's around here somewhere, though it's always hard to spot a dwarf in a crowd." Penley gave the room the most cursory of glances, then shrugged. "Well, never mind that. What matters is that your artifacts are an absolute hit.

"Everyone is so excited to see them. I haven't had an opening night this electric since Gunderson's living art piece on the movement of mountains. No one can stop talking about these pieces, the sense they evoke of time as an organic experience intersecting with a construct of the sentient, subjective mind, the weight of their presence in a lightweight age."

"And that's good?" Heather asked.

"Darling, it's utterly marvelous." Penley took hold of Heather's arm, and this time she didn't resist. "Let me introduce you to some people. In the absence of the artists themselves, their living descendant is the belle of the ball tonight."

"I don't want to meet people."

"But they want to meet you, and that, my dear, is all that matters."

Penley dragged Heather away into the crowd, leaving Lucy alone with her champagne.

There were so many people at the far end of the room. It didn't seem worth fighting through the crowd to the Tolderai artifacts. If she wanted to, Lucy could arrange a private viewing with Heather once all of this was over. Instead, she decided to take the opportunity to look at the other works.

The nearest one to her was, at first glance, one of the most conventional in the gallery. A traditional oil painting of a rural landscape, caught within a gilt frame, it could easily have been a nineteenth-century work, perhaps something from Europe that had arrived with the other immigrants on America's shores. Except that, when Lucy looked more closely, she started to see less traditional details.

A cellphone poking from the pocket of a peasant farmer. A beer can discarded among the leaf litter at the foot of a gnarled old oak. The slender line of a radio mast rising over the thatched roofs of a village. There was even a bar code in the black and white pattern on one of the cows. She laughed in delight as she caught more of those details, hidden from the casual eye.

"Not bad, is it?" The voice made her turn to see Gruffbar standing next to her. A champagne glass looked particularly fragile in his hand. "Not exactly original, but it's cleverly done, and the brushwork shows attention to the history of the craft."

"I thought you were here to see the Tolderai artifacts?" Lucy said.

"I got a look, and I have to say, it's impressive craftsmanship. I wasn't sure, given who the Tolderai are, but they had some gift for industry."

"Don't put it that way around Heather. She'll give you one of her glares."

"That's guaranteed whatever I say. Might as well at least be honest."

"Is that a good motto for a lawyer?"

"I've heard worse."

"Thank you for your work on this. I don't think it would have happened without you."

"Your payment is all the thanks I need." Gruffbar looked around. "Though I'll admit, this is a nice bonus. I've even managed to pick up some more work. That's the good thing about people who can afford original art. They can afford legal representation too."

"Looking to set yourself up as the go-to lawyer for L.A.'s magical art scene?"

"Why not? There's good money in it, and it feels good to work with people who make things. Plus, I already have some relevant contacts."

"You have, haven't you?" Lucy's mind went back to the magical street art that had been causing problems in the past few days. There had been more moving pieces, more attacks on anyone defacing the paintings, and more for the Silver Griffins to cover up. "I have something else I want to ask you about. This probably isn't the time, but could I come by your office tomorrow?"

"Is this a Silver Griffin thing?"

"Yes."

"Then I can't really say no, can I?"

"I suppose not."

"I have a free slot at eleven. Will that do?"

"Perfect."

Gruffbar grunted and handed his empty glass to a passing waiter.

"You've really taken the buzz off my evening, Agent Heron."

"Sorry to hear that."

"Think I'll go talk to someone who can't arrest me."

Lucy laughed. "Fair enough. Have fun."

As Gruffbar disappeared into the crowd, Heather reappeared, an empty glass in one hand and a collection of business cards in the other.

"These people." She waved the cards. "Why do they think I care about them?"

"Because they think you're here to sell art."

Heather snorted. "Well, they're out of luck."

She stuffed the cards into the empty glass and swapped it for two full glasses from a passing waiter.

"Here." She handed one to Lucy, who was only halfway through her first glass.

"Coping mechanism?" Lucy asked.

"Something like that."

Lucy looked more carefully at Heather. She was frowning, as usual, but there was a gleam in her eyes.

"You're having fun, aren't you?"

"I'm not hating it as much as I thought. They've all said good things about the artifacts, and they're treating them with proper respect. It's the first time I've seen outsiders show such recognition for my people. It's good to see the tribe getting its due."

"So maybe this wasn't a bad idea, after all?"

"No, you were right." Heather smiled. It wasn't a big smile, but it was there. "L.A. might not be the forest, but it was worth moving here."

"Well then, here's to L.A." Lucy raised her glass. "And to the art of your ancestors."

"The ancestors." Heather chinked and took a drink. "Now I should get back in there. They keep asking questions, and I don't trust Penley to get the answers right."

CHAPTER TWENTY-TWO

"Two of you?" Gruffbar looked up from behind his desk. "I feel outnumbered."

"We could fetch your pet ogre from downstairs," Jackie said. "Get him to stand behind us with a wrench, even the odds if I get out of hand."

"Are you going to get out of hand?"

"No, she isn't." Lucy closed the door of Gruffbar's office, muting some of the noise from the auto shop below. "And we do have an appointment, remember? Or did last night's champagne wash that detail away?"

"Oh, I remember. It takes more than bubbly elf tonics to get a dwarf drunk." He waved a hand. "Take a seat. We might as well get this over with, whatever it is. But before we start..." He placed his phone on the desk and pressed a button. "You don't mind if I record the conversation, do you?"

"Why, you worried we'll lock you up?" Jackie asked.

"I want to make sure I'm not misrepresented."

"But if you incriminate yourself, I bet the recording will

mysteriously get corrupted."

"You think I'm going to incriminate myself?"

Lucy held up a hand to cut off whatever Jackie planned to say next.

"It's not that sort of conversation," she said. "We're not investigating you, and now you have that on record."

"So what is it about?" Gruffbar lit a cigar with a chunky Zippo lighter. It had a skull embossed on one side, the top of its head turning into a gearwheel.

"Do you have to do that?" Jackie waved away a trail of smoke.

"You're not paying clients, so I don't have much reason to keep you comfortable."

"But you know what that does to your lungs?"

"I'm a lawyer, not a doctor, but I've seen the public health commercials. I'm still happy to take my chances."

"Perhaps we could get back to the point?" Lucy said. "Then we can leave you to get on with your work."

"Suits me."

"We're hoping to pick your brains as someone with connections in the magical underworld."

"I wouldn't say that I have connections to any kind of underworld. That sort of thing could tarnish a lawyer's reputation."

"Let me rephrase the request... You know a wide range of people in different walks of life, including some who, rightly or wrongly, have had encounters with the law."

"Sure, that sounds like a description of a lawyer to me."

"And you also pay attention to art in the city."

"Sure. It's a cliché, but I like things that people make, whether it's a good motor or an oil painting. Humans take this stuff for granted, but dwarves, we appreciate the work that goes in."

"Great. Do you know much about street art?"

Gruffbar leaned back and blew a long plume of smoke toward the ceiling. He tapped ash into an ashtray, then peered with apparent interest at the end of his cigar.

"Street art is a slippery term. I assume you're not talking monumental sculpture or the murals that corporations commission when they're trying to look hip?"

"Not sculpture, but it's possible that the person we're looking for might have worked on paid murals. I don't know what else those artists do."

"You're after a graffiti artist?"

"Graffiti is a slippery term."

Gruffbar laughed. "All right, you got me there, agent. You're looking for someone who works with spray cans?"

"That's right."

Lucy explained the paintings that she and Jackie had seen and de-spelled, with Jackie occasionally adding details. There was no point hiding the existence of magical street art. Rumors were all over town. Lucy had even heard guests talking about it at the gallery the previous night, disputing whether it was all the work of a single artist and speculating how much it would cost to buy a piece of their own.

One of them had referred to the artist as "Magical Banksy," and Lucy was worried that a label like that might create a sense of legitimacy, encouraging whoever was making these paintings. The Silver Griffins needed to get a lid on this fast before the mundane world sat up and paid attention.

"There's a signature on these murals," Lucy said. "At least the ones we've looked at. The letters V and X. I don't know if that's initials or the artist's full tag, but given your interests, I thought you might know. Do you have any idea who it might be?"

Gruffbar took another long drag on his cigar and stared up at the ceiling as if trying to read something there, browsing through the pages of memory as they unfolded across his mind.

"V and X…" He tapped his cigar over the ashtray. "It's certainly distinctive and easy to spray. Just a few quick lines. You know anything about this artist beyond those letters?"

"We think they might be short," Jackie said, leaning forward in her seat. "Could mean a Willen, a gnome, even a dwarf…"

She gave Gruffbar a pointed look.

"I thought you didn't suspect me of anything?"

"You're part of the dwarf community. You're more likely to know someone there."

"Be careful, agent. Racial profiling is an ugly business. There are dwarves all over this city, from a thousand different communities and a hundred different clans. Just because we all look the same to you, that doesn't mean we're related."

"I didn't mean—"

"Oh, I think you did, or you wouldn't have said it." He raised an eyebrow. "You should be more careful who you work with, Agent Heron."

"I'm sorry, okay?" Jackie waved apologetically. "It's just

that you asked what we know, and short is one of the few details we have."

"Some humans are short."

"You're right. I'm sorry."

"What can you tell me about the art?"

"It's magically empowered."

"And it's very good," Lucy added. "This VX has a real talent, both for the design of their murals and the fine details. Honestly, it's a shame they're adding magic because otherwise, we could leave this for people to enjoy."

"Or for the city authorities to paint over?"

"Anyone who does that is taking their life in their hands. Some of these paintings are getting really dangerous, attacking people who get too close, causing hurt and fear."

"Which is why you want to stop them?"

Lucy shook her head. "Sadly, we'd have to do it regardless. You know the rules about publicly visible magic."

"I do." Gruffbar ground out the end of his cigar. "And I don't know anyone with the initials V and X, at least nobody with artistic talent or living in this town."

"Might you know something if there was a reward?" Jackie asked sharply.

"Agent Kowal, what sort of unscrupulous monster do you take me for?"

"A lawyer."

"Well, that stereotype's fair, at least. But it won't help you. I wouldn't know more if you came in with a sack full of gold and dumped it out here on my desk, though for that, I might do some investigating on your behalf."

"We do our own investigating, thanks."

"Of course you do, and you probably have other investigations to work on, so if we've finished here?"

"I think so." Lucy stood and extended a hand. "Thank you for your time, Gruffbar. If you do think of anything about this artist, give me a call."

"Of course, Agent Heron." He shook her hand, then nodded at Jackie. "Agent Kowal, I'd say it was a pleasure, but…"

"But lawyers are always honest?"

"Not always honest, but we never lie."

"Not even that one?"

"See you around, agents."

The witches headed out down the iron stairs and across the auto shop. As they went, the mechanics paused in their work and stared at them. Their expressions were just short of outright hostility.

"Anywhere people are suspicious of me, I get suspicious of them," Jackie said as they emerged onto the street.

"We can investigate the auto shop later if you really want. For now, we have an artist to catch."

"And we're no closer than we were an hour ago."

"Shame. I really thought Gruffbar might be our best bet."

"That guy is never anyone's best anything."

Back in the office, Gruffbar stopped the recording on his phone and backed the file up to cloud storage, then tapped another icon to bring up a folder full of photos. He had another like it full of his favorite machines he'd seen around L.A., and one of the best buildings, solid ones with good foundations or unusual features.

This time though, he opened the folder of street art and

flicked through it. He smiled as the images scrolled past, pieces that had caught his attention down the years. Ones that made great use of color, were particularly well laid out, or that made effective use of unusual locations. That was the extra beauty of street art, its defiant relationship with its environment. It was why the corporate-sponsored stuff, the Nike paintings and the Banksy wannabes decorating the walls of investment banks always felt so flat and lifeless. Criminality was part of the craft.

There they were, pieces by VX down the years, from her early works with their crude but striking layouts, through the period when she'd refined her detailing, to the recent, magically infused works. He used "she" and "her" cautiously, as he'd only heard rumors about the person behind the mask, but enough of those rumors said female for him to believe it.

What he had said to Lucy and Jackie was true. He didn't know anyone with the initials VX, partly because he'd never met VX and partly because he didn't know if those letters were initials. But he knew enough to know that he didn't want the Silver Griffins getting in the way of work this good.

He scrolled through his contacts until he reached the number of a forger turned street artist who he'd helped with some previous charges. The guy answered the call within seconds.

"Gruffbar, what's up, man? Are the Silvers after me again?"

"Don't worry, they're not after you, at least not as far as I know. But I need you to get the word out to another artist, someone going by the tag of VX…"

CHAPTER TWENTY-THREE

The next morning, Lucy was up bright and early, but not for the sake of work. Following a hearty breakfast and a drive north out of the city, she hiked along a woodland trail through the Angeles National Forest with Charlie and the kids. Buddy excitedly yapped as he tugged on his lead, trying to escape Charlie's grip and run off to explore the trees.

"Calm down, Buddy," Charlie said. "Remember what happened last time you got loose here? We were hunting you for an hour."

"I don't think that's much of a deterrent," Lucy said. "He liked playing hide and seek."

"Well, don't tell him, but I brought some doggy treats. Hopefully this time, I can lure him back if he gets away, instead of chasing over every hillside for a mile around."

"I don't think you need to worry about that. He can't get half as far as he could when he was a bloodhound."

"Maybe not, but he can still be pretty agile when he wants to be. I'm not taking any chances."

The whole family was in good spirits as they made their way along the trail. It was a beautiful day, with the sun shining and the birds singing to each other in the trees, perfect weather to be out and about.

"Did you magic this up?" Charlie asked Lucy in a stage whisper. "Get your big powerful bosses to make the sun shine just for us?"

"Don't be silly, Dad," Ashley said. "We all know that the Silver Griffins aren't that powerful."

"Oh really? Then why doesn't it ever rain when we go out hiking on the weekend?"

"Because if it was raining, we wouldn't go out. You're reversing cause and effect, and you know it."

"Well, that's me told." Charlie laughed. "If I wanted to get away with things like that, I shouldn't have raised such smart kids, huh?"

"Or Mom shouldn't have."

Eddie had charged off down the trail with Dylan in close pursuit, playing at dinosaurs. Now the two of them ran back, and Eddie had a look on his face that was all too familiar to Lucy.

"Cookie?" he asked.

She laughed.

"What makes you think I have cookies?"

"You always have cookies," Dylan said. "Plus, the house smelled of them this morning."

"All right, yes, I have freshly baked cookies as part of our lunch."

Eddie made a face, but Dylan was more pragmatic. He looked at his watch.

"It's nearly twelve o'clock," he said. "We could look for somewhere to stop for lunch."

Eddie's expression brightened. "Lunch cookies?"

Lucy and Charlie laughed.

"Fine," she said. "Start looking for somewhere we can stop and eat."

Eddie and Dylan raced off down the trail again, enthusiastically hunting for a suitable spot.

"Don't you want to go with them, sweetheart?" Lucy asked Ashley.

"No, thank you, Mom. I'm happy just walking."

"Is this because of how heavy your backpack is?"

"No. Well, maybe."

Ashley shifted the strap of her bag, and something *clanked* inside.

"Did you need to bring all that with you?"

"How else could I work on my robot?"

"This is supposed to be a day off, sweetheart. Some family time."

"Eddie changes shape during family time. I think I should be able to make robots."

"I could argue with that logic, but I won't."

Eddie came running back along the trail. "Found it!"

He grabbed Lucy's hand and dragged her, laughing, along the path. Soon, they turned off the trail into a clearing where Dylan sat, his backpack next to him and a smile on his face.

"See, perfect," he said. "Now, about those cookies…"

Lucy started unpacking her bag, which held a lot of the picnic things. By the time Charlie, Ashley, and Buddy caught up, she'd spread a blanket on the ground, with plates and cups, sandwiches, and cookies. Soda, chips, and fruit merged from Charlie's bag to complete the feast.

"No cookies until you've had sandwiches," Lucy said as the kids reached for one particular tub. "That applies to you too." She glanced at Charlie, who drew his hand back guiltily.

They sat and ate in the sunshine while the birds sang around them and the wind blew gently through the trees. It was one of the most peaceful, beautiful moments that Lucy had experienced in a long time. She wished that there was some way she could make it last forever when she realized that there was—or at least there was a way to make the memory last.

She brushed crumbs from her fingers, then took a sketch pad and a pencil out of a pocket in her bag and started drawing the scene. With a few strokes, the outline of the trees and the trail took their place on the page, followed by the beginnings of her family.

"Draw dinosaurs?" Eddie climbed into her lap.

"No, sweetheart, I'm drawing us and the scenery around us."

"Oh." Eddie nodded sagely, then shook his head. "Needs more dinosaurs."

He reached into her bag, took out a pencil, and made to add to the picture.

"Hey, this is mine!" Lucy laughed. "If you want to add dinosaurs to a picture, why don't you start one of your own?"

She took another sketchpad from her bag and gave it to Eddie.

"Colors?" he asked.

"Sorry, I only brought pencils."

"Okay."

He climbed out of her lap, laid the sketchpad down on the ground, and set about carefully drawing a battle between two large, clawed lizards.

"Can I have a go?" Dylan asked.

"Sure." Lucy tore a few pages from her sketch pad and handed them to him, along with a pencil. "Sorry, I don't have another spare pad. Does anyone else want to join?"

To her surprise, Ashley looked around with interest. In between bites of her sandwich, the girl genius had been assembling something out of her string robots, something that was currently incomprehensible to Lucy.

"Yes, please," she said. "This could be a useful test."

"Guess I might as well join in too," Charlie said. "It would be a shame not to when you're all having fun. But given my talent level, I might team up with Eddie, so he can make my pictures look better."

He took a pencil and crouched next to Eddie, adding spikes and scales to the dinosaurs.

For a long while, they sat quietly eating cookies and sketching. Lucy expanded on the picture she had already begun, adding detail to the trees and bushes around them, tweaking the images of her family to show them drawing. That was another part of the moment she wanted to keep: Eddie and Charlie cuddled up together while they drew, Ashley with her machine in front of her, and Dylan with a look of intense concentration on his face. She could never fully do them justice, but she wanted to capture their spirits as well as she could.

Ashley's machine *whirred* and *clicked* as she adjusted it. Strands of silvery metal took hold of the pencil, then lowered it until it touched the page.

"Draw tree," Ashley typed into the tablet she used to control the robots.

"TREE," the machine wrote in blocky letters, stabbing through the page a couple of times along the way.

Ashley went into the programming and made some adjustments, then tried again.

"Draw tree."

This time the machine at least managed a drawing: one large blob with a line sticking out of the bottom. She adjusted the parameters again and pointed the program toward more online resources showing how a tree should look.

"Draw tree," she tried again.

For a moment, nothing happened, then the pencil started moving. It darted frantically back and forth across the page, scritching and scratching. Ashley expected to see a tree shape emerge from the abstract lines, like when her mom drew. After a few minutes, she realized that things were happening the other way around: the machine was trying to draw a tree in so many different ways at once that all it was making was a big, dark mess. She hit the stop button, and it went still.

Meanwhile, Dylan was facing frustrations. Art wasn't one of his favorite classes in school, despite his friends' enthusiasm for their current comics project, and his mind tended to wander to magical things when he was supposed to be learning to draw. Now he wished that he'd been more attentive since his picture looked nothing like what he wanted. Magic was usually good for whatever he wanted to achieve, but today his attention to magic was getting in the way.

Then he had a flash of inspiration. He checked that no one was walking along the trail below them, then pulled out his wand and tapped his pencil. "Ducere lignum."

The pencil started darting across the page, creating an image of a tree. Sure, he hadn't used his hand to draw it, but he'd used his magic, so it counted as him drawing, right? Next, he would add some other trees, some bushes, a cookie, and then see how well the wand could draw people he knew.

Eddie and Charlie weren't worrying about whether their art looked right. They were having too much fun making it look cool. As well as dinosaurs, they'd included an elephant, a bear, and a giant spider, with a few stick figure trees in the background, to create a sense of scenery.

"How about if we add a shark?" Charlie said, whispering so as not to interrupt the others.

"Silly Daddy." Eddie shook his head. "No sharks in woods."

"What if it's an underwater forest?"

Eddie's eyes went wide at the wonderful novelty of that idea. Then he nodded vigorously.

"Shark and octopus." He started drawing tentacles.

After a while, Lucy glanced at her watch, then blinked in surprise. She knew that she had lost track of time, but not how badly. They had been here nearly two hours. She was amazed to see that everyone was still contentedly drawing. Even Buddy seemed happy dozing in the sun.

Quietly, she packed away the picnic things. When the others got bored, they could get moving again. For now, she was happy to see them enjoying nature and creativity together, without a care in the world.

CHAPTER TWENTY-FOUR

Heather led the Underfoot Brigade deeper into the earth, out of the concrete tunnels that lay under L.A. and into the deeper places she and the Tolderai had dug. The entire Brigade had insisted on coming along, not wanting to miss out on this field trip. She had been surprised by that. Given the voluntary nature of their schooling, there were usually a few Underfoots missing from any lesson she ran, but apparently the Tolderai's forest caves had a special appeal.

"This isn't the way we went before," Twylan said.

"No, we're going to a different cave," Heather said. "We have a growing number of forest caves, spread around under the city. This is the best one for today's lesson."

Up ahead, a light was glowing. The Underfoots kept their torches and light spells on, but that more distant light with all its promise of seeing something special drew their attention. They moved faster, eager to get there, and chattered excitedly to each other.

The tunnel opened into a wide cavern. The first of the Underfoots stopped inside, only to be pushed aside by the others as they spilled out of the tunnel. Soon, everyone was standing and staring around.

"It's amazing," Twylan said.

The forest was so much more impressive than the last one, like nothing else she had ever seen. The cavern itself was at least fifty feet high, creating plenty of space for the trees to grow. Instead of building an artificial ceiling to hold the roof up, the Tolderai had grown one, using magic to weave roots and vines into a dome that was perfectly solid and yet still bustled with life. Flowers and leaves hung from it, birds flew between them, and insects buzzed between the branches.

The trees themselves were a mixture of different types, most of them with green leaves, though some had the red of maples or shades that were closer to silver or yellow. They stirred in a breeze that blew in from root-lined ventilation tunnels high in the walls. Although they had only been growing down here in the dark for a short time, some already bore fruit. As Twylan watched, a squirrel bounced along a branch, shaking the pears that hung from it, and leapt to the next tree over.

Between the trees, the undergrowth varied. Some patches were thickly overgrown, with stands of ferns and tangles of vines. Others had short grass, patches of moss, or leafed plants that exuded sweet scents from underfoot. A series of magical lights suspended in root cages that glowed with the warm, welcoming light of a summer sun illuminated everything.

"Today, we're going to be talking about ecosystems," Heather said. "But I want you all to pay attention to that part, so first, you have half an hour to explore. Be back here in thirty minutes sharp, or this will be the only time we come to the caves."

That was enough to get everyone's attention. They looked at watches and phones and a few set alerts, determined to follow the rules if the rules would bring them back here.

Leontine was the first to take off and explore, launching himself into the air with a flap of his wings. He soared up into the treetops and away. Twylan and Kix took a more gentle approach, ambling together down the herb-planted space between the trees.

"This is lovely," Kix said in a soft voice.

"I know," Twylan said, equally quiet. "It's like something out of a fairytale."

"Do you think this is what real forests are like out beyond L.A.?"

"Some of them, maybe, though I haven't seen many pictures that are as good as this."

They walked toward the far side of the cave, paying attention to the landmarks as they passed. Theoretically, the cave wasn't big enough for them to get lost in. They should have been able to make for a wall in any direction and then walk around the outside. But the walls had quickly vanished from view, and they didn't want to take any chances on getting back in time.

Twylan drew a deep breath as the scents of sage and rosemary joined the clear smell of tree sap.

"This reminds me of that book we were looking at in Carol's class, the one about the art of historical gardens. Remember how some of the rich people would have their gardeners bring in plants from all over the world?"

"Yes!" Kix said excitedly. "And they'd organize them into different sections, to represent different places or ideas, or because it was more visually pleasing."

"That's what this feels like—plants from all over the world. Except that instead of laying them out along themes and ideas, they're all jammed in together. It's a jumble of different pieces. Amazing pieces, but chaotic."

Kix laughed. "I suppose that's the Tolderai for you. They're not interested in asserting order, only jamming as much life in as possible."

Their route brought them to the center of the forest. The ground here was damp, and it ran down into a pool at the heart of this small, green world.

"Is it weird that I didn't think about water?" Kix said.

"I didn't either. I suppose, with it being underground, I just assumed that the roots would find water from somewhere."

"It's another spell, like the lights, see?" Kix pointed at the surface of the pool. Ripples were running out from the center as the water rose from the depths in a slow, constant stream, creating something like a small fountain in the middle of the pool.

"It could be a machine, like the ones people have in their gardens."

"Really?"

Twylan laughed. "No, of course not. This is the Tolderai."

They took off their shoes and socks and walked into the shallows. The water was cool, clear, and refreshing. Even here, plants were growing, and a frog hopped across lily pads at one side.

"This is the most perfect thing I've ever seen," Kix said.

"Not perfect." Twylan pointed between the trees. "Look."

They waded back out of the pool and over to the thing she had spotted, a plant dying in the shade of the trees. Its leaves had turned brown, and it was wilting, fading into the soil.

"What happened to it?" Kix asked.

"Maybe it isn't getting enough light? Or it can't compete with the other plants here for food and water."

"That's such a shame. Should we move it?"

"Why not?"

They didn't have any tools to dig with, but the soil was soft and crumbly beneath their fingers. They scooped dirt out in a ring around the plant, then lifted it out, roots and all, careful not to damage the already weakened leaves. Then, with equal care, they dug another hole, close to the edge of the pool. They lowered the root ball into that hole and patted the soil into place.

They paused to look around.

"I bet Carol wasn't involved in setting up this forest," Kix said. "It doesn't look like an artist's work."

Twylan laughed. "You're right. She would have used some of the lessons from that book."

"Or at least laid things out so that the smaller trees were at the edge. Then we could see over them to the taller ones."

"Lots of layers, like in a landscape painting."

"And with these different colored trees, you could set up some lovely contrasts. A band of something silvery breaking up the deeper greens, perhaps reds and oranges around the edge."

"She would have laid the undergrowth out differently as well, to create paths and ways through. Then people could appreciate it all more easily."

Twylan glanced at her phone.

"We should get back. Time's nearly up."

They washed the soil off their hands in the pool, put their socks and shoes on, and headed back along the route they had taken into the woods.

"We could rearrange this for them," Kix said. "Make it more visually pleasing. It would be a good way to show how much we've learned. I think Carol would like that."

"I think you're right." Twylan smiled. "Should we talk to Heather about it?"

"No, let's keep it as a surprise. That way, it will be even more special."

They were emerging from the trees, and as they did, Leontine came down to land beside them.

"What are you two talking about?" he asked.

"Oh, nothing," Twylan said. "How was it up there?"

"Amazing. This whole place is fantastic."

"Isn't it?"

They joined the rest of the Underfoots gathering around the tunnel mouth. Heather did a headcount and, apparently satisfied, raised her voice to address them.

"I hope you all enjoyed that, but now it's time to focus. I have another guest teacher for you." She ushered a young wizard into view. He had a blond ponytail, a thin goatee, and a nervous smile. "This is Nathaniel Oakmantle. As well as being a Tolderai, Nathaniel has a doctorate in ecosystems, in which he researched reforesting projects. He's going to talk to you all about what we're doing here, how it works, and what it teaches us about the living environment." She took a step back and then, when Nathaniel didn't say anything, gave him a nudge. "Get on with it."

"Um, hi." Nathaniel waved a hand. "So, let's start with trees..."

Nathaniel started talking, but he wasn't as interesting as Carol or as forceful as Heather. At the back of the group, Twylan and Kix turned their attention away from him and started whispering to each other.

"When can we start?" Kix asked.

"How about tomorrow night?"

"Brilliant. I already have an idea for how to rearrange the trees."

CHAPTER TWENTY-FIVE

Charlie knocked on the door of the house. It was a strange, isolated place, in the hills outside L.A., one that combined turrets, arches, and balconies with solar panels and a wind turbine on the roof. It looked like the creation of a mad inventor, or possibly seventeen of them all working at cross purposes, trying to build different versions of the house. Just looking at it, he felt sure that they'd reached the right place and were at the home of a magical.

"It's certainly something." Ringo stared up at the building. "Something that must have cost a lot of money. This guy can afford to pay our fees."

Charlie knocked again, then noticed the bell pull hidden among the complex carvings around the door. It looked like a leg protruding from one of the semi-naked classical figures that someone—for reasons he would never understand—had thought were perfect to be sculpted around a door frame. He pulled on it, and a bell gave a dull *clonk* somewhere inside.

"I'm coming. I'm coming."

The muffled and distant voice emerged from beyond the strange carvings. The door swung open, and a man appeared. He wore workman's boots, tweed trousers, a tie-dye t-shirt, and a gold chain with a clock hanging from it. Whisps of gray hair protruded from beneath a large tartan beret.

"Are you Mister Mulvers?" Charlie asked when he finally got over the extraordinary outfit enough to find his words.

"Certainly am," said the strange-looking man. "And you are?"

"Charlie Heron and Ringo Fuller, from Green Machine Conversions. You asked us to come out and make some changes to your car?"

"Oh, the magical green men!" Mulvers exclaimed, clapping his hands together.

"I suppose you could call us that, yes."

"In that case, give me a moment to fix my image. You know how it is, got to put on a display in case of mundane callers."

Mulvers flexed his hand, magic sparkled between his fingers, and the air around him shimmered. He started to shrink as layers of illusion peeled away, and Charlie realized that this must be why his clothing choice was so odd: it wasn't real, but a hurried illusion, and one that had probably gone wrong somewhere along the line.

Except that the clothes didn't change. As the last of the magic dissipated, a gnome was left standing in front of them, still dressed in his previous extraordinary combination of clothes, but at half the height.

"Let me show you the collection." Mulvers led them

down the steps, along a gravel driveway, and around the side of the house, to a building that looked more like a sixteenth-century stable block than a modern garage.

"Collection?" Ringo asked.

"Oh yes, the job isn't only one car." Mulvers grinned and waved a hand. "It's all of these."

A whole row of cars sat in the broad building, each one unique. There was a Porsche, a Rolls Royce, a Mini Cooper, even a Ford Model T, the granddaddy of modern motor cars.

"Looks like you've made some modifications of your own." Ringo approached the first car in line. It was a DeLorean, a strange enough vehicle in itself, with its distinctive doors that lifted. But it was made even odder by the changes that had taken place. There were lights on the wheels, two short smokestacks protruding from the hood, and a row of tiny windmills on the roof.

"I dabble," Mulvers said, spinning one of the windmills. "Mostly for fun, though sometimes for effect." He patted one of the smokestacks. "This one, for example, can be powered by exotic fuels, while the Mini over there can fly if you cast the right spells into the engine. Not flight spells, obviously." He chuckled and shook his head. "What a thought."

Charlie opened the door of the DeLorean and peered at the controls. There were far more runes than on the average car. There was also a raised seat and an extension on the steering column so that Mulvers' height wouldn't get in the way of driving.

"Are any of them normal?" he asked.

"What is normal?" Mulvers asked. "Hurtling around the

country in a steel box powered by burning prehistoric remains could hardly be considered normal, could it? Yet here we are."

"I mean, have any of them not been modified already?"

"Oh no. I hate boring cars."

Charlie didn't think that anyone could ever consider a DeLorean boring, especially when you considered the potential for *Back to the Future* impressions, but it wasn't his place to criticize a client. He raised an eyebrow at Ringo, who shrugged.

"We've never worked on a pre-modded car before," Ringo said. "This might take longer than normal."

"I understand." Mulvers patted the hood of the DeLorean. "I wouldn't want a rush job."

"It might be more expensive," Ringo added.

"Fine by me." Mulvers winked. "My family is on the loaded side. The others waste their money on things like investment banks and construction companies, but what's the point of that? Live rich, die rich, have no fun along the way? No, I'd much rather spend it, and if that means you guys can make my gas guzzlers run green, then that's a win for everyone except Aunt Gladys, who we should all ignore."

"Okay then, I'll bring the van around."

While Ringo went to fetch their vehicle, and with it all the materials and tools, Charlie looked over the machines they would be adapting.

"Which one has the fewest modifications?" he asked.

"Hm, probably the Mini."

"The flying Mini?"

"Apart from that, it only has five or six changes. Barely touched it."

Again, words clearly meant something different to Mulvers, but Charlie wasn't going to object.

With a crunch of gravel, the van came around the corner. Ringo parked, got out, and started taking tools from the back.

"Mind if I watch you?" Mulvers asked. "It's always a pleasure to see craftsmen at work."

Again, Charlie exchanged a look with Ringo. This job already wasn't what they had expected, but it was a lot of work, and they might be willing to work differently for that.

"Sure," he said. "They're your cars. You should get to see what we're doing."

Together with Ringo, he levitated the Mini a couple of feet above the ground, then laid it on a set of blocks they'd made to ensure they could access the parts they needed. The underside of the Mini was a strange place compared with the cars they had worked on before, but they set to it with enthusiasm, answering Mulvers' questions as they went along.

"What rune is that? Why the exhaust pipe? Did you try any other materials for the filters? What if I had a car with five exhausts? Would you put the same spells in every one?"

The chattering gnome added entertainment to the day as they stripped out the underside of his car and reassembled it with added magic and mechanical materials. Once everything was back in place, they took the Mini off the blocks, set up sensors around the exhaust, and turned the engine on.

Charlie frowned as he looked at the readings. "That's not right."

Ringo joined him. "Recalibrate the sensors."

They pressed a series of buttons and tried again, then tested their van just to be on the safe side. The results were clear. What had worked on two dozen other vehicles wasn't making a bit of difference to Mulvers' car.

"Let's try again," Ringo said. "Maybe we set something up wrong."

His tone was as doubtful as Charlie felt, but they levitated the car again anyway, set it on the blocks, and stripped out their original work before installing the spells and parts again. This time, they kept the car on blocks while they ran their tests. It still hadn't worked.

"Must be interference from the other mods," Ringo said. "You got any idea which one could cause this?"

"Me?" Mulvers shook his head. "Heavens, no. I just tinker at changes until they work, got no real idea how they interact with each other."

"Well, let's try something different." Charlie scratched his head. "Perhaps if we move the filters up so they're not right next to those purple crystals. I could also put the runes on the outside of the pipe as well as the inside to reinforce the spells."

It took the best part of an hour, the unfamiliar configuration making even minor changes more difficult than they should be, but by the end, everything was in place.

"Let's give it a go." Ringo started up the engine, then

went around to the rear with their sensor array. He shook his head. "Still as bad as ever."

"This is clearly going to be a tough one," Mulvers said. "I'll go make coffee. You boys keep tinkering."

Three coffee breaks and an impromptu picnic lunch later, they were no closer to a solution than they had been at the start.

"I'm sorry, Mr. Mulvers, but I don't think we can fix the fumes on your cars," Charlie said. "If this is the trouble we have with the simplest one, we might never get the rest fixed."

"Nonsense," Mulvers said. "You're bright guys with a good product and fighting spirit. I have every faith in you."

"But it doesn't work!" Ringo flung his wrench down in the gravel. "Your mad tinkering is getting in the way of all our spells."

"It is rather, isn't it?" Mulvers wiggled his eyebrows. "Here's the thing, though. To me, fixing up a car is more an art than a science. You can't just engineer your way out or pick an answer from an instruction manual. You have to play around and find what works. If it gets me the master-piece I want, I'm happy to pay for your time and materials while you keep tinkering. You'll get there in the end."

"And if we don't?"

Mulvers shrugged. "Then I'll still have paid you. What do you say?"

"We have other clients," Charlie said gently. "People waiting on our services. Not to mention our day jobs."

"And I'm happy to be fitted in around all that. Now, what do you say?"

Charlie looked at Ringo. It had been a long, frustrating

day, but even in their failures, they'd learned a lot about magically modified cars and came up with ideas to refine their work. Plus, Mulvers was willing to keep paying…

"Fine." Ringo picked up the wrench. "We'll be back, but I'm finished with this madness for today."

CHAPTER TWENTY-SIX

"Where we going?" Eddie asked. He'd been busy thinking about dinosaurs when the family set out from home, and it was only five minutes later that he realized he had no idea what was going on. This sort of thing could lead to situations he'd rather avoid, like a trip to the dentist or getting stuck wandering around the supermarket. If he needed to start raising objections, now was the time to do it.

"We're going to visit my friend Ellis," Lucy said. "You remember him. He's the one who came over for dinner with Sarah."

Eddie made his thoughtful face. It helped when he was trying to remember things. "Red shoes?"

"Yes, that's him."

"Okay." The man with the red shoes had been funny. This could be a good trip out. Plus, there were muffins in the box Eddie's mom was carrying, and he had high hopes for eating some of them later.

Their route took them down toward the southern end of Silver Lake. They were in no particular rush, so they took their time, letting Buddy sniff at trees and lampposts, exploring what other dogs lived around here, and looking for squirrels he could chase. The squirrels in the trees above watched Buddy in silent suspicion.

The house they were heading for was on a quiet street. It had an overgrown front yard, and some of the external paint was flaking off. It didn't exactly scream dream home.

"Al would never let us get away with this," Charlie said as they walked up the driveway. "He'd be at the door every day, offering advice on how to make the place more presentable, suggesting ways to get the plants under control."

"Maybe Ellis doesn't have an Al of his own," Lucy said. "Or maybe he hasn't had time to act on that advice yet. After all, he's only been here a few days."

"You think Al would take that as an excuse? Al was round within hours of that plank falling off our gable. I hadn't even noticed there was anything wrong."

"Are you complaining?"

"Definitely not! He helped me fix it too. But maybe next time he needs a project, we could point him this way."

Lucy shifted her box of muffins, balancing them in one hand, and knocked on the door with the other.

"One second," Ellis called from inside. There was a clattering, a *thump*, and some muffled muttering. Then the door creaked open to reveal Ellis. For once, he wasn't wearing his combination of dark suit, red tie, and matching sneakers. Instead, he was dressed in loose overalls, their material new but already spattered with paint stains. "Howdy, Herons. Come on in."

He took a step back, and there was a crinkling as

plastic sheeting shifted under his feet. It stretched all across the living room floor, and like Ellis, one corner was heavily stained, though the rest of it was pristine. That was also the one corner of the room that had been painted.

"Might want to steer clear of that part," he said, gesturing with his brush. "It's where I've been working."

"Just got started, huh?" Charlie said, looking at the patch of yellow against the walls' old off-gray.

"This morning, yep," Ellis said. "Reckon it's a couple of hours' work well done."

"A couple of hours?" Charlie stared incredulously at the small painted area.

"He probably had to clean the walls first," Lucy said. "Then lay down this sheeting, get the things together…"

"No, that was just painting time," Ellis said, looking around. "Should I have gotten further?"

"Not necessarily," Charlie said, rapidly trying to walk back his words. "I mean, this is probably your first time decorating a house, right?"

"Sure is. Never had a place I could do this before. Gotta say, it's harder than I expected. Folks on the how-to videos, they all look clean and orderly, and they race through this stuff, but it's taking me forever, and, well…" He gestured down his paint-spattered front. "You can see how clean I am. I mean, how does anyone do this without spattering themselves?"

Lucy glanced at the brush sticking out of a can, coated with paint up past the bristles.

"Maybe we could help," she said. "Speed things up."

"I'll go fetch a few things." Charlie headed out the door.

"This is mighty kind of you," Ellis said, "but you don't have to join. I've got this."

"It's what friends are for." Lucy held out her box. "And they're also for providing provisions. How about if you stop for coffee and cake, and we can start again when Charlie comes back?"

Charlie returned half an hour later, bringing a car full of coveralls, brushes, rollers, and all the other accouterments of interior decoration. By then, there was one muffin left for him and a wide spray of crumbs across Eddie's chin.

"We can get started while you have coffee." Lucy pulled coveralls on over her other clothes.

"That's okay," Charlie said. "I'll save my muffin for later."

"Better guard it closely then. Eddie has his hungry dinosaur look on."

She'd had time to talk with Ellis about his designs for the house and develop a plan to bring them about. With the organizational efficiency of a trained manager and, more importantly, an experienced mom, she handed out paint-brushes, rollers, and the tasks to go with them.

"Charlie, you can do the ceiling in here while Dylan and Ashley help Ellis with the walls. Eddie and I will clean the walls in the other rooms so they're ready when you finish. We'll take Buddy with us to keep him out of the paint."

"Can I use my robots?" Ashley shook her backpack.

"Can they paint?"

"If I program them right."

This was more about involving the kids than getting much out of them, and playing with robots was always a good way to involve Ashley, so Lucy nodded. Then she grabbed some cloths and a bowl of soapy water and led Eddie and Buddy into another room.

"We're going to make this into game," she said. "What sort of supervillain could we defeat by washing the walls?"

Eddie looked thoughtfully down at the water, then popped a soap bubble.

"Lex Luthor," he said.

"Perfect. So, we're helping Superman to beat Lex Luthor by washing Lex's microrobots off the walls. We've got to get every inch of the wall, or the robots will grow back, so you need to be really thorough. Can you do that?"

Eddie nodded, dunked his cloth in the water, and dribbled soap bubbles across the floor. "Ready."

While Buddy napped in the corner of the room, Lucy and Eddie set to work. Obviously, he could only reach low places, so Lucy started high, figuring that she would work her way down to meet him. But when she turned with half the walls already cleaned, she noticed that Eddie had barely moved an inch.

"Are you all right there, sweetheart?" she asked.

"Being thorough," Eddie said. "Getting all the robots."

He was moving his cloth in tiny, purposeful strokes only a fingertip wide. Any concerns Lucy had that she would have to go back over his work vanished. This was, as Eddie had said, very thorough indeed.

With that room done, they headed to the next floor. Lucy smiled as laughter drifted up the stairs. The others were having fun, and if the occasional *clunk* or shout of alarm indicated that things weren't going completely smoothly, at least the work was getting done without anyone getting annoyed.

She finished by washing the walls in the master bedroom, one of the few with any furniture in it, a double bed with Ellis's suitcase sat next to it. At least he'd done that much moving in. She hoped that he would get a closet once the decorating was done, rather than living out of a suitcase forever. Habits were fine, but you could go too far. She wrung out the cloth, looked around at a job well done, and headed down the stairs.

The first sign she saw of the chaos below was a stain on the floor right by the bottom of the stairs. She stopped on the bottom step, holding back Eddie and Buddy, and looked around.

No one could deny that the walls had been painted. In fact, they were so thoroughly painted that it was dripping off in places, or running in slow trickles to the floor. But the painters were also quite thoroughly painted. Dylan's dark hair had gained yellow highlights, Ashley was spattered down her front, and Charlie looked like he'd walked into a wall. Even Ashley's robot had changed color. They waved their brushes at her enthusiastically.

"What happened?" she asked.

"We got the job done," Ellis said proudly. "Pretty fine, right?"

"You missed a bit," Lucy said, pointing to one corner and then to a patch of ceiling. "And one there. How did you manage that when you've got so much on yourselves?"

"We were having fun," Charlie said. "Competing for who could do their bit quickest, or make the funniest shape, or hold their brush in the strangest way while still painting."

Lucy laughed and shook her head. "You'd never get away with this if Al was in charge. And look at the state of you all! The paint's even got under the sheets, onto the floor."

"Dang." Ellis looked down. "Does that mean I need a new floor too?"

"Let's not get carried away." Lucy looked at them and reconsidered those words. "Let's not get carried away again. Now, none of you move."

"But..."

"No buts." She drew her wand. "Someone needs to clear up this mess."

She waved her wand through the air and started to chant. Like a scene from *Fantasia*, the brushes lifted into the air, then marched neatly out the back door, followed by the cans of paint. Soapy water fell like rain on the paint-spattered decorators, then evaporated once they were clean. With a gesture from Lucy, the plastic sheets crumpled into a heap, revealing the paint spots on the floor. Another spell washed those away. At last, the Herons and Ellis stood, clean and dry, in a room where the only reminder of decoration was the smell of fresh paint.

"What about the bits we missed?" Ellis asked, pointing at the ceiling.

Lucy waved her wand again, and the paint rearranged itself, filling the gaps. Every wall was now perfectly covered.

Exhausted by the magical effort, Lucy sat on the bottom of the stairs.

"I could do with a cuppa," she said.

"You've earned it." Ellis went to put the kettle on. When he came back in, he looked around happily. "This is mighty fine work. Thanks for your help, Herons, but maybe I should use magic for the other rooms. It feels like cheating, but…"

"What's the point in having magic," Lucy said, "if you don't cheat with it once in a while?"

CHAPTER TWENTY-SEVEN

Gruffbar sat back in his chair, boots up on the desk, reading through the fine print of a contract. This was a good one. He admired the skill of the other lawyer, his ability to sneak possibilities in through the way the clauses interacted. A lesser lawyer might have missed it, but to Gruffbar it was like seeing the gears in a machine slot together, each doing nothing, but together creating a machine that would grind down anyone who opposed it. Oh yes, this was the work of a craftsman, and as the lawyer for the other side of the deal, it was Gruffbar's duty to tear it apart. He picked up a pen and started crossing out clauses.

A noise made him look up. Someone was shouting down in the auto shop. That usually meant a dissatisfied customer, and Gruffbar had earned the occasional week of free rent by sorting out disagreements that went too far. It was always worth a look to see what was going on.

He walked around his desk, opened the door, and stepped out onto the top of the iron staircase. By the entrance to the shop floor, someone was arguing with Gunther, a brave thing to do given his intimidating bulk. Their face stayed hidden at first, but then Gunther shifted, and Gruffbar saw Heather Fields, her face knotted up in fury.

"It's his professional office!" she snarled at Gunther. "Of course people can go there to see him."

"People who have appointments," Gunther said. "People who don't attack my staff."

"Your man was in the way." Heather gestured toward a mechanic who stood off to one side, clutching his stomach.

"He says he got out of the way."

"Oh, he got out of the way all right, so that he could grab my—"

"Hey!" Gruffbar shouted, hurrying down the stairs. "There's no need for trouble here. Ms. Fields, why don't you head up to my office, and I'll sort this out." She stomped off up the stairs, and Gruffbar turned to the mechanic. "Seriously?"

"It was just—"

"Don't pull that shit, man, especially not on my clients." Gruffbar turned to Gunther. "Sorry. Is this gonna be a problem?"

"Not for you." Gunther glared at the mechanic. "But we're gonna have some words about workplace harassment."

It wasn't the response Gruffbar had expected, but he wasn't going to complain. He hurried up the stairs and closed the office door behind him.

"Sorry about that," he said. "Can I offer you something? A whiskey, maybe, or a coffee?"

"From your plastic pollution machine?"

"I have some chamomile tea that only needs hot water and a teabag, no plastic."

"You drink chamomile tea?"

"Some of my clients are elves."

"Well, I don't care about those clients." Heather flung a magazine down on his desk. "I care about this."

Apparently, the inappropriate mechanic wasn't the only thing making Heather angry. Gruffbar sat and flicked through the magazine, trying to work out what was winding her up. It was a locally produced 'zine from a collective based in the arts district, poorly spell-checked but with some striking visuals. Among them were photos of bowls in a familiar style, as well as prints and t-shirts that imitated their pattern.

"Is this Tolderai work?" he asked.

"No! They're ripping us off."

"Ah, I see."

Gruffbar took out his phone and pulled up pictures of the artifacts Heather had loaned to Penley's gallery. The bowls in the magazine weren't an exact duplicate, but there was an undeniable similarity of style. Reading the magazine more closely, he learned that this was the whole point. The artists were trying to capture the spirit of these ancient artifacts, which they referred to as "the style of an age more authentic than our own, more grounded in the realities of dirt, sweat, and the forest's song," whatever any of that meant. Gruffbar seriously doubted that the members of a hip art collective knew anything about dirt and sweat, except for the dirt and sweat they saw on TV.

"This isn't the only one," Heather said. "I saw a kid

selling t-shirts with our pattern on them and someone painting them on the side of their house. You have to stop this."

"I do?"

"You're our lawyer!"

"So you're hiring me again?"

"Of course I'm hiring you again! Why else would I be in a place that stinks of petrol fumes?"

"Some people like it."

"Some people are idiots."

She glared at him. Gruffbar held his tongue. He didn't need his clients to share his tastes or even be polite about them, though it helped. What he needed was for them to pay, and Heather had shown that she could.

"You're saying that you want to defend your intellectual property?"

"No, I want them to stop copying our art."

"Same thing."

Heather pressed at her temples with her fingers. "This sort of nonsense makes my head hurt. It was so much easier when we spent all our time tending to trees."

"Let's start at the beginning. How long have people been doing this?"

"A few days."

"Since the gallery opening?"

"Exactly! They didn't even wait a week, just started ripping us off."

"And I presume that this undermines your profits from your people's work?"

"Penley is still paying us."

"Not that, the ancillary profits."

"The what?"

Gruffbar drew a deep breath. It was like trying to explain supercomputers to a gerbil.

"Your people's art is very hot right now. It's new, it's exciting, people want to see more of it. This is a chance to sell prints, photos, t-shirts. Have you not considered that?"

"Of course not."

"Well, if you're not meeting a market demand, someone else will."

"Stop the legal talk and explain it properly."

"That wasn't law, that was economics."

"Do I look like I care?" Heather loomed over his desk, hands gripping the edge tight, glaring down at him. "Make it go away."

"It's not that simple."

"Make it simple."

"I can't!"

Now he was on his feet too, glaring up at her, shouting back. Someone knocked on the door.

"You all right in there, Gruffbar?" Gunther called.

Gruffbar drew a deep breath, then sank back into his seat.

"Nothing to worry about," he called back. "Just a difference of perspectives."

He took a bottle from a desk drawer, poured generous slugs of whiskey into a pair of glass tumblers, and slid one across the desk to Heather.

"Sit down and drink that."

"Why?"

"Because I need you to calm down and listen. I can

make the chamomile tea instead if you prefer, but that stuff tastes like—"

Heather knocked back the whiskey and sank into her seat, which exhaled a cloud of dust. "Get on with it."

"By my beard, woman, you don't make this easy." Gruffbar sipped his drink. If he'd known she was going to chuck it back like that, he would have given her the cheap stuff, but it was too late now to avoid that waste. "People like what your ancestors made. Is that all right with you?"

"Of course. It's good art."

"Great. Well, when people like something, they want more of it. Some of them want their version, so they can feel like they own a piece of beauty. Some want to wear it to signal their taste to the world. Some just want to look at variations on the theme, like when you get into *Law and Order* so you watch a dozen different versions because it's not as good as the original, but it's as close as you can get. That make sense?"

"Yes." Heather grabbed the bottle and poured herself another shot. This time she sipped it, to Gruffbar's relief. She was still frowning, but he felt like he was making progress.

"So, that's what's happening with your artifacts. People love them. They're making art inspired by them, painting murals in that style, wearing t-shirts to show how cool they are for noticing the hip new thing. This wouldn't happen if the art wasn't good."

Heather sipped her drink and nodded. "I understand. You're trying to persuade me to see this as a compliment to my ancestors."

"Well, it is."

"So I should just accept it?"

"I didn't say that."

Now they were into more comfortable territory. Gruffbar could see the opportunities for profit lining up. The souvenirs. The licensed imitations. The ticket sales from a tour of the original artifacts. Then there were the conversations to be had with people like this art collective, the threats to take imitators to court, and what those imitators would pay to avoid it. Sometimes the law just needed to be a threat, the gleam of a blade in the dark rather than the plunging of a knife into someone's back.

And of course, as the Tolderai's lawyer, he would take his cut of their cut of any profits. This trend might not last, but he was more than ready to ride it to the bank.

He rubbed his hands together.

"The market won't let you stop this completely, but you can profit from it. Control the reproductions and imitators so that you get your cut. This is a golden opportunity."

"No." Heather set her glass down on the desk.

"I already told you, we can't stop it, so this is the best we can do."

"No, now that I understand, the best we can do is nothing."

Gruffbar sank back in his seat. "What do you mean?"

"I was angry at people for imitating us, but you're right. It's a compliment and a sign of our influence. That's a difficult thing to adjust to, but one we can make use of. I should accept it and let it flower."

"You can make money off it while it flowers."

"And limit its growth? No, I would rather see how this

thing scatters its seeds and what they grow into. We can decide what to do with them later."

Gruffbar could feel the profit draining out of his future, like blood running from his veins. It was heartbreaking.

He looked at the magazine again. Some of the art in there wasn't bad, and who knew what the current generation of artists could make from the Tolderai style. This might lead to good things. He just wished they could be profitable for him.

"Once you relinquish control, stop protecting your IP, you can't take that control back," he said, one last attempt to get Heather on board. "Better to assert your intellectual rights now. You can always let go later."

"No, I've decided." Heather stood. "Thank you, Gruffbar. You've helped me to understand the world better."

"Just doing my job." He reached for the whiskey bottle. "My bill will be in the mail."

CHAPTER TWENTY-EIGHT

Twylan and Kix sat in Twylan's room in the Underfoot Brigade's home tunnel. Like most of the Underfoot dwellings, they'd built the room from waste materials, with walls constructed from abandoned boards and plastic sheeting, the furniture collected from dumpsters. Twylan had put in a lot of effort to make the place a home, with posters, offcuts of wallpaper, and faerie lights strung across the walls. From humble beginnings, it had become more homey than the solidly built rooms of many other teenagers.

The two of them sat on the bed with books scattered around them. They had been to the public library and taken out as many books as they could relating to garden design. There were beautiful picture books with large, glossy full-page photos, how-to books with guidance on laying out and plant a scenic garden, and dry, academic books filled with theory. Each filled them with excitement.

"Look at this." Twylan held up one of the biggest books. A double-page spread showed a managed forest where rows of trees in different colors created a striped pattern. "It's how I imagined arranging the trees."

"We should layer them," Kix said. "Use height as well as color, and put some of the more striking colors further back, so they don't overwhelm the rest. What do you think of this?"

She held up a sketch, bringing together the ideas they had been working on. Art and design were Kix's areas of expertise, having grown up in a family of tailors and fashion designers, and her gift showed through now.

"It's brilliant," Twylan said. She looked around at the other books they had gathered. "Do you think we should read more of them, to see what else they suggest, before we go and make any changes?"

Kix looked at the books.

"There's an awful lot there."

"It could be useful."

"We have a design that works, right? We don't need to know any more."

"You're right." Twylan closed her book. "Let's do it."

Leaving the books where they lay, they set off out of Twylan's home and down the Brigade's main tunnel, past the homes of their friends and companions.

"Where are you two off to?" Siltor asked, pausing in the middle of a new illusion.

"Oh, just going for a walk," Twylan said, as innocently as she could. They had decided not to tell anyone else what they were doing in case others wanted to get involved. The more people knew, the more likely it was that the secret would get out, spoiling the surprise for Heather.

Siltor gave them a curious look. "Seems to me like you're up to something."

"You know what they say about people who are up to something," Kix said.

"No, what?"

"Takes one to know one. So what are you up to, Siltor?"

"Nothing! Got to go now."

He hurried into his home.

"Well, now I really want to know what he's up to," Twylan said once she stopped laughing.

"Do you want that enough to stick around here?"

"No, let's go do this."

They hurried down the tunnel into a narrower one at the far end and deeper into the network that ran beneath L.A. Following the route Heather had taken them along a few days before, they headed deep into the ground, past the end of the concrete tunnels, and into the deeper dark the Tolderai had carved below.

Even before they reached the forest chamber, they could sense it coming. The air smelled different, there was a fresh taste on their tongues, and the soft twitter of birds and insects echoed through the lifeless dark. By the time they reached the forest, they were already giddy with anticipation.

To their relief, no one else was around. Even in the absence of magicals, artificial sunlight shone down, bathing the trees in its warm glow.

Kix pulled the design out of the pocket of her sequined dungarees.

"Where should we start?" she asked.

"Let's go to the pool. Then we'll be in the middle of things."

Herbs gave up their scent as the two girls made their way through the shadows beneath the trees to the pool that irrigated the cave. Here, the earth was soft and damp, a perfect place to start digging plants up and shifting them around.

"Show me again," Twylan said.

She surveyed the diagram, then held out her hands.

"I'll lift things. You move them. You're more likely to get them into the right places."

"That means you're doing all the heavy lifting."

"I know, but I have the power for it." Twylan tapped her cheek below where magical light flared from her eyes, leaving sooty marks across her skin.

"All right, but be careful."

Without meaning to, Kix took a step back. She had seen what could happen when her friend let her full power fly, and it could be as dangerous as it was powerful. Beneath Twylan's gentle demeanor there was magic that could level office blocks.

Twylan looked around, then raised her arms and chanted. The words hung in the air, power emerging around them, magic spilling from her eyes and flashing around her fingertips. The air was electric, leaves and blades of grass standing on end, and insects flung around in a rising wind.

The trees shook and started to rise. One by one, spreading out in an ever-widening circle, they lifted from the ground, roots and all, and hung in the air. Twylan hovered too, lifted by the currents of her power, slowly rotating with the flow of magic.

Kix closed her eyes for a moment, picturing the design they had planned, then opened them again and began. Using her magic, she pushed the floating trees to the left and right, back and forth, rearranging them into neat, color-coded groups. They spread out at her direction, forming lines and circles, smooth avenues down which people could walk. A flick of her hands propelled dirt out of the ground, making holes for the roots to fill, then refilled them once the trees had sunk into position.

With the trees in place, they started rearranging the other plants. First came the bushes and ferns, then areas of grass and herbs, and finally layers of moss. Some formed smooth curves, while others settled into a checkerboard pattern, a touch they had borrowed from a Tudor gardening book.

By now, Kix was sweating from the strain of the work, her magic almost entirely spent. She didn't know how Twylan could do what she did, pumping out ten times the power but still keep going. She was a powerhouse, and she had it all under control.

Trembling with exhaustion, Kix approached her friend where she hung in the air, eyes blazing like twin suns, and tugged on her skirts.

"You can stop now, Twylan. We're finished."

The light in Twylan's eyes flared, then faded. Her feet settled on the mossy ground, then she sank to her knees, eyes dull, and stared into the clear waters of the pool. "I'm exhausted. Wish we'd brought snacks."

"Who says we didn't?" Kix pulled two large chocolate

bars from her pocket and handed one to Twylan. They unwrapped them and ate in weary silence, staring around at the results of their work.

The forest looked even more beautiful than before. Where there had been a wild medley of unordered and untamed plants, now there was a pattern—an aesthetic, a sense of something behind it all. Individual plants stood out against the contrasting leaves of their neighbors or combined to create larger areas of a single shade. The patterns of low plants marked out routes between the trees, flanked by lines of herbs, flowers, and ferns.

"We did good," Twylan mumbled around a mouthful of chocolate.

A movement between the trees made them look around. Heather Fields appeared, scowling and cursing under her breath. She stopped when she saw Twylan and Kix.

"You two?" She looked around at the rearranged forest. "Did you do this?"

"Oh, yes," they said in unison.

"Why would you do this?"

"To make it look better," Twylan said. "You put so much effort into the plants, but not the layout. After all the art lessons, we thought we could help out. Do you like it?"

Heather pressed her hands against her face and let out a muffled growl.

"I don't think she likes it," Kix said, her voice quivering with the same nervousness that Twylan felt.

"I know that you did this with the best of intentions," Heather looked at them again, "but now I have to undo it all."

"Why?" Twylan's heart sank. Had all their effort been for nothing?

"Because the design of gardens isn't only about how they look, it's about how the plants grow. It's about giving each of them the right soil, the right light, the right drainage. It's about how they go together.

"It might have looked wild, but I planned this place out in a purposeful way, to give every plant the best chance of flourishing so that it could become something self-sustaining. You've undone a lot of that."

"But it wasn't working," Kix said. "Plants were dying. We saw them."

"That's part of how a forest works." Heather crouched on the mossy ground in front of them. "Weren't you listening to what Nathaniel said? Plants dying and rotting, others springing up to take their place, that's the cycle of nature. It's what keeps a forest healthy. Without it, we'd have to keep coming in here with manure or chemical composts or who knows what else. We planned that death and decay."

"I'm so sorry," Twylan said. "We had no idea."

"And you didn't think to ask?"

"We wanted to surprise you."

"You certainly did that." Heather rubbed her eyes. "It was a... I don't know, a thoughtful gesture. But you've put form before function. That's fine with art, where form is the function. It can even work for fashion. But for a forest, function has to come before form." She pulled out her wand. "Come on, let's put this back how it was, then I'm taking you for a catchup lesson on how ecosystems work."

CHAPTER TWENTY-NINE

"New coffee time question," Jackie said. "If you could meet any witch or wizard, real or legendary, from any time in history, who would it be, and why?"

They walked out of Starbucks, Jackie carrying a coffee and Lucy a steaming cup of tea, and headed for Lucy's SUV.

"I don't know," Lucy said. "Merlin, maybe? He must have seen all sorts of things. Castles, battles, kings, random women waving swords out of ponds. His stories would be great. How about you?"

"Probably one of those witches from the fairy tales, like the one who lived in a gingerbread house. I have serious questions about the structural integrity of a place like that."

"So you want to become a mythical building inspector?"

"I'd have other questions too, including how you get an oven big enough to put annoying kids in. Or annoying adults."

A pigeon flapped down to land on Lucy's shoulder. She

untied the ribbon around its leg and unrolled the message from underneath.

"No time for inspections now." She held up the slip of paper. "There's another one of those paintings."

Jackie groaned and climbed into the vehicle. "How many is that today?"

Lucy dropped the message, which turned into a heap of wriggling worms for the pigeon to feed on, got in beside Jackie, and started the engine.

"Three so far, but it's only lunchtime. I'd be amazed if this is the last one."

They set off through the traffic as fast as they legally could. Some days Lucy wished that they had the powers of the mundane police so they could race through the city streets, lights and sirens blaring, but it was probably a dangerous option. Besides, they hadn't missed a magical outbreak yet.

That "yet" hung in the front of her mind, the sword of Damocles forever hanging over the heads of the Silver Griffins. It would only take one big miss to reveal the magical world while keeping it hidden relied on success after success after success. This week, with a growing number of incidents around the city, it was getting harder to keep up those successes.

They turned into Rampart Village, then down a back street. At least this time the painting was somewhere relatively inconspicuous, unlike the earlier one at a busy intersection. There shouldn't be much of a crowd.

"I see our problem." Jackie drew her wand.

Up ahead, three cartoon bears stood in the middle of the street. The biggest one was holding a bowl and spoon, while the little one had a blanket draped around his shoulders. They had a cute, Disney-esque design, with big eyes and rounded bodies, but their open mouths revealed rows of pointed teeth and dagger-like claws extended from their fuzzy paws. They had two teenagers backed up against a wall.

Lucy hit the brakes, and the SUV screeched to a halt a dozen feet from the nearest bear. Both witches leapt out, wands at the ready.

The big bear turned toward them and flung his bowl away. It shattered against the wall, spattering the whitewash with a layer of porridge. He roared, and even that had a cartoonish effect, blowing Lucy's hair around.

Before she could act, the bear charged at her, claws waving. She leapt aside, waving her wand as she went. "Agglutino."

Glue clung to the bear's foot, sticking him in place. He swung around, swiping at her with his paws. One caught her on the backswing and knocked her against the wall.

"Renuo!" Jackie exclaimed.

The magic vanished out of the bear, and it collapsed into a paint stain, but now the other two were on Jackie, the middle bear grabbing her hand and trying to take her wand while the little bear leapt on her back and wrapped an arm around her throat.

"Help!" Jackie croaked.

Lucy stumbled to her feet. Her head had hit the wall, and now the world was spinning around her. She raised her wand, but it was hard to aim straight.

"Renuo," she said.

A counterspell shot from her wand, but whatever it hit, it wasn't one of the bears.

"Right a bit," Jackie said as she struggled to get the little bear off her back. The other one had wrenched the wand out of her hand and was waving it around, growling and trying to make it work.

"Renuo!" Lucy said, letting fly again.

"I said right. Your right. The other direction."

Lucy swung back. Her vision was starting to clear, her thoughts coming together. The bear with the wand pointed it at her, and magic swirled around the tip.

"Renuo," Lucy snapped.

Her counterspell collided with whatever the bear had cast, and the two spells vanished in a flash of magic.

"Renuo!"

At last, the magic hit the middle bear. Like the big bear before it, the creature collapsed, hitting the ground as a brown paint stain.

Jackie was on her knees, face pale. The little bear had its arm around her throat and was squeezing tight.

"Renuo."

For a moment, the little bear stood staring at Lucy, its expression of thwarted rage made almost endearing by its big eyes and rounded ears. Then it went the way of the other bears, leaving a long stain down Jackie's back.

Now it was Jackie's turned to stumble uncertainly to her feet.

"Thanks," she croaked, rubbing her neck. "That would have been a lousy way to go, choked to death by an extra from *The Jungle Book*."

"What was that?" asked one of the teenagers the bears

had been menacing. He had a set of marker pens in his hand. Behind him, the remains of a mural were still visible, including a woodland clearing and a perfect thatched cottage, like something out of a fairy tale. Fluffy white clouds littered a blue sky above, and the sun was smiling down, all of it achieved in spray paints.

"Nothing you need to worry about." Lucy pointed her wand. "Never was, never will be."

The expressions on the faces of the two teenagers went dim, and their hands hung loosely by their sides.

"Let's get them out of here," Lucy said, "then we can have a proper look at the painting."

They walked the two youths out of the back street and down the road a little way, then sat them down on a bench. It seemed like a safe area, somewhere they could be left until they came to their senses, the memories of the past half hour wiped away. Then Jackie and Lucy went back to the scene of the crime.

"More magical art." Jackie shook her head. "Just brilliant. Who is this joker?"

"Not the same one we were looking for before." Lucy pointed at the bottom right corner of the painting. Instead of the letters VX, the signature was a cartoon image, a smiley face with horns. "Now we have multiple magic users applying the same techniques to their art. No wonder we're getting so many calls."

Jackie picked up one of the teenagers' abandoned marker pens. "Self-defense again?"

"Looks like it." Lucy pointed at a spot near the middle of the painting, where someone had been scrawling over the image in ink. "We have an F, a U, a C, and presumably that's the point at which daddy bear decided that he'd had enough."

"I'd get pissed off too if someone tried to write that on me."

"Is there anything they could write that you wouldn't object to?"

"Probably not, but the lack of imagination adds insult to injury. This was probably a cute painting, then some idiot comes along, and all they can think of to add is a swear."

"You almost sound like you sympathize with our magic artists." Lucy raised an eyebrow. "That's not like you."

"Oh, it still pisses me off that they're wasting our time like this, but it's a bit more understandable when this is the other side."

Even after de-spelling the bears, there was still magic in the painting, so they countered that too to be on the safe side. They'd barely finished that when another pigeon landed on Jackie's shoulder.

"Great," she muttered. "Another one. Come on."

They got into the SUV, and Lucy hit the gas, following the directions Jackie gave her. They rushed past the dazed teenagers, still sitting on their bench, and down several more streets, toward a row of shops where someone had reported a lion behind a liquor store.

"It's not like there's even a pattern." Lucy swung them around a corner. "These things are popping up all over the place, in all sorts of styles. If they were working in one district, we would know where to look for the ringleader. If they were hitting specific targets, we could look for a cause or a motive. But it's everywhere, every day."

"Got to admire their persistence." Jackie pointed. "Down there."

They pulled up at the end of an alley and leapt out. Sure enough, down by the dumpsters, a tramp was lying on the ground, pants around his ankles, with a purple and gold lion looming over him.

"What do you think he was going to do to the painting?" Lucy asked.

"Seriously, you can't work that one out?"

"Oh."

"Oh indeed."

The lion looked up as the two witches approached. It tried to growl, but the magic hadn't given it a voice, just a really menacing expression. It charged toward them, teeth bared, muscles tensed, sunlight glittering off the flecks in the metallic paint.

"Renuo!" they chanted in unison.

The lion exploded in a shower of purple and gold, a fine rich mist that filled the alley with a smell of paint.

"I liked the style of that one," Lucy said. "The look was distinctive."

"I would have liked it a lot better if it wasn't attacking us." Jackie gestured down the alley. "You go pick that guy up and give him his 'never was.' I'll clear out what's left of the painting."

"Why don't I get to deal with the painting?"

"Because you're better with people."

There was a flutter of wings, and two pigeons swept down out of the clear sky.

"We'd better do this fast," Lucy said. "It looks like it's going to be a long day."

CHAPTER THIRTY

Ashley, Dylan, and Eddie sat in their den beneath the Heron family home. More and more often, this was where they came to at the end of the day, instead of hanging out in the back yard or watching TV in the living room. They'd set up the den perfectly for their entertainment, there was no risk of being spotted doing something odd, and they were allowed to practice their magic and to invent. It was the perfect space.

Ashley sat on a beanbag with her string robots spread out in front of her. Four of them were linked together, three forming a tripod and the fourth hanging down between them, moving a felt tip pen across a sheet of paper. Others lay nearby, waiting for her to add them when she wanted to try something new.

That was the joy of the string robots. They were adaptable in a way that poor old Octo, now gathering dust in the corner of her lab, hadn't been. Octo was useful as a reconnaissance device, and he could provide support in a fight, but there were lots of other situations where he was completely useless. Ashley wanted a robotic system suitable for any circumstance that she could rearrange for whatever was needed. The strings promised to provide that solution if she could get them to work.

"What are you doing?" Dylan looked down at the robots. He had his hand outstretched, a pebble floating in the air two inches above his palm.

"What are you doing?"

"Practicing control without concentration. It was Twylan's idea. I have to keep this stone floating for as long as possible, without it shooting up into the air or whizzing off on its own, while I do other things."

"Does it shoot off often?"

"No, but you know how that window broke yesterday…"

"Oh."

"Yeah. So anyway, I need distractions to test myself against, so what are you doing?"

Ashley hit stop on the tablet that controlled the robots, then pulled out the piece of paper they had been drawing on. She held it up for her brother to see. It was a mess.

"I'm trying to improve the fine movements of my robots. They need to be able to learn new tasks without me programming every detail."

"Why?"

"Try to give me instructions to pick up a pen."

"Okay, um, lower your hand…" Dylan watched carefully as Ashley followed his instructions to the letter, but not the intention. "No, further, until you reach the floor. That's better. Now move right. Again. Again. No, not like that, you've knocked the pen away."

"Like what, then?"

"Um, up again...No, not that far!" Dylan blew a raspberry. "Okay, I get it. Detailed instructions are hard."

"Exactly. So I need software that can learn, that can work these things out for itself. Drawing seemed like a good way to fix that, but it's creating extra complications."

"Why don't you show me? Sometimes talking to someone else helps."

Ashley put a new piece of paper under the drawing robots, then set them off again.

"They're supposed to be drawing a tree," she said. "But look..."

The string arm swung one way, sketching the first line of the tree trunk, but as it swung back, another line crossed that one at the wrong angle to add to the tree.

"Momentum makes the arm swing in ways the robots haven't planned for. They see what's happened, but they can't stop it, and they can't work out another solution."

The pen was still moving, but for almost every movement that set down a tree feature, another added a random line. The more the robots drew, the more erratic those lines became and the worse the intended lines connected. Any hint of a tree disappeared beneath the other mess.

"I've tried the control software in all sorts of different configurations, but none of them works. It's so, so... Urgh!"

Ashley flung her hands up in the air.

Dylan looked at his sister with concern. She was normally so calm, so rational, but this was really bothering her. He wanted to help.

"Could I add some magic?" he asked. "Like Dad using magic and technology together to fix up cars."

Ashley shook her head. "This is a robot project, not a magical one. I want to fix it with science."

"Have you looked at other people's robots?"

"That won't help. No one else is making robots like these."

"Maybe you don't need to look at things like yours. Maybe you need to look at something different to help you find a new perspective. Sometimes, when I get stuck on my homework, I try to—"

Suddenly, the stone hovering above Dylan's hand shot away as if an invisible hand had thrown it. It flew through a doorway and down a tunnel, and there was a crash at the far end.

"What that?" Eddie leapt to his feet, then the air around him shimmered, and he turned into a fierce guard dog, ready for trouble.

"My bad," Dylan said. "I'd better go clear up."

He headed off down the corridor with Eddie at his heels, tail wagging.

Ashley stared at her robots, willing inspiration to come, but however much she strained her brain, nothing new emerged. She'd tried out every idea she could come up with. Maybe Dylan was right. Perhaps it was time for someone else's ideas.

She picked up the tablet again and opened a browser window, then searched for the phrase "string robot." The first few pages of results looked distinctly unpromising, so she switched to image search, where she could at least see what was happening at a glance.

The results here were equally uninspiring. There were robot arms tying strings to show off their programs, diagrams showing the wires operating robotic hands, a robot playing the guitar, even robot puppets held up by strings. None of it was even slightly like what she was after. Where were the other great scientists and engineers pushing the boundaries of how robots worked? Where were the pioneers?

Several pages in, still nothing had inspired her. She looked down at her set of robots, which were still valiantly trying to draw a tree, creating an ever darker mess on the paper.

Art had inspired her to run these latest tests, so maybe it could inspire a solution. She added "art" to the search phrase to see what string robot art might look like beyond the mess she was making.

The results were even more irrelevant. Half of them had nothing to do with robots. They were just pictures drawn with string, some of them portraits of famous people, others cartoon characters or abstract patterns. The crisscrossing lines created patches of darkness against lighter backgrounds, and some of them held each other in tension, making shapes beyond simple straight lines.

Ashley stared at one of the images. It was a string portrait of Einstein, one of history's greatest geniuses reduced to a novelty. It was sad. Then she noticed the article it was attached to. A robot had created this art, working out the optimal thread path to replicate an image using only straight lines of string. There was an ingenuity to it, using an algorithm to find the logical solution to an arbitrary problem.

She looked at the strings in the picture again, intersecting each other in such a way that simple straight lines created an image of history's greatest genius.

Then it hit her. Intersecting lines. Crossing strings.

She took three more of her string robots and, with mounting excitement, fixed them into place on the existing arrangement. Each one ran from a leg of the tripod down to the central string. Instead of one robot controlling the pen, there were now four.

The programming was more complex, of course, but sometimes complex was good, like the task of teaching a robot to draw Einstein. She typed away while the others came back into the room, the stone floating above Dylan's hand again, and kept typing while they read and played games. She was still at it when they left and when Dylan returned twenty minutes later to say that dinner was ready.

"I've got it!" Ashley grabbed his sleeve. "Look!"

She slid a clean sheet of paper under the assembly of interconnected string-shaped robots, then hit a command on her tablet. The strings lifted the pen into the air, then dropped it at a corner of the paper. They dragged it across the page, but this time, when they reached the end of the line, the pen didn't swing back. It lifted off the white sheet, shifted an inch to the side, and descended to start scribbling in the outlines of leaves.

The picture was rough, childish, more like Eddie's efforts than Lucy's, but it was clearly a tree. A minute later, apparently content that it had done its work, the robot assemblage stopped drawing and lifted the pen off the page.

"Well done, girl genius." Dylan ruffled his sister's hair. She frowned.

"That's not very tidy," she said.

"Neither is this place. Look!"

All around were the discarded sheets from failed drawings, the messy masses of would-be trees from the robots' earlier struggles. They lay around where Ashley had been working, like pale leaves fallen around a giant tree.

"It's art," she said. "It's supposed to be messy."

She tapped one last button on the tablet. The strings disengaged from each other and fell limp on the floor. Ashley gathered them up and put them away in the box where they belonged before gathering the papers to go in the recycling bin.

"I thought it was supposed to be messy?" Dylan was grinning.

"It was, but I've had enough art for today. Let's go get dinner."

CHAPTER THIRTY-ONE

The tattoo shop had an old-fashioned bell above the door. It rang as Lucy stepped inside, followed by Jenkins.

"Receptionist's off today," someone shouted from a back room. "Gimme a few minutes, and I'll be with you."

It wasn't the first time Lucy had been in a tattoo shop, but only because of the five others they had already visited that day. The novelty hadn't worn off yet, and she walked up to a big board of designs with an undiminished sense of curiosity.

"Did you ever consider getting one?" she asked as she looked at the suggested designs. There was something for everyone—dragons, flowers, Celtic crosses, samples of fonts for people who wanted to wear their words on their skin.

"Never interested me," Jenkins said. "If I'm going to get my body modified, it'll be for extra mental processing, improved memory, or possibly super speed, not just to look different."

"Does that mean you would consider getting one of these magical tattoos?"

"Absolutely. But not until I understand how they work."

"You wouldn't have one yourself yet, but you were willing to put them on Nigel?"

"We have to make progress somehow."

The shop was an odd mix of old-fashioned and ultra-modern. The front room held polished wood seats with padded leather, posters of tattoo designs in elaborate gilt frames, and a mechanical cash register. A glance over the counter revealed a modern white plastic card reader, and as the bead curtain at the back shifted in the air-conditioned breeze, it revealed glimpses of a starkly hygienic workspace with white walls and a tiled floor. A buzzing like a dentist's drill emerged from that room, setting Lucy's teeth on edge.

"What do you think?" she asked. "Could this be our magical tattooist?"

"Possibly. I can't tell until I see more of the person or their workspace. Really, Agent Heron, is this how you normally do your job, trying to jump to conclusions before you have the evidence? Because if it is, I think I should go back to the lab. I don't want to take part in fieldwork if it makes a mockery of science."

"Don't worry. We're not going to start arresting people based on speculation. I only wanted your first impression."

"My first impression is that it's a tattoo shop, and anything else will have to wait for evidence." Jenkins peered over the counter, looking for anything that might pass for a clue. Then he started lifting the picture frames away from the walls, looking to see if anything hid behind them. He bounced as he moved around the room, a ginger-haired streak of nervous energy.

"Are you all right out here?" Lucy asked. "I know it's been years since you've been in the field, other than during the case with the Knights. Maybe we should have started small."

"Oh no, I'm absolutely fine, Agent Heron. More than fine. There's something exciting about being out here, at the pointed end of the Silver Griffins' work, facing the criminals and miscreants that you tackle daily. Do you think that we might get into a fight or some sort of chase?"

"Maybe. You have to be ready for anything."

"Excellent, because I've brought a few gadgets just in case." He rummaged around in his bag, then started holding out objects for her to see. "Runically reinforced shock baton for knocking out supernatural threats. Flying pills, in case we have to chase down a winged fugitive. Expanding caltrops, in case we need to prevent someone chasing us. What else did I bury in here…"

Lucy stared in bewilderment as Jenkins waved his outlandish devices.

"It's great that you came prepared," she said, "but don't you think that this is overkill when we already have our wands?"

"Overkill is still dead. Unless you're facing a necromancer, of course. Then death starts coming out the other side."

"Well, keep those hidden. For all we know, this is an ordinary tattoo parlor with an ordinary tattooist."

The bead curtains at the back of the store rattled, and two people stepped out. One was a young woman in leather trousers and a sleeveless Clash t-shirt, with a layer of clear plastic wrapped around the skull freshly tattooed on her upper arm. The other was a man with a shaved head and piercings through his nose and lower lip.

"Remember, keep it clean and dry for now," he said. "Apply the lotion, and if you get any itching, give me a call."

He pulled the card reader out from under the counter and took the woman's payment.

"See you next time," she said, then headed out, the bell ringing as the door eased shut behind her.

"Hi there," the man asked, smiling at Lucy and Jenkins. "I don't think we've met before, have we? I'm Tom." He held out his hand.

"Lucy." She shook the hand. "And this is Toliver."

"Cool. You don't meet many Tolivers." Tom smiled. "First time getting ink, or just first time coming to me?"

"I'm wondering about getting my first tattoo," Lucy said. "But I'm nervous about the whole thing. I thought going around some tattoo shops and seeing what they're like might help, and it might help me work out who to go to."

"I totally get it. Too many people rush into this and end up with an artist whose style doesn't suit them." He gestured toward the bead curtain. "You want to come in back, have a proper look around? It might help lay your fears to rest."

"That would be brilliant."

He led them into the back room. There were a couple of large, padded chairs, like luxury versions of the ones from a dentist's surgery, and a stool next to each one. A tattoo gun lay on a tray next to one of the chairs.

"You Scottish, Lucy?"

"English, but the Yorkshire accent seems to confuse a lot of people over here."

"Yorkshire like York, like in the Wars of the Roses?"

She laughed. "That's one of the county's claims to fame, yes."

"Cool. I got into reading about that stuff after watching *Game of Thrones*. History gets real gnarly sometimes, you know?"

"Oh yes." Lucy looked around the room. The problem she had here was the same one she'd had at all the other tattoo places they had visited so far. She didn't know what she was looking for. Without any experience with tattoos and tattooing, she couldn't spot what counted as odd or out of place. It was all down to guesswork and trying to see as much as possible. Fortunately, Jenkins was proving to be a good distraction.

"Is this what you use to draw on people?" he asked, picking up the tattooing gear.

"Would you mind putting that down?" Tom asked. "It's pretty much my livelihood."

"It doesn't seem very efficiently designed. Couldn't it have more needles?"

Tom took the tattoo gun out of Jenkins' hands and laid it down on the tray. "Maybe you'd like to look at some designs?"

"Yes, that could be interesting."

Tom pulled a folder out from under a table near the back of the room and opened it for Jenkins to see. "These are all works I've done in the past five years."

"The anatomy's wrong on that horse, you know."

"Well, it's about the art, not the science."

"Apparently, yes. How long do these take to put on someone?"

"Depends on the design. Some of them take several days' worth of work."

"All to change the pigments of your skin? That seems excessive."

"Look, buddy, it's great that you're here supporting your friend, but maybe you could show some manners?"

"I only said—"

"I heard what you said, and I caught the tone too."

"I really don't think—"

"Please excuse Toliver." Lucy came over to intervene. "He usually works alone in a lab, and he doesn't get out much. His social skills aren't what they could be."

"My social skills are perfectly functional. It's the rest of society that is ridiculous."

Tom laughed. "Okay, I get it. Tell you what, mister lab man, do you want to see the chemical side of what I do?"

"Yes, that sounds interesting."

Tom led them to a wooden cupboard in the corner of the room. It mostly consisted of drawers, each a few inches deep, and when he pulled one of them open, there was a tinkle of glass.

"My inks," Tom said proudly. "Custom mixed for clearer colors, among other benefits."

Jenkins took one of the bottles out of the drawer and peered at it.

"Interesting. What goes into this green?"

That started a long conversation about chemistry between the two men, which Lucy could only partly follow. It was still telling. It seemed that Tom was committed to the science of his work, to doing things better than others had done them before, to doing it his way.

More importantly, as she took a bottle out of the drawer and peered at it, she felt a tingle of magic. Something more than ordinary chemicals infused the ink. She picked out another from near the back and felt magic there too.

"Those are for my special tattoos," Tom said. "Ones to help people feel empowered."

"How do they help with that?"

Tom laughed. "Trade secret." He took the bottles from her, put them back in their place, and closed the drawer. "Have you got any more questions?"

Lucy glanced at Jenkins, who waggled his eyebrows at her, then stared significantly from Tom to the drawer. Fortunately, Tom was looking at Lucy, not him.

"No, I think I've seen everything I need to."

"Cool. The bell just rang, which means my ten o'clock is here."

"We'll get out of your way." Lucy smiled. "Thanks so much for letting us have a look around."

"My pleasure. If you decide to go ahead with that tattoo, you know where to find me."

They walked out, past a large man in a biker's outfit, and into the street. The bell rang as the door closed behind them.

"Why didn't you arrest him?" Jenkins asked. "There's magic in those inks and his needle gun."

"I didn't notice that part."

"That's because you didn't touch it. Honestly, how do you field agents get anything done? It's a good thing I'm here with you."

Lucy decided to let that one slide. "He's definitely our lad, but that doesn't mean we should arrest him yet."

"Why not? He's using unlicensed magic!"

"True, but that doesn't mean we have to lock him up. I have the beginnings of a better idea."

CHAPTER THIRTY-TWO

VX strode down the street in the pre-dawn gloom, her backpack *clanking* as the spray cans knocked against each other. She didn't have to carry the ladder today. Double-Rezz was doing that for her. If she'd wanted, she could have given the paints to someone else to carry too, offloading the weight onto any of the half-dozen street artists who trailed her, eager to learn more about her techniques. That felt like cheating. She had to carry her cans and do some of the grunt work that went into making art a reality.

They stopped in front of a billboard, one that VX had been eying for months. She hadn't dared to use it until now because the road beneath it got busy and there wasn't enough sidewalk space for her and the ladder. Now she had assistance, and she could try things she wouldn't have before.

The team members who could pass for humans put on high visibility jackets and safety helmets, while the others pulled up hoods and masks and started setting up cones along the stretch of road beneath the sign. A couple of tools added to the sense that real work was happening here, that there was good reason for closing off a lane of a road that would be busy once the pre-work traffic started to appear.

VX set up her stepladder and climbed up to face the billboard. It currently held an advert for perfume, or possibly for a car. It got hard to tell the difference once you got into the abstract adverts of high-end brands.

There were downsides to working on a space like this, and prime among them was impermanence. Whatever VX did now, it would be gone soon. Admittedly, a lot of her work didn't last long because people didn't appreciate it enough to protect it or keep it in place, but this time destruction was guaranteed. This was prime advertising space, and someone else would have it booked for their poster soon. Even if they didn't, the paper would slump and fall away far faster than a brick or concrete wall. But permanence wasn't everything, and this was certainly a good spot to get her work seen.

"We're all set, boss," Double-Rezz said.

"I told you, don't call me that. We don't have bosses and workers. We're a free collective."

"Sorry, VX."

Her following of small-time artists turned to watch as VX pulled out her first paint can. As she shook it, her magic started flowing into the paint. This was part of the whole process now, not something she added near the end. The magic and the art were one, and that unity opened a whole realm of possibilities.

She pressed down on the top of the can, and the paint

started to flow. Browns and yellows first, then muted blues and greens, as she marked out the central image of her new piece, a spray-paint reproduction of the Mona Lisa.

She had spent so long staring at images of that painting, studying its structure and style, absorbing the essence of Da Vinci's masterpiece, that she barely had to think to know where the paint should go. A long pale curve here for the edge of her exposed skin, darker for the shadow under her chin and that fall of hair, a delicate line to mark out where that elusive smile should be. Behind her, the disjointed scenery and a sky that faded almost to white as it neared the ground.

Here was where the magic came in. Spray painting didn't lend itself to blended colors or subtle gradations, but her powers gave her more control. She could hold particles of one color in the air while she sprayed another, releasing them slowly to mix like oil paints on a palette. She could keep them from drying and swirl them around on the surface where they had landed, further blending the colors and blurring the line between one area and the next.

She could use magic as a funnel to direct the spray into specific shapes or onto smaller areas. As the magic and the paint flowed, she wondered why she hadn't been doing this for years. Magic could enhance art in so many ways.

Her followers excitedly chattered as they watched her. Some of them were friends of Double-Rezz. Others were artists who had tracked her down through their efforts. All were eager to learn, and she was happy for them to watch what she did, to learn whatever they could. Art was for sharing.

With the central image done, she moved out toward the

edges. She wasn't standing on the ladder anymore. She didn't need to. The magic lifted her into the air like it lifted the cans around her.

She and her tools floated before the painting in progress like bees hovering at the mouth of a flower, waiting to taste the sweetness that lay within. Except that she was the flower, the producer casting the sweet nectar of art across Los Angeles.

To the left of that first image of the Mona Lisa, she painted another version. This time the colors were brighter, the setting more modern. Lisa wore a hoodie instead of a Renaissance dress, and her hair was bleached blond with the roots showing. Behind her, instead of a calm rural scene, there was a bustling city shrouded in smog.

Beyond that Lisa came another, a future Lisa, a cyberpunk model in Goth clothes with microchips embedded in her shaved skull and a smartphone clutched in her hands. A striking figure in black and silver, dark yet shining, her background a collage of web pages and computer code. This was the image that had inspired the whole piece, a tribute to a sci-fi novel that VX had read when she was in high school. This was the Mona Lisa of a broken electronic future.

Now VX floated the other way, to the right of the original painting. Here, she made Lisa a figure from deeper in history—a woman draped in furs with a mammoth roaming the plains behind her, freshly emerged from Africa. Her fingers showed stains from picking berries, and there was a napped flint in her hand.

Beyond her, the last one, the Lisa who would really get

them talking in the magical art circles. Mona Lisa of Oriceran, an elf with glowing skin and violet eyes, her beauty outshining even the original. Magic sparkled around her fingertips.

To mundane viewers, she would be a flight of fancy, a figure inspired by folklore and storybooks. To the magical authorities, she was a provocation, a direct statement of their presence in the world throughout its history, a defiant pressure against the shroud of secrecy behind which they lived. Because what was the point of art if not to provoke?

VX hung in the air, her cans around her. Now came the details, and with them a reversal. Instead of the magic directing the paint, the paint directed the magic. Spellcraft rode into the picture on the back of the sprays, bringing it to life. As VX touched up the smiles of all five Monas, those smiles came alive, stirring ever so slightly, mischievous and playful. Painted eyes blinked down at the artists below. A few touches of white brought a river to life in the background, and it started to flow as if it was real water.

"Yo, that is the bomb," Double-Rezz said, his tone hushed with awe.

Sparks flew around the head of the cyber Mona. The power light blinked on modern Mona's phone. These weren't things that VX had planned. They emerged as she painted. What she hadn't even imagined before now became obvious.

"It's like riding a wave," VX said. "You can't control it. You have to let it carry you. If you're willing to do that, you'll go to places you never even dreamed of."

Her cans clattered to the ground, and she floated back,

still suspended in the air, taking in the whole of the painting. She had been so busy making art about other things before, about society or politics or the destruction of the environment. This channeling of magic had given her a new purpose, a desire to make art that turned in on itself, that said something about the medium as well as the world.

"High art made with low materials," one of the others said. "I love it."

VX drifted down until her feet settled on the ladder, then she climbed down to the sidewalk. It was lighter now, and traffic was starting to go past. Some drivers glared in annoyance at the coned-off section of road. None seemed to have noticed the reason for it.

"I want to do more," VX said.

"Meet at the same place tomorrow then?" Double-Rezz asked.

"Not tomorrow, right now." Her body tingled with magic, and her mind buzzed with the thrill of creation. "We've got the cones, we've got the high vis, you can use them to distract people while I work."

The others looked at each other.

"In broad daylight?" one of them asked.

"Yes, in daylight! We have to do more. We're turning this city into a living gallery, a place of magic and majesty. If we stop, the authorities will have time to de-spell the paintings, to wash them off or paint over them. If we keep going, we can overwhelm the authorities, ensure that people see the art. We can brighten the whole city. Are you in?"

"Hell yes." Double-Rezz grabbed a bag and started stuffing paint cans into it. "I know another advertising board that loads of people see, where we could set up again."

"There's a wall near my house that would be perfect for something like this," another artist said.

"But what if people see us?" another one asked. "Not all of us can show ourselves."

"You won't have to." VX waved her hand over one of the cans of paint, then sprayed it up into the air. As the droplets settled, they transformed, imbued with powerful magic. They landed on the artists, and one by one, they disappeared. "Now you're the color of the city. It'll only last an hour or two, so make the most of it. It's time to show L.A. what it can be."

CHAPTER THIRTY-THREE

After several days of working on Mulvers' modified cars, Charlie was finally starting to get used to his client's fashion sense. Purple Crocs, leopard-print pants, a Hawaiian shirt and a top hat might not be most people's idea of a coherent look, but by Mulvers' standards it was almost restrained. The top hat meant that Charlie could even keep track of where Mulvers was over the top of the Mini, despite the gnome's stature.

"I have to say, it's a pleasure to watch you boys at work," Mulvers said. "The ingenuity. The commitment. The sheet audacity of trying to work the unworkable in two ways at once, to make secret use of magic on publicly driven cars and to dispose of the bleak and billowing fumes that blight our roads and cities, it's really fantastic."

From out on the driveway came the sound of cursing and gravel being kicked around.

"Still think we're so fantastic?" Charlie asked.

Mulvers chuckled. "I've uttered a profanity or two in

my time. It's a sign of the passion you and Ringo bring to your work."

"Well, I should go check what he's getting passionate about now."

Charlie walked out of the garage, past the Mini and all the other cars stored with it, to where Ringo stood in the wide driveway, pieces of dismantled engines scattered around him. He was glaring at one piston and another lay at his feet. Grease covered his hands and his wand, which lay on top of one pile of parts.

"Still not working, huh?" Charlie asked.

Ringo shook the piston in the air.

"I swear, this is the dumbest idea we've come up with so far. Cutting out the crap at the point where it creates the fumes? We're going to slow down the car, gum up the engine, and get nowhere fast while crud still pours out."

"You know what, it's your can-do attitude that makes you such a pleasure to work with."

"I expect the attitude from your wife, not from you."

"Sorry, she's not here. I'm filling a gap in the market for Ringo Fuller-related insights."

Ringo snorted and turned the piston over in his hand.

"Look, this is from one of the spare engines that Mulvers bought so we could run tests. I engraved the pistons with sigils, and they held the spells well enough, but..."

He pointed at a crack running down the piston.

"Fractures?" Charlie whistled. "We're lucky it didn't blow."

"One of the others did."

"Oh."

"Yep. So that's one more plan out the window."

Ringo flung the piston down in disgust, and it *clanged* against the other one lying on the ground.

Charlie surveyed the pieces of machine scattered across the gravel driveway, the engines and other mechanical components from half a dozen Minis. Money really wasn't an object where Mulvers was concerned. He wanted greener versions of his beloved collection of modified cars, and he was going to do whatever it took to make that happen. It was still a great learning opportunity for Charlie and Ringo, but the whole business felt increasingly unreal.

"The problem isn't only the interactions," Ringo said. "Although that's bad enough, all those different spells interfering with each other. The biggest problem now is where to put anything new.

"There are so many odd spells and bits of weird tech jammed inside that machine that there's barely a spare surface for us to put a rune on. We can try engraving on pistons or embedding it in filters, but then you're undermining the physical strength of those components. And there are places we simply can't put the magic or the mechanical components we've relied on."

Charlie scratched his head. "There has to be a way we can do this."

"No, there doesn't. Some things aren't possible. Money and wishful thinking aren't always the solution rich people think they are."

"They've always worked for me." Mulvers had emerged from the garage. He was smiling as he usually did, but that relentless cheeriness was starting to rub Ringo the wrong way. He gritted his teeth and glared at their employer.

"Could you give us a few minutes, Mr. Mulvers?" Charlie asked. Frustrating as the job was, he didn't want to lose it, especially when they had already invested so much effort into their work. And Mulvers was so good-natured, in his weird way, it would be a shame to disappoint him, never mind to see him knocked flat by an enraged bounty hunter turned mechanic.

"I'll go make coffee," Mulvers said. "You boys always come up with great ideas when I do that."

He bustled off, whistling as he went.

"Seriously." Ringo shook his head. "There's too much, and there's that guy."

"Remember, he's paying us well to do what we enjoy."

"I know, but still." Ringo shook his head.

"Let's go through this again. Tell me what we can't do."

"We can't use our usual setup. We learned that the first time." Ringo started ticking off the possibilities on his fingers. "We can't shift it up along the undercarriage because it interferes with the speed spells. We can't fit the mechanical parts into the engine. We can't replace them with spells in there because they either get disrupted by the other magic or break the pistons. And after the strawberry Jell-O incident, we're not doing anything with the fuel tank.

"Short version, there's nothing we can touch inside that car that will make the damnedest bit of difference."

"Fine, how about on the outside?"

"You want to staple magical devices onto the outside of a Mini? You don't think that might draw some attention when he drives it around town? I don't mean to be a downer, but I think it could get awkward if your wife carts our client off to Trevilsom because of work we've done."

"All right, so it was a dumb idea, but maybe we have to try those now."

They walked into the garage and around the Mini, looking at the machine and its modifications, both men hoping that some bolt of inspiration would arise.

"Look at this." Ringo picked at a piece of flaking paint and shook his head. "All we've done is damage. This thing is gonna need a respray once we finish."

"Maybe we should offer that as part of our service: one free magical respray with… every… mod…"

Charlie's words trailed off as he stood staring at the car, one hand resting on its roof.

"You all right, man?" Ringo asked.

"I've got it," Charlie whispered, as if afraid that speaking too loud would break the idea. "I know how we can make this work."

"She certainly looks great." Mulvers ran a hand over the hood of his car. "Good of you boys to deal with all the dings and scratches as well as the fumes. You sure you've got it this time?"

"Oh, we're sure." Charlie opened the door. "Give her a quick drive around the grounds. We've rigged pollution meters to the exhaust and readouts on the dashboard so you can see the results for yourself."

Mulvers got in, started the engine, and roared off down the driveway. He turned off onto the lawn and across the wide grounds of his house, then lifted into the air, making the most of his Mini's other modifications. The little car soared high above the rooftop before coming back around to land on the gravel with a *crunch*.

"You boys really are marvels," he said. "Either that or you rigged those pollution sensors."

"Don't worry, sir, we're in this for the good we can do, not the money," Charlie said.

"Though we do still need to be paid," Ringo added hastily. "Got to cover the bills somehow."

"Of course, of course." Mulvers patted the steering wheel. "How did you do it?"

"With this." Charlie held up a can of paint. "There was no way to fit the mechanisms in the car, and spells on the inside caused interference. So instead, we came up with an alternative solution, one that's entirely magical, and infused it into your new paint job."

Mulvers laughed. "You made a paint-on spell?"

"Something like that, yes."

"Ingenious, utterly ingenious." Mulvers got out and looked over the car admiringly. "But what if the paint gets scratched? Will that stop the spell working?"

"It might impair it a little, but someone would have to really go to town to stop it working at all. And we'll leave you some spare paint for touch-ups so you can keep the car in top condition."

"I can't argue with that." Mulvers looked toward his garage. "Can you use this miracle paint on the other cars as well?"

"The principle holds, but the spell's sensitive, so they'll each need a separate mix, which means that we can keep with their current color schemes too. By the time we finish, your collection won't only run cleaner than they ever have, they'll look better than ever too."

"I knew you'd work it out in the end."

While Mulvers went to make a celebratory coffee, Charlie and Ringo packed away their tools and leftover paint.

"Now we have the paint. Is it going to be the best approach every time?" Ringo asked.

"I think so," Charlie said. "It was a pain to create, but it's easier than what we were doing before. Crazy to think that we had to go through all these complications to end up with something simpler."

"Guess it's like Mulvers said at the start, this business is more an art than a science. We needed something to force us into getting creative."

CHAPTER THIRTY-FOUR

Summoned by the doorbell, Lucy rushed down the hallway to the front door, fixing her earrings as she went.

"On my way!" she shouted, then laughed at herself for providing excuses seconds before she opened the door.

Jackie and Sarah stood on the doorstep, Sarah in a new summer dress, Jackie in smart jeans and a sparkly top.

"Ready to go paint the town red?" Jackie asked.

"Not quite." Lucy let them in and closed the door behind them. "Dinner ran overtime because Eddie was telling us about all his favorite animals, in detail, with models made out of mash. Give me a few more minutes."

"See, this sort of thing is why I don't want kids," Jackie said. "Imagine having to wait for a toddler to finish their dinner any time you want to go anywhere. And I'm assuming that mash made quite a mess for you to clear up."

"Charlie's turn for that tonight. Besides, it's totally worth it. Eddie is far better dinnertime entertainment than the latest TV show."

"And apparently, parenting deadens your cultural tastes as well."

Lucy led her friends into the living room. The kids were in there, but for once the TV wasn't on. Instead, they were all busy with paper, pencils, and crayons.

"Hi, guys." Sarah sat on the sofa between Ashley and Dylan. "What are you up to?"

"Animals," Eddie called from the floor.

"Really?" Jackie folded her long legs under her to sit beside him. "What sort of animals?"

"Lions and tigers and bears and elephants and—"

"Sounds like you have a whole zoo there."

"No, jungle."

"Eddie doesn't like putting animals in cages," Dylan said. "He's probably worried that we'd do it to him."

Eddie looked at his brother in shock. "No cage!"

"Like we could ever contain you. You'd turn into a mouse and run out through the bars."

"Mouse!" Eddie dropped his pencil and made a face. The air shimmered around him, and the little boy disappeared, replaced by a dormouse. The tiny creature twitched its whiskers, looked up at Jackie with darkly soulful eyes, then scrambled up onto her lap.

"Fine, you can sit there." She stroked the mouse on its head. "But try not to put holes in my new jeans with your claws."

Lucy bustled back into the room, carrying a bottle of white wine and two glasses.

"Sorry, I'm still not ready yet," she said. "Would you like a drink while you wait?"

"That would be lovely, thank you," Sarah said.

"Might as well get started," Jackie added, holding out her hand.

Lucy poured them each a glass of wine, then hurried back out.

Ashley descended from the sofa to a place on the floor. She laid out her paper, then started pulling lengths of silver string from her pocket, setting them up in a framework above the paper. To Jackie, who hadn't seen the string robots before, it was a strange sight, these broad threads stiffening into rods as Ashley set them in place, then clinging together to create a sort of scaffolding. Others hung down over the page, clutching a pencil between them.

"What's all this, kiddo?" Jackie asked.

"My new robots," Ashley said. "They're designed to combine in various configurations so I can deploy them in diverse environments for different purposes. The same technology could be useful in construction, rescue, reconnaissance work, anything with the right programming."

"This doesn't look much like a rescue."

"I'm using art as a way to refine the fine controls and programming systems. Because it's precise and variable work, it's a good way to do precision testing."

"Ah, of course. What little girl isn't interested in precision testing?"

"Most of them." Ashley looked at Jackie. "You'd be amazed at how little most people care about science."

Jackie laughed. "I might not be amazed, but I appreciate your passion, kiddo. Why don't you show me how it works?"

On the sofa, Dylan was showing Sarah his picture.

"I'm trying to draw the Tolderai settlement from the archaeological dig I helped on," he said. "Real archaeologists do this to help people understand what the past was really like, how people lived."

"That's lovely." Sarah looked over his shoulder at the picture. "Is that one of their houses?"

"Yes, but I can't get the door right." Dylan frowned and tapped his pencil against the page. "I did one before that worked, but now it won't go right."

"Do you still have that other one?"

"Would you like to see it?"

"I'd love to."

While Dylan dashed out of the room, Eddie the dormouse scrambled off Jackie's lap, grabbed the corner of his picture between his teeth, and started dragging it across the carpet toward Sarah's feet.

"Maybe you should change shape, sweetie," she said. "It'll be easier to show me if you can carry it."

The air around Eddie shimmered, and the mouse became a monkey. He grabbed the picture, jumped onto the sofa, and climbed up onto the back. From there, he leaned over Sarah's shoulder, waving the picture in her face.

"It's hard to make out details this way." She laughed. "Why don't you sit next to me so I can see it properly?"

Eddie slid down the back of the sofa and placed the crumpled sheet in Sarah's lap.

"So this is an elephant? And that must be the lion?"

Eddie ooked and jumped up and down in his seat in excitement.

Lucy came back in, looking a lot calmer than she had been before.

"Right, everything that needs clearing up is cleared up. I'm ready to go."

"Give us a minute," Jackie said. "I haven't finished my wine yet."

"And Eddie's showing me his art. Have you seen the claws on this tiger? It's ferocious!"

Dylan reappeared, carrying an armful of drawings.

"I couldn't find the right one," he said, "but these show other bits of how the ancient Tolderai lived."

"Sounds fascinating." Sarah patted the sofa on the other side of her from Eddie.

"Looks like we're going to be here a while," Lucy said. "I'll go get a glass."

"Hang on there!" Jackie held up a hand. "It's ladies' night, remember? There's tequila out there waiting for me."

"We have wine and comfortable seats, which is more than we'd get in half the bars," Sarah said. "I'm happy to stay here if Charlie doesn't mind."

"I'm sure he'll be fine with that," Lucy said. "Shall I go grab snacks?"

"Wait, wait, wait." Jackie frowned. "It's easy for you two to stay in. You're loved up already. How am I supposed to meet someone if we don't go out?"

"You were going to ditch us?" Lucy asked, slapping her hands to her cheeks in mock shock. "For some random stranger?"

"On ladies' night?" Sarah shook her head. "Shame on you, Jackie Kowal."

"Urgh, fine." Jackie flung her hands in the air. "Obviously, I wasn't going to ditch you guys. We can stay in and have a quiet night."

"Not a quiet night." Lucy held up Eddie's picture. "A gallery night featuring the work of some of the L.A.'s finest young talents. It doesn't get much more cultured than that."

Lucy disappeared into the kitchen, from where there was a clatter of cupboards opening and a rustle of snack packets.

"Hey, kids," Sarah said, "would you like to show us more of your pictures?"

"Sure," Dylan said, looking through his pile of drawings. "I can tell you all about the dig."

"I could show you how the robot has been improving," Ashley said. "I've kept sample sketches along the way for the scientific record."

"Ook!" Eddie leapt off the sofa and went to rummage in a pile of papers.

Soon, the three witches were seated on the sofa, bowls of chips and cookies parked between them, sipping their wine, while the kids waited eagerly to one side, clutching their favorite pictures. At the witches' feet, Buddy sat with his tail wagging back and forth, basking in the lively pleasure of his humans. He didn't need to understand what they were doing. It was enough to know that they thought it was fun.

"Which of these Picassos is up first?" Jackie poured herself a fresh glass of wine.

"The one with the nearest bedtime," Lucy said. "Come on, Eddie."

Eddie, back in the shape of a small boy, walked to a

place in front of the TV and held up one of his pictures.

"It's a hippopotamus." He took time over "hippopota-mus," sounding out each syllable of the word. "In a river."

"I love the choice of colors." Sarah got into the spirit of an art show opening. "The contrast of gray and blue evokes the sharp contrasts of the riverbank environment, where land and water meet. The dividing lines of black felt tip marker accentuate dichotomies."

She waggled her eyebrows at Jackie, challenging her to join the art appreciation game.

"There's a startling energy to the penmanship," Jackie said, more than willing to play along. "Many people might have chosen to work with straight lines, but the artist's zigzags and scribbles create something more vibrant, something filled with movement and potential. The animal truly comes alive." Jackie *clinked* her glass against Lucy's. "What do you think?"

"I think that it's a bold experiment in form and layout. By placing the animal off-center, Heron creates a sense of imbalance in our world. He reminds us that nature is unstable, constantly changing, unwilling to be bound by our conventions of art and beauty, our obsessions with balance and symmetry." Lucy laughed. "There we go. I didn't waste my education."

Across the room, Ashley leaned over to whisper to Dylan. "They're weird."

"That's grown-ups for you," he whispered back. "You want to show them your pictures, right?"

"Of course."

"Play along with the game then. Humor them."

Ashley nodded. "Smart."

"See if you can grab the cookie bowl when they're not looking. Those are oat and raisin. We shouldn't waste them on adults."

Eddie finished showing off his pictures, then went to curl up in a chair, rubbing a hand sleepily across his face.

"That was lovely, sweetheart," Lucy said. "You're making our evening very entertaining."

"Who's next?" Sarah asked.

Ashley stepped forward, pictures at the ready. "A new artist," she announced. "The natural inheritor of Da Vinci's tradition of art and machines: a machine that draws."

"Bravo!" Jackie waved her wine glass. "Bring on the robot art."

CHAPTER THIRTY-FIVE

A pigeon fluttered across the road and landed on Lucy's Rivian, which sat in a Starbucks parking lot.

"Not another one," Jackie muttered and sipped her coffee. "Magical graffiti, right? It's all we've done for days, rushing to these places where the pictures are seen, fighting off whatever's popped out of them, getting rid of the magic, then wiping everyone's memories. The city's going mad with magical art."

"This one's different." Lucy read the message after she took it off the pigeon's leg. "Weird plants in a souvenir shop."

"Thank goodness." Jackie climbed into the car. "If I see one more spray paint portrait come to life, I'm going to scream."

Lucy took her seat, started the vehicle, and drove them through the mid-afternoon traffic toward the scene of the trouble.

"Why do you always end up driving?" Jackie asked. "You drive like an old lady."

"We're always in this old lady's car, that's why."

"We could use my car."

"Your car is a gas-guzzling mess that's going to fall apart any day now."

"Fair point. Maybe I should get Charlie and Ringo to take a look at it. How much do they charge for cleaning up the fumes?"

"I don't know, but I'm sure they'll give you mate's rates."

"I do not want to mate with Ringo Fuller."

"Ew! Why did you even put that image in my head?"

Jackie laughed. "Got to keep myself entertained somehow."

They pulled up down the street from the L.A. public library.

"Wait, that souvenir shop?" Jackie said as they hurried toward the library's gift shop. "Isn't that going to get a lot of attention?"

"Get ready with your 'never was,'" Lucy said. "I expect we'll need it."

A cop stood outside the gift shop, glancing nervously up and down the street.

"Are you the specialists Captain Jones was sending?" he asked as Lucy and Jackie approached.

"That's us," Lucy said. It was always easier to deal with a magical situation when someone in authority was aware of the magical world. They didn't see this sort of support often, but it was a relief in a busy week to have a little pressure taken off them. "Have you been able to keep the public out?"

"Except the ones inside already," the cop said. "The

captain told me to leave them there?" He seemed confused by the situation. "Are you, like, botanists?"

"Something like that."

"I figured you'd have tools and sprays and things."

"Sometimes all the tools you need are in here." Jackie tapped the side of her head. "Now, we're going to sort this out. Don't let anyone else in, okay?"

"Sure thing."

"Seriously?" Lucy whispered as they walked inside. "All the tools you need are in here?"

Jackie grinned. "It sounds smart, stops people asking questions nine times out of ten."

"And the other times?"

"That's when we wipe their memories."

The gift shop was a neatly ordered space with shelves of books, cards, and ornaments, most of them themed around the library, its contents, and the sights of L.A. One section looked distinctly different. Creepers ran from the shelves, out across the walls, floor, and ceiling, twitching and waving their leaves. Flowers bloomed, dropped their petals, and bloomed again. Something like a Venus flytrap snapped at the store worker and three customers who stood nearby, staring at it.

"Not your average souvenir," Jackie said.

"This is so weird," the store worker said. "We didn't have any plants here last night, and now..." He jumped back to avoid the creepers as they grabbed at his ankle. "It's like being trapped in some fantasy jungle."

"Don't worry," Lucy said. "Help is here. If you could all back away from the display, then turn this way..." She waved her wand. "Never was, never will be."

They all went slack, faces blank, arms hanging by their sides.

"Don't you think we should have come up with a plan first?" Jackie asked.

"And discussed our magical plan in front of them?"

"Fair point." Jackie, her wand raised and ready, took a few steps closer to the display. "There's something else in the center." She waved her wand. "Subvolo."

There was a rustling of leaves and half a dozen items lifted off the shelves, summoned by Jackie's levitation spell. They floated over to her and hung in the air.

"It's a bunch of pots," she said. "Maybe they're nothing to do with the plants?"

The plants seemed to disagree. The creepers strained to reach Jackie and Lucy while the Venus flytrap snapped viciously at the air a few feet from them.

Lucy plucked one of the pots out of the air and rolled it over in her hands, examining the decorations around the outside. They were an abstract, geometric design containing several very familiar details.

"I might know what's behind this." She put her wand away and pulled out her phone. "Give me a minute."

The phone rang for nearly a minute before Heather answered.

"Lu, is it urgent?" she asked. "I'm in the middle of a lesson."

"Fairly urgent, yes. You know the patterns on that scrying bowl you let Penley put on display?"

"Yes."

"Can they act as magical conduits?"

"Of course. They wouldn't be much use for scrying otherwise."

"So they could have different effects if rearranged in new ways?"

"Potentially. Although in the hands of anyone other than a Tolderai, there's only a one in a hundred chance you'd get a useful arrangement."

"One in a hundred is enough, given how many people have started imitating your art."

"Oh. Shit. Do you need me to come deal with it?"

"No, we've got this."

"That stupid dwarf, I never should have agreed to—"

"This isn't your fault. Accidents happen."

"Everything was easier when we stayed hidden away."

"But it wasn't as much fun, right?" Lucy looked around. The creepers were growing, trying to reach the bowls. "Got to go. I'll see you soon."

"Well?" Jackie asked as Lucy put her phone away.

"Tolderai-style magic in the bowls."

"That's why plants."

"Exactly."

"So how do we solve it?"

Lucy looked at the bowl again. The design was beautiful, carefully interweaving Tolderai concepts with a more modern aesthetic. The world deserved to contain art like this. Tourists deserved a chance to take it home, a souvenir of L.A. But that wasn't going to happen.

She flung the bowl down, and it shattered on the floor, pieces scattering all around. The plants waved their creepers, then lashed out at her. The Venus flytrap stretched to the end of its stalk and latched onto her wrist.

"Ow!" Lucy tried to wrench her arm free, but the plant was stronger than it looked.

Jackie muttered a spell and a glowing blade emerged from the end of her wand. "I'll cut you out."

"Don't bother with that." Lucy battered the plant with her wand. "Deal with the bowls."

Jackie grabbed the floating bowls out of the air one by one and flung them to the floor. As each one shattered, the plants trembled, and some of their leaves fell. By the time there was only one bowl left, the Venus flytrap had let go of Lucy, and the remaining creepers had curled in as if the plant were hugging itself. The whole thing trembled, and two flowers blinked like big, sad eyes.

"Sorry," Jackie said. "We can't have you doing an Audrey Two impression in the public library."

She flung the pot down. It shattered, and the plant collapsed.

Quickly, the two witches used magic to gather up the remains of the pots and plants and bundled them away through a portal for future study at Silver Griffins HQ. By the time the shop's inhabitants started to recover their senses, the shelves were back in order, books and cards spread out to take up more space.

"That's weird," the store employee said. "I thought we had something different on that shelf."

"The vendor recalled them," Lucy said. "You just sent them off, remember?"

"Oh yeah, of course."

The witches headed out and sent the cop on his way with thanks.

"What now?" Jackie asked. "Do we go around collecting

up all the Tolderai-inspired art, in case any of it goes rogue?"

Lucy shook her head. "It's everywhere. We can't possibly track down every piece. Definitely not while we're still chasing magical street art."

"So we're too busy coping with this to fix it?"

"It's starting to feel that way, isn't it?"

"Damn right. When's the last time we had a spare hour to go chase leads, to work out who's making all this magical art?"

They walked back toward the SUV. Both witches groaned as they saw the pigeon perched on the roof.

"Can't we at least do something about the Tolderai part?" Jackie said. "Put out a PSA or shut down some artists' workshops or something?"

"A PSA, seriously?"

"Fine, a spell. We do a big spell to stop all the plant magic in L.A."

"The Tolderai live for plant magic. We'd get lynched by Heather."

"I'm willing to take that risk, given the alternative."

Another pigeon fluttered in. It looked suspiciously like it had two messages tied to its legs.

"Actually…" Lucy stopped, hand outstretched toward the pigeon. "Maybe we could do something like that. Not stopping all plant magic, but stopping all the magic using those symbols on the bowl."

"Why not go for all the art-based magic while you're at it?"

"That's it!" Lucy laughed. "It's not a long-term solution, but it could stop the Tolderai imitators from accidentally casting magic for the next few months. By then, the fashion for all things Tolderai will wear off. We'll be able to track down the remaining imitators and stop any spell-casting designs."

"If only we could do that for the street art too."

"Why not? Like you said, shut down all art-based magic in the city. We won't be busy chasing our tails anymore, and that'll give us time to investigate. By the time the spell runs out, we'll have caught the perpetrators."

"Can we do something that big and powerful?"

"I don't know, but we have to give it a shot." Lucy grabbed the pigeons and stuffed them in the back of the car. "Come on, let's go talk to Applegate."

CHAPTER THIRTY-SIX

There weren't normally many Silver Griffins in the office close to midnight. It was one of the most magically powerful times of day, which meant that anyone still on duty would be out and about, catching ghosts, containing overexcited shifters, and dealing with the other magicals that came out at night.

Tonight was different. Tonight, every Silver Griffin in L.A. was in the building under Griffith Observatory, and except for a single duty officer handling the phones, all of them had gathered in the Special Equipment and Weapons firing range.

"Is it me, or does this not feel very mystical?" Ellis asked. "If we're gonna go for magic this big, shouldn't we be standing in an ancient stone circle, or at least some-where with a view, where the storm clouds can come in, and the lightning can flash dramatically?"

"Maybe a forest," Jackie said. "Somewhere dark and brooding, with bats flapping past."

"Or at least a grand hall," Lucy said. "With massive

stone walls, gargoyles staring down at us, and a mosaic floor decorated with eldritch runes."

"Yes, well, if you can find the budget for that, I'm more than happy to spruce the place up," Roger Applegate said. "Although I might consider spending the gargoyle money on a new computer system instead. For now, this is the largest room we have and one custom-built to deal with unusual magics, so unless anybody has a better idea, we should probably get started." He picked up a gnarled wooden staff that was leaning against the wall. "Is this thing strictly necessary?"

"Not exactly." Jenkins looked up from a checklist on a clipboard. "You could use something in bone instead."

"That sounds a bit necromantic. I don't want to be standing in the middle of the circle while people ask whether I'm the bad guy. Best to stick with oak, eh?"

"Plus it would take us a few weeks to source that much mammoth bone, carve the parts, and piece it all together."

"Mammoth bone?"

"Magic on this scale can be very sensitive. The details matter."

Applegate sighed. "I suppose you're right. That's why I have to wear the robes as well, is it?"

He turned on the spot, and the robes he was wearing over his suit swirled around him. They were sky blue with silver trim and pictures of stars and moons sewed on. They made him look like a kid in a "my first day at wizard school" fancy dress outfit.

Jenkins and Nigel eyed each other, and both stifled a grin.

"Oh yes, those are necessary," Jenkins said. "Totally serious. No joking. Vital to the whole thing."

"If you say so. I'm amazed at you boys' ability to throw this ritual together so quickly."

"Thank you, sir."

Jenkins waited a moment while Applegate walked to the center of the circle, then whipped out his phone and took a photo of the ridiculous robes.

"Sir, you forgot your hat!" Nigel waved a pointed velvet monstrosity with a huge, floppy brim.

"You're going too far," Jackie whispered. "He'll work it out."

"Ssh!"

"Oh, if I must." Applegate grabbed the hat and shoved it onto the top of his head. "This had better be worth it."

"I promise," Jenkins said, taking another photo, "it will be."

For all of his messing around, there was an edge to Jenkins' demeanor. He had put a huge amount of effort into preparing this ritual and got almost no sleep over the past couple of days since Lucy had come to him with her big idea. Now the moment of truth had arrived, and every Silver Griffin in L.A. was preparing to take part in something he'd prepared. He was about to have the biggest success of his career or a very public failure.

"It'll be fine." Lucy put a hand on his shoulder. "No one understands applied magic better than you."

"True, true, true." Jenkins nodded. "But I don't usually work on this broad a canvas. What if I've scaled it up incorrectly, or picked the wrong runes, or—"

"Take a deep breath. And another. Now, distract your-self, talk to me about something else."

"I can't think about anything else!"

"Then focus on some detail, like, are there limits on the spell?"

"Of course! Every spell has its limits. In this case, we purposefully inserted some to bring the magical power target back within reasonable bounds."

"So, what are those limits?"

"The most important is an exception. The spell will stop any magical art from working in L.A., but not within thirty feet of its creator. While the artist is nearby, the spell is too connected to their power for us to overcome by brute force. It's a simple matter of math, you see..."

He kept talking, explaining power ratios, magical quotients, and the interference value of external variables, none of which meant anything to Lucy. She nodded and smiled and let him talk about topics he could master until calm descended over him again.

A bell chimed.

"Time to begin," Applegate called.

The assembled witches and wizards gathered in a series of concentric rings around the regional manager. Jenkins had painted runes on the floor at Applegate's feet, and the gusts from his flapping robes made the flames of a dozen melting candles flicker.

"Wands please," Applegate said.

Lucy, standing between Jenkins and Jackie, drew her wand, as did everyone else. They held them loose in their hands, as instructed by Jenkins in the pre-ritual briefing, ready for what was to come. Then, at a nod from Applegate, the witches and wizards started to chant.

The chanting was a whisper at first, a soft hissing of voices in the dimly lit hall. Those sounds echoed back, growing in power as they did, and the witches and wizards raised their voices in response. The sound grew, took on a rhythm and a tune, like the voices of monks praying in some ancient monastery.

A clock struck midnight, and Applegate's rich, deep voice emerged from the throng.

"We gather at the witching hour,

"When we are at the height of power,

"When magic's strong and matter weak,

"When spells will find the path they seek.

"We come to cast the Griffin's net

"Across the city where it's set

"To hold back art where magic's been

"And make sure magic stays unseen."

The chant continued, and as it did, the runes on the floor started to glow. The Griffins raised their wands and channeled their power through them, the magic streaming into the room until the air was thick with it, like a cloud that Lucy could feel pressing against her skin, tingling like static.

She held out her wand and tapped its tip against Jackie's. A line of power stretched between them, glowing and pulsing. Then she turned the other way and tapped against Jenkins's wand, creating another thread. Turning around, she made a third connection to the witch behind her in the next layer of concentric circles. One by one, lines appeared connecting witches and wizards, a spider's web of enchantment.

Applegate raised his staff. The head blazed with power, and as it rose, so did the web. It floated up and expanded until the whole of the ceiling was covered in its strands.

The room shook. Lucy glanced around. Everyone else took this in their stride, assuming it was part of the plan: everyone except Jenkins.

"What's happening?" she whispered.

"I knew we should have done this somewhere else," he whispered back.

"Why? What's going on?"

"There are magics built into the walls of this room to stop experiments from breaking out. I thought I'd set up the spell so it would safely pass through them, but if something snags..."

He went pale as a lump of plaster fell from the ceiling.

"If something snags, then what?"

"If something snags, we could bring the whole building down on our heads."

Lucy went pale as well.

"Is there something we can do to stop it?"

Jenkins shook his head. "Too late now. Just hope and pray that—"

There was a sound like thunder, then the web vanished into the ceiling, and the building stopped shaking. Jenkins exhaled.

"Got away with it."

In the center of the circle, Applegate was still reciting the vocal of the spell, a long string of words designed to bind the magic in place. Other Griffins stepped forward and placed objects in front of him: a smoldering cone of incense, a unicorn's horn, an origami dragon made from a page out of an old spellbook. Applegate touched each one in turn with his heavy oak staff, and each one crumbled to dust as the power within it was drawn away.

Then the final offering—a pot of paint and a delicate artist's brush.

"Bought them from the wargames store," Jenkins whispered. "They have some really good materials these days, and I thought that—"

"Ssh!" Lucy hissed. She could feel the power still growing, and she wanted to see this moment, to mark it into her memory. One of the most powerful spells the L.A. Griffins had ever cast, and she was here for it.

Applegate touched the paint and brush with his staff. A glowing net formed around them, different from the one that had disappeared into the ceiling. Instead of a hazy glow, its strands had sharp, clear edges, like the bars of a cage. It tightened around the paint and the brush.

"Decipula," Applegate said.

The magic turned for a moment to iron bars, then vanished, taking the paint and brush with it.

Applegate chanted again, and the witches and wizards joined him. The magic spun around them, rushing around in ever-faster circles, a rising tornado of power. It tossed their clothes and hair wildly about and almost lifted the lightest of them off their feet.

Then Applegate slammed the head of his staff against a gong. A single note rang through the air. The wizards and witches fell silent. The magic was gone.

"It's finished," Applegate said. His voice was hoarse

from chanting loud enough to be heard over the rest. "We need a test."

Lucy pulled a paper and pencil from her pocket and stepped into the circle. Her colleagues all held their breath, watching and waiting. She drew a picture of a horse, then cast an enchantment on it. The horse became animated, throwing its head back, flailing its forelegs in the air.

"It didn't work," someone whispered.

"Wait," Jenkins said sharply.

Lucy handed the page to Applegate. The horse kept moving. Then she stepped away. A gap formed in the circle and she walked out. When she was thirty feet from her starting point, there was a collective gasp. She looked back. The horse had gone still.

"Congratulations, Agent Jenkins," Applegate said. "You did it. L.A. is safe from magical art."

CHAPTER THIRTY-SEVEN

Sarah shook out the picnic blanket and laid it on the grass. A little farther away across MacArthur Park, ducks were swimming on the lake, and people were walking past, some hurrying to get from place to place, others taking their time to relax and enjoy the calm surroundings. There were executives in suits, moms with strollers, teenagers with a skateboard in one hand and a cellphone in the other. The whole place felt alive.

She sat on the blanket and started taking things out of her bag. A tub of sandwiches, a bag of chips, homemade brownies, cups, and a bottle of sparkling juice. She laid it all out on the blanket while the sun shone down and people wandered past, chatting happily to each other.

"Well, this here is a fine surprise." Ellis smiled down at her. "When you said to meet here, I figured we'd be going to some nearby restaurant, not chowing down on the grass."

"I thought this would make a nice change," she said.

"It's certainly a fine thought, though I have to admit,

I've been eating on the floor a lot lately. Really need to get myself a table."

Sarah laughed. "I don't think that a picnic in the park is the same as sitting on your hard dining room floor, eating takeaway with one of the two forks you own."

"Hey, I have six forks now! Went and bought myself a cutlery set last night."

"That's very civilized of you, but now the barbarians have arrived, and they demand that you sit and give them a kiss."

"I don't see how I can resist a demand like that." He leaned in to kiss her, and for a long moment, the rest of the world receded for both of them. Then he sat on the blanket beside her and peered into the sandwich tub. "What have we got here?"

It turned into a slow sort of meal, neither of them eager to get to the end, and both still more excited to talk and listen to each other than to eat the lunch they had supposedly met up for.

"Look." Sarah pointed with a corner of brownie. "There's an artist down by the lake."

"At least we can be sure he ain't gonna be using magic."

"The ritual worked then?"

"Oh yes. It's been quiet all day. Not a single call out for a moving painting, no pictures springing off walls and attacking people. It wore everyone out so much that we're taking the day to recover and regroup. Tomorrow, we start talking to artists and street wizards, trying to work out who was behind all of this."

"Does that mean that you have the afternoon off?"

"Technically, I ought to be doing paperwork, but I ain't

been in the department long enough for any to pile up. So yeah, my time's pretty free."

"That's good timing because I'm not on shift this afternoon. We could really draw this picnic out."

"Sounds good to me."

They kissed again, taking longer over it this time. Nothing in the world could rush them.

When they returned to their food, the artist was still at work. He'd set up a seat opposite his and invited people to sit there while he drew their caricatures. Those who liked them paid him for his trouble and walked away with the picture at the end. Those who didn't... After a moment's thought, Sarah realized that she hadn't seen anyone leave unsatisfied.

"Stay here," she said. "I'll be back in a moment."

Ellis ate a brownie and watched as she skipped off down to the lake, then returned with the portrait artist in tow.

"This is Johnny," she said. "He's going to draw us and our picnic to commemorate this moment."

"Sounds good to me." Ellis sat up straight.

"No, no." Johnny waved him back down. "Slouching was good. It captures the picnic mood."

Sarah sat beside Ellis, and they kept eating while Johnny drew them.

"This feels kind of weird," Ellis said. "Having someone watch me while I eat."

"It is, isn't it?" Sarah said. "But it'll be worth it."

Their conversation became awkward and halting. It was hard to relax and be cozy with each other when a stranger was staring at them, silent and serious as his hand darted back and forth across his sketch pad. Fortunately, Johnny was very good at his job, and his task was to provide quick sketches, not detailed masterpieces. After a few minutes, he tore the front page from his pad and handed it to them.

Ellis laughed in delight. Johnny had exaggerated features on both of them but to different effects. Ellis's beard had become extra small, his sneakers extra large, his posture so laid back he was sinking into the ground. In short, he looked absurd. Sarah, on the other hand, somehow looked more lovely than ever, with big eyes like a manga character and a radiant smile.

"My freckles!" she exclaimed as she pressed her hands to her cheeks. "They're not that bad!"

"It's a cartoon," Ellis said. "It ain't the real you, though I think he's done a fine job of capturing your spirit. How much do we owe you, Johnny?"

"Oh, the lady paid already."

"Well then, consider this a tip." Ellis handed over a twenty. "Thank you for your fine work."

When Johnny was gone, the two sat gazing at the picture together while they finished off their lunch.

"You really think he's made me look good?" Sarah asked.

"You always look good, but yeah, I'd say he's brought out the adorable side."

"Well, if you say so..." She seemed doubtful but didn't say any more.

With the picnic done, they packed away the cups, tubs, and blanket and gathered their litter to go in a trash can.

"What now?" Ellis asked.

"My original plan only went up to here," Sarah admitted. "But since we both have free time, why don't we take a walk back to your house, and you can show me your new forks?"

"Well, that's mighty forward of you," Ellis said. "But how could I say no?"

The walk from MacArthur Park to Silver Lake wasn't the prettiest in the city, but Ellis wasn't bothered by that. All that mattered to him was spending time with Sarah. They walked hand-in-hand, and he felt like he was drifting on clouds instead of trudging along the concrete sidewalk.

While his attention was mostly on her, he couldn't help noticing every piece of street art they passed, and each spray can image on the corner of a building. The past few weeks had made the Silver Griffins vigilant around those pictures, expecting every one to spring into life, but now they were still. Any that had started as magical were now only decoration. The world was at peace, at least his corner of it.

"I'm really glad you decided to move here." Sarah squeezed his hand. "Not that it wasn't exciting before, getting as much of you as I could before you rushed away again, but I'll take quantity alongside quality if I can."

"Calling me quantity makes it sound like I'm putting on weight." Ellis patted his belly. "Do I need to cut back on the big picnics?"

"Not that I've noticed, but I'd love you either way."

"And I'd love you regardless of my belly."

Sarah laughed. "What about if my freckles spread, so I was mottled all over?"

"I think the freckles are cute. They're one of the things about you I love."

"Really? And what are the others?"

"Oh, just about everything."

Eventually, after a few diversions into shops and some pauses for kisses and passing traffic, they reached Ellis's street. His house still stood out, the front yard overgrown, paint peeling off one side of the gable.

"Have you thought about what you're going to do with this yet?" Sarah ran a hand over some of the bushes that threatened to overwhelm the path to the front door.

"The yard?" Ellis shook his head. "That's way down the list. Gotta get the inside livable first, then make the outside properly weatherproof so there's no risk of something falling. Then, and only then, it's time to think about plants."

Inside, the living room was still mostly bare although a bean bag faced a television propped up against one wall.

"Seriously?" Sarah shook her head. "You got a TV before you even got a sofa or dining table?"

"Someone at work was getting rid of it. Didn't seem right to let it go to waste."

"All right, I'll allow it. Why don't we go shopping on the weekend? I can keep you company and save you from terrible style choices while you furnish this place."

"I reserve the right to stick with my terrible style choices, but other than that, you're on."

"I suppose decoration should wait until you have some actual furniture."

"I have one bit of decoration already."

"You have?"

"I have now." He opened her bag and took out the carefully rolled-up cartoon of the two of them eating their picnic in the park. "This is taking pride of place on the wall over there."

"Seriously?" Sarah laughed. "You don't have to do that. There must be nicer things you'd like on your wall."

Ellis shook his head. "I've spent my whole adult life switching between rentals and hotel rooms. I've had plenty of time around the sort of decoration that could count as nice or perfectly tasteful. I don't want that anymore. I want personal. I want to be surrounded by things that matter to me."

He waved his wand, and a frame appeared around the picture.

"Do you even have a hammer and nail to hang it up with?"

"Why would I need that?" He waved his wand again, and a hook appeared on the middle of the wall. He walked over and carefully hung the picture from it, then took a step back and smiled. "My first decoration in my new home. Maybe it ain't the finest art, but it's perfect to me."

Sarah slid her arm around him. "Me too. I hope there are plenty more soon, all the happy memories we can make."

CHAPTER THIRTY-EIGHT

Lucy pulled up in the street outside the building site and glanced at the time on the dashboard. She was running late already, but she couldn't ignore this call. She would just have to deal with it quickly and then get on the road to school.

She got out of the car, stuffed her wand into her back pocket, and opened the gate in the chain-link fence. There were traces of magic on the padlock and chain that lay on the ground. Someone had broken in by magical means.

The site was being turned into apartments, as so often happened with empty urban space. Concrete slabs had started rising around a central pillar and steel frame, but they were gray and featureless, without the windows or external cladding that would turn this into something people might want to live in. The ground was churned-up dirt and scattered rubble, the outcome of heavy vehicles and heavy construction.

A sound came from the center of the site. The roar of an enraged animal sounded like it was real and present, a beast stalking through the urban jungle, except that it kept cutting off abruptly, like the end of a recording.

Lucy emerged around one of the concrete slabs and saw a wide-open area. Two workmen in high visibility jackets and hard hats stood frozen stiff as statues, one with a look of fear, the other with a hand held out as if angrily admonishing. Near them was a Willen, most of his short, furred body concealed by baggy jeans and a loose hoodie, but with his rodent snout protruding from under the hood. He held a can of spray paint and magic glistened around his claw as he tapped the side of the can.

Thirty feet away, on a stretch of concrete wall, was a picture of a lion. It had been painted in purple, red, and gold, the bold colors glowing in the warm light of evening, a stark contrast with the cold, dull gray all around.

"What is this bullshit?" the Willen said. He took a few steps toward the painting, and it sprang into life, the lion reaching off the wall to claw the ground in front of it, growling as it did so. When the Willen stepped back, the painting froze, the claw went back to a flat image of paint, and the beast's voice fell abruptly silent. "Did you do this?"

The Willen turned angrily to the frozen men. He raised the spray can, and his hand sparkled with magic again, adding something dark and dangerous to the paint.

"It wasn't them." Lucy stepped out from where she had stood concealed and held up her Silver Griffins identity amulet. "Agent Heron, badge number 485. We've put a stop to magical art in this city. Unless you want to spend the rest of your life in Trevilsom, I suggest that you put down the can and step away from your victims."

"Screw you, lady." The Willen took a step toward the

painting, which came to life again. "You can't go censoring art. My buddy here will protect me."

With a growl like a rising storm, the lion stepped off the wall and prowled toward Lucy. It bared its teeth, and its claws gleamed against the broken ground. It was the perfect embodiment of predatory ferocity, swathed in purple and gold.

"I don't have time for this," Lucy said, "so let's skip to the end." She pointed her wand at the Willen. "Subvolo."

The Willen squeaked in alarm as the magic lifted him into the air and levitated him across the building site toward Lucy. As soon as he was thirty feet from the wall, the enchantment on the lion broke. The paint hurtled back onto the concrete, becoming flat and inert again. The closest thing to life left in it was the eyes, which the Willen had painted with a particularly convincing gleam.

"You won't get away with this," The Willen sputtered.

"I was going to say the same to you." Lucy held him flailing futilely in the air while she pulled out her phone and called the Griffins transport room. "Hi, it's Agent Heron, badge 485. I have a captive in need of urgent transport to HQ... No, I can't bring him in myself. I'm on my way to something... Does it matter what? The important thing is... Fine, for the record, I'm going to a PTA event at my kid's school, and if I don't turn up, that will raise lots of awkward questions. It's our job to avoid awkward questions, so could you please... Thank you." She hung up and pocketed the phone. "Don't worry. You'll be out of here soon."

"This ain't gonna work," the Willen said. "When VX

realizes what you people have done, she'll lose her shit. She will crush you."

"I'm not too worried about being destroyed by a lone graffiti artist," Lucy said. "Although if she wants to try, that would be super helpful. It'll save me the effort of hunting her down." She considered it for a moment. "Is that my plan now? I feel like that could be my plan."

The air shimmered, and a portal appeared, a black void in a ring of golden magic.

"Off you go." Lucy waved her wand, and the Willen vanished through the portal, which promptly vanished. "Now, to finish clearing this up."

She unfroze the two construction workers, who looked at her in bewilderment.

"What the…" one of them began.

"Never was, never will be." Lucy waved her wand, and they both went slack, their memories of magic and moving art fading away. "When you recover, you'll remember seeing that painting of a lion and deciding that you need to wash it off, okay?"

She hurried back to her car, chaining the gate shut on her way out, and headed off down the road. She wasn't going to have time to go home now. The auction would have started already. She would just have to hope that the other parents were also wearing jeans and Converse.

There was a single spot free for parking down the road from the school. She pulled in, grabbed her bag, and rushed inside.

Annie the admin looked up from behind her reception desk and smiled. "Sports hall."

"Thanks." Lucy rushed past.

The doors were closed when she reached them, but she heard voices inside. She eased a door open and slipped in.

The hall was full of parents and staff, sitting in neat rows of folding chairs. They held cardboard disks with numbers on them, the PTA's improvised equivalent of the paddles used at professional auctions. At the front of the room, Principal Reyes stood on a stage. He was dressed more smartly than usual, with his sleeves rolled down and a bow tie around his neck. With one hand, he held up a picture made during the paint and sip evening. With his other hand, he was gesturing to people in the audience.

"Come on, we can go a little higher," he said. "Remember, you're not just buying this fine art. You're also buying new equipment for the school. Do I hear sixty dollars? Thank you there in the middle of the room. Anyone going above sixty? Sixty-five maybe? Yes, thank you. And seventy now! We've got a bidding war going on." A ripple of laughter ran through the audience. "Seventy-five, perhaps? Yes, and eighty, eighty-five... Any more above eighty-five? Going once, going twice, sold to Mr. Murphy for eighty-five dollars."

There was a round of polite applause as the winning bidder went up to collect his painting. During the distraction, Charlie turned in his seat in the back row and gestured to the empty spot next to him.

"How much did my picture raise?" Lucy asked as she slid into the empty seat.

"It didn't yet," Charlie replied. "Lots of people were saying nice things about it during the exhibition part of the evening, so they've saved it for near the end."

"Really? But I didn't even have time to finish!"

"People like that it's a simple sketch. Apparently, it has life and authenticity."

"You mean smudges and shaky lines."

Charlie laughed. "Just be grateful that people are interested. Some pieces barely sold at all, even though it's for charity."

"Quiet, please!" Reyes called. "Now it's time for our penultimate picture of the evening, by the PTA's very own Kelly Petrie."

Kelly stood and waved to the crowd while Reyes held up her painting for everyone to see. It was fine, but Lucy felt as if she could have done better if she'd had time to get to the paints.

"What am I bid for this fine still life in oils?" Reyes asked. "Who'll start me at twenty dollars?" A disk shot up. "Thank you over there. How about twenty-five? Yes, we have twenty-five. Thirty even, though Max, I'm not sure you should be bidding on your wife's painting." Everyone laughed. "Who wants this more than Max? Thirty-five over there. Forty. Forty-five. Fifty…"

The bids kept coming, and a sense of excitement rose, encouraged by Reyes.

"That's a lot of money for Kelly's amateur art," Lucy whispered to Charlie.

"It's good for the school," he whispered back.

"I know, but…" Lucy sighed. "You're right, no buts. If it raises the money we need, I'm happy for her to win this time."

"Two hundred dollars!" Reyes exclaimed. "Our highest bid of the evening by quite a way. Any more for any more? No? Then going once, going twice, sold to Mrs. Sanchez for two hundred dollars. Thank you all for your bids, and let's have a big round of applause for the artist."

Kelly stood and waved again. Somehow, she managed to spot Lucy in the crowd and gave her a smug, triumphant look. That bid had crowned Kelly as the school's art queen.

"And now, our final lot." Reyes held up Lucy's picture. "A finely detailed and evocative still life in pencil, by Lucy Heron. Lucy, are you here?"

Lucy stood, blushing, gave a hurried wave, and sat back down.

"Not showboating for your adoring fans?" Charlie whispered.

"When that's all I managed?" Lucy shook her head. "I'll sit here and try not to die of embarrassment."

"Starting at twenty dollars," Reyes announced. "And there's the bid already. Who'll give me twenty-five? Yes? Thank you. How about thirty?"

Lucy saw Charlie's hand twitch, about to make a bid and push the price up.

"Don't you dare," she hissed. "I don't want people to think I only earned anything here because of my husband."

"I want to contribute."

"Then we'll donate later. Now keep your hands still, or I'll freeze them in place."

She turned her attention back to Reyes, caught off-guard as she heard the bids.

"We're at one-eighty. Who'll give me one-ninety? Yes, one-ninety… And two hundred! Anyone want to go higher, give us a new record for the evening?"

"Two-twenty," someone called.

"Two-forty," came the reply.

"Two-sixty."

"Two-eighty."

"Three hundred!"

Reyes looked around the room.

"Going once at three hundred," he said. "Going twice… Sold for three hundred dollars to Ms. Flemming. Thank you very much for your generosity. Now let's have a big hand for the artist."

Lucy stood again, still blushing although with very different feelings this time. She hadn't dared to think so highly of her work, but other people loved it. Apparently, where art was concerned, she still had what it took to make a splash. A roar of applause washed over her.

"I can't believe it," she said as she sat back down next to Charlie.

"I told you, lots of people liked it. Life and authenticity."

People had started getting up to leave. Max waved to the Herons as he walked past, but Kelly stalked by without looking at Lucy, her nose thrust into the air.

"You're grinning," Charlie said.

"Just happy to have helped out the school," Lucy replied. "Honest."

CHAPTER THIRTY-NINE

"What you doing?"

The sentence sounded less like coherent words than a string of grunts. Dylan looked up from his drawing to see Jeff Barr standing over his table, an ugly sneer on his face.

"My work," Dylan said. He glanced around the room. The art teacher must have stepped outside because Jeff never bothered anyone when an adult was watching. Like all the most experienced bullies, he knew how to pick his moments almost as well as he knew how to pick his nose, something he was doing right then and there.

"Looks like scribbling to me." Jeff pulled out his finger. "Like a baby did it." He grabbed a pen and scrawled across Dylan's page. "See, just like a baby."

Dylan glared, but Jeff only laughed as he dropped the pen next to the paper.

"How's your work going, Jeff?" Sofia asked. "I bet your stickmen are real Eisner winners."

"What?" Jeff turned her way.

"The Eisners, they're an award for comics, though the

only way you'll win anything is if they base a monster on you."

"Want me to improve your work too?" Jeff reached for the pen, an ugly expression twisting his face.

"Want me to kick your shins until they're one big bruise?"

Jeff clenched his fist and glared at Sofia, but he didn't make a move against her. For all his tough talk, she'd taught him why it wasn't wise to mess with girls, especially ones who took their inspiration from superheroes.

"Teacher's coming," Jeff said. "Guess I'll go work. Later, losers."

Jeff stalked off across the classroom. Lance picked up the abandoned pen and put a lid on it.

"That guy wouldn't even make a good monster," he said. "He's too unoriginal."

"I don't know. I think there's a place for a pig-faced supervillain in my story," Dylan said. "Everybody else in it is based on someone real, so why not the bad guy?"

He sat back and took a look at the images he had drawn so far for this comic. They started with the hero, of course, a superpowered witch who flew around town stopping magical accidents and keeping everyone safe. He'd made sure that she didn't look anything like his mom, that she had a different name and did some things differently, like flying on a broom and not enjoying cookies, but the core of her was still there, for anyone who knew what they were looking at.

He found it hard to describe the feeling that came from presenting his mom, and other people from his life, in this way. The world of magic was one he normally had to keep secret, a vital part of him hidden from the world. It wasn't only the thrill of revealing it, however subtly and covertly, that had enthused him for this project. It was the feeling that the magicals he knew deserved more credit.

They'd saved the day dozens of times, thwarting powerful criminals, smog monsters, crusading knights, and a host of other threats, but most people had no idea that they were there. The school thought his mom was an insurance investigator, a job where even the title sounded boring. It was cool to think that, in some small way, this piece of work would give her and her colleagues the credit they deserved.

"That's good work, Dylan," the art teacher said, looking over his shoulder. "Now, think of the colors you want to use. Bold, simple design choices can help make a superhero stand out."

She walked around the table to look at the others' art.

"This is excellent, Sofia," she said. "Can you tell me a bit about it?"

"Sure." Sofia hesitated for a moment while she got the pieces of the story together in her head. "I wanted to do something different because there are so many superhero comics already, so I'm writing and drawing an epic fantasy."

"You mean like the *Odyssey*?"

"More like *Lord of the Rings* except not everybody in it is a dude. This is the hero, her name's Talarel, and she's a magician. She can use her powers to control the world around her, summoning storms or digging tunnels so she can hide safely under the ground."

"I can see the storm," the teacher said, looking at the

image of the windswept young woman, with her robes flapping and leaves flying around her. "You've given her a great sense of power. Who else is in her story?"

"This is Runs on Air, an elf." Sofia pointed at another picture, where a slim figure stood with a bow in one hand and a flame in the palm of the other. "He's a hunter, but he also makes illusions. His fire's not real, but people will think it is, so they'll get scared, and, um, I don't know, maybe that's how he'll chase off the bad guys?"

"Ingenious. Who are these cute little guys down here?"

"Those are the three mice, Fee, Spear, and Bob. They follow the heroes around, watching them, learning from them."

"Fee, Spear, and Bob, huh?" The teacher looked around the kids at the table and smiled. "Well, sometimes it's fun to put a part of yourself into the story, even when the rest of it is wildly unreal. It can bring in grounding emotions, even through little mice."

She moved on to look at other people's work. That was how it went with teachers. Between thirty kids, they could only ever give one a few minutes of their time.

"You turned us into mice?" Lance leaned in to look at Sofia's page. "Seriously?"

"Would you have preferred it if I left you out?" she asked sharply. "Or if I made you into an ugly, warty rat, giving everyone diseases?"

"Hm, I guess not. But I want to play myself in the TV adaptation."

"How are you going to play a mouse?"

"Same way as that guy played Gollum in the *Lord of the Rings* films. I'll wear a green suit with dots on it, and I'll make perfect mouse movements, then they'll do a digital model over the top." He pulled his hands up beneath his face like a rodent with its paws at the ready. "See, perfect mouse."

"All right, you can be in the TV version. But I want Twylan to play Talarel."

"Can Twylan act?"

"She won't need to. Talarel's based on her, remember?"

"Just don't tell Siltor if they make a version of his character on TV," Dylan said. "I think his head might explode with pride."

He looked down at his work. Jeff's scribble was still there on Dylan's page, marring the work he had done. It ruined one of the pictures of the witch, where she was rescuing people from a magical explosion. Dylan had been looking forward to showing this to his mom once he finished, and he didn't want Jeff to have spoiled it.

He looked around the room, making sure that no one was watching, then touched his finger to the page.

"Deleo," he whispered and let magic flow through his finger. There was a soft glow at the tip as he ran it along Jeff's scrawl, wiping it away. When he finished, the picture was back how it had been.

"Could you do your pictures like that?" Lance whispered. "Like, use magic to make them perfect? Find a spell that made all your drawing super realistic and dynamic and cool, that got rid of all your mistakes and made it awesome? Because if I could, that's what I'd do."

Dylan shifted uncomfortably in his seat.

"I tried it a bit," he admitted. "I found that I could use magic to make pictures. But it did it so well that it didn't feel like my drawings anymore. And it took the fun out of it. Drawing lets me do something different instead of casting spells all the time. I want art to be a thing I do for me."

"Even when we have to do it for school?"

"Especially then, because otherwise, it's cheating. Then I'm no better than Jeff."

A serious silence settled across their table. "No better than Jeff" was one of the worst things they could imagine.

"So you don't think art and magic should mix?" Sofia asked.

Dylan shrugged. "I don't know. There are probably cool ways to do it, but I don't know them, and I'm okay with that. Art has a magic of its own, you know? The way you draw a line, and suddenly ink and paper seem like a person. The way images come alive and stories unfold. It doesn't need spells. It's amazing the way it is."

"I like that," Sofia said.

"You would," Lance said. "You're really good at art. Me, if I had magic, I'd use it all the time."

"Then it's a good thing you don't because you would make such a mess."

"Maybe that could be my main villain," Dylan said. "The man who shouldn't have magic." He grinned at Lance. "Looks like you're going to be in all our comics."

Lance sighed. "I preferred it when I was only a mouse."

CHAPTER FORTY

Lucy and Sarah stopped outside the door of the tattoo parlor. Inside, a woman was shouting, and though they couldn't make out the words, the anger of her tone was all too clear.

"Do you need to go in and stop the fight?" Sarah asked.

"Not unless it gets magical," Lucy said. "Or it seems like someone's going to get hurt."

"Oh good. I really don't want to get caught up in someone else's mad mood."

"You wouldn't have to go in with me."

Sarah looked at her friend and shook her head. "You know I would."

The door burst open, the bell wildly clanging as it jolted, and a woman in leather pants and a sleeveless t-shirt walked out. She stopped in the doorway and looked back, one finger pointing at the skull tattoo on her other arm.

"This is bullshit, Tom," she shouted. "She promised me more than just a pretty picture, and you'd better make good on that promise."

Then she stormed away, and the door swung shut.

"Coast's clear," Lucy said. "Are you ready?"

"Sure."

"Then let's do this."

Together, they walked into the shop. Tom, the tattooist Lucy had met on her previous visit, leaned against the counter, his head in his hands. At the sound of the bell, he straightened and offered them a brittle smile.

"Ladies. How are you doing today?"

"Fine, thank you." Lucy gestured toward the door. "We saw your other customer leave, or more accurately we heard her. Is everything all right?"

Tom's smile became even stiffer.

"It's fine. Just a little trouble with some of my inking supplies. There's a certain sort of person who's never satisfied, you know?"

"Disappointment must be hard to accept when you're making permanent changes to your body."

"Oh, yes. That's why I get so much business doing cover-ups. When people make a mistake with a cheap tattooist, they end up having to pay twice, so they can get someone like me to fix it." He gave Lucy a quizzical look. "You've been here before, right, but with a different friend?"

"Well remembered. I guess artists get good at remembering the details of faces."

"I'll take the compliment, but it was the accent that gave you away." He drew a deep breath, and some of his tension dissipated. "So, you've decided to go ahead with the tattoo?"

"Not exactly."

"Ah, so you want to ask some more questions, maybe get an idea of how it would look?" He took a narrow felt tip pen out from under the counter. "If you want, I can sketch something quickly on your arm, give you a better sense of what it'll look like. Unless you're not going for the arm, of course. That's where most people start, and it's what I recommend if you're not sure, but some people have a specific vision in mind, want to hide it from relatives, or are after something more intimate."

Sarah raised an eyebrow. "You mean like—"

"No!" Lucy said. "Neither of us wants to know."

"Lucy, I work in a hospital. I'm not going to get grossed out because someone has a picture of a lizard on their—"

"La-la-la I'm not listening!"

"Okay, okay, I'll stop!" Sarah exchanged a look with Tom. "My friend's English. You know how they get about these things."

"I'm not prudish. It's just that everyone has a limit, and I don't want to think about needles in certain places."

"I'm not jumping to any conclusions," Tom said, "but that is what a prude would say."

"I've listened to punk rock, I've read The Wasp Factory, I just, you know..."

"Come from the land of tea and stiff upper lips."

"No! Well, yes, but also... Oh, enough of this, let's get to the point." Lucy pulled out her Silver Griffin amulet and waved it at Tom. "You know what this is, right?"

He stiffened, but to his credit, his face stayed calm.

"Not sure I do. Is that the design you're after for your tattoos?"

"So you don't know anything about magic?"

"I've done some fantasy art for my clients, gave a guy a full back wizard once. I can do it again if you really want."

"Listen, sunshine." Lucy planted her hands on her hips and glared at him. "I'm with the Silver Griffins, and I am onto you. I've seen the magic inks you have back there and the magical tattoo gun.

"I had to clear up the mess when you gave some plonker super strength, and he trashed a perfectly decent pub. By rights, I should have hauled you in days ago. So this is your last chance. Fess up, play the good little wizard, or you'll be making your tattoos with ballpoint pen ink and a pin from the Trevilsom prison inmates' workshop. Got it?"

Then came the silence. It was a special silence, one that always came the moment after Lucy laid out a criminal's options while he tried to work out just how stuffed he was. It was a silence so tense it could have seen a therapist for a year and still been popping stress balls at the mention of her name.

"Just hypothetically," Tom began, "if I was using some sort of magic in my—"

"Prison workshop it is." Lucy pulled out her wand.

"No, wait!" Tom took a step back, hands raised. "I confess, okay? I did it! I've been putting magic in my tattoos. I'm not much of a wizard, but my grandma taught me a bit, and I realized it works best for me when I put it in ink. So that's what I do, weak magic in a limited way, just a little augmentation."

"A little augmentation? That wanker you gave super strength to went full Hulk proving how tough he was."

"That was a test, trying to push myself further than

normal. I shouldn't have done it. I admit that, and I won't do it again."

"You shouldn't have been doing it in the first place. What else have you put out into the world?"

"Just a few little augmentations. I made someone faster, helped a lady with her memory, some boosts to charisma, nothing too weird." He hesitated. "I mean, except for the one I let fly."

"You gave someone the ability to fly, and you didn't think that might be a problem?"

"I mean, maybe. What have they done with it?"

"I don't know, and that's the whole problem!"

Lucy flung her hands in the air in exasperation. It was like trying to talk to one of her kids when they were in an obstinate mood. The guy knew he'd done wrong. He even knew how and why. He just really, *really*, didn't want to admit that actions had consequences.

"I don't want to go to Trevilsom," he whimpered. "Please, isn't there another way?"

"Fortunately for you, this time there is." Lucy placed her hands on the counter and leaned forward right in his face. "Because I am a good Griffin, a helpful Griffin, a Griffin who persuaded her boss that sometimes reform is better than retribution. Do you want to hear my lovely plan?"

"Yes, please."

Lucy took a step back and pointed at Sarah. "This is Dr. Smith."

"Hi." Sarah waved. "Nice to meet you."

"Dr. Smith runs a clinic for magicals. She also works in a busy hospital. She meets a lot of people with long-term medical problems. Sometimes she and her fellow practitioners can't solve those by normal means, or the person can't afford their treatment. Now you're going to fix their problems."

"I am?"

"You are. Maybe someone's suffering nausea from cancer treatments. You'll give them a tattoo that takes the sickness away and lets them live with their discomfort.

"Maybe someone else has a crippled leg. You'll create a tattoo that restores strength to it. Not the sort of crazy strength you gave that other idiot, but the sort that will give them a normal life. Perhaps you'll even work out tattoos to fend off diseases for the immune-compromised or to help addicts stay clean."

"I guess, sure, maybe I can do that. As long as it's enhancing people's bodies and minds, that's what I've been doing."

"Good. Now, this next part is important. Whatever you do, you won't get to brag about it. Most of your patients won't know about magic, can't know about magic. As far as they're concerned, it's all psychosomatic. You're giving them a way to focus, to overcome their problems. You're providing good luck charms, not spells, understand?"

"But they will really be spells?"

"Yes, of course, that's the whole point." Lucy frowned. "I'm starting to worry that you might not be smart enough for this."

"I am, I swear!" Tom said. "It's all just a lot, you know. And, well, there's a problem…"

"Go on."

"My magic's stopped working."

"Really?"

"Yeah, just the last few days. It all seems fine while the customer's in the chair, but the minute they walk away, the magic stops working. I think I'm losing my touch."

Lucy considered telling him the truth about the Silver Griffins' ritual, the suppression of art magic, the wider events he had somehow stayed oblivious to. But he didn't need to know. He just needed to cooperate if he was going to help sick people.

"Don't worry about that," she said. "I know for a fact that the magic will start working again in a few weeks." Or, more accurately, the ritual would wear out then, but that was still in things he didn't need to understand. "Until then, your tattoos will work as long as they're around you, which means you can safely practice the new designs you'll need. When time's up, one of us will give you a call, and Dr. Smith here will start sending you patients. Patients who you'll tattoo free of charge, of course."

"But I—"

"Is it even real ink in prison, or do they make it from boot polish and ashes?"

"Free tattoos for sick people. Got it."

"Good lad." Lucy patted him on the shoulder. "Look at how you're turning your life around. One minute the criminal, getting busted by the Griffins, the next you're doing vital service for community members. You're an inspiration to us all." She opened the door, and the bell rang out with its clear chime. "It's a good opportunity I'm giving you, Tom. Don't waste it."

CHAPTER FORTY-ONE

"I can't believe we're going to the forest again," Twylan whispered to Kix as they walked along the tunnel, near the back of a crowd of excited Underfoot Brigade students. "I thought that Ms. Fields would never let us back after last time."

"I know," Kix said. "Do you think there are more things we broke that need fixing, and she's taking us back to do it?"

"With the whole class?"

"Maybe we messed up so bad it will take everyone to fix, and they'll all hear about what we did, and we'll be humiliated in front of everyone, and, and, and..."

"Take deep breaths." Twylan patted her friend gently on the back. "Otherwise, you're going to hyperventilate."

Kix nodded sharply, then drew a deep breath and another, her little body heaving with each one.

"What's gotten into you two?" Leontine asked, looking over his shoulder at them. "You've been having weird whispered conversations all week."

"Nothing," Kix said sharply. "Why would anything be the matter? Nothing's wrong, everything's good, nothing to see here."

Twylan shook her head and tried not to laugh as her friend committed the least convincing cover-up since Watergate.

"Now I know something's going on." Leontine turned to face them. Unlike many of the other Underfoots, he couldn't produce magical light, so instead, he had a flashlight to illuminate his way down the tunnels, and he shone it in their faces. "What's this all about?"

"We tried to do something nice in the underground forest, but it did more harm than good." Twylan stroked Kix's shoulder as the gnome struggled to bring her breath under control again. "Remember that it was a nice thing, Kix, and Ms. Fields understands that we didn't mean any harm."

"Is this why we're going there now?" Leontine stared at them accusingly. "Are we going to have to clear up your mess?"

"We did that already." Twylan frowned thoughtfully. "At least, I'm almost sure we did. If not, then I guess we'll find out in a minute."

"Then what's all this about?" Leontine asked.

"Probably another lesson. Now get moving. We're falling behind the rest."

They hurried after the others in the class, and a few minutes later emerged in one of the forest caves. It wasn't the same one they had been to before although it was similar in many ways. The ceiling of woven roots and living vines. The swath of trees occupying most of the space with leaves in dozens of different shades of green, yellow, and silver. The undergrowth between them, ranging from dense tangles of briars to springy moss to clusters of brightly colored flowers.

The air was fresh and delicately scented, and there was a gentle chirping of birds. A magical approximation of sunlight streamed down from the ceiling.

Like the other cave, it had a chaotic sort of loveliness to it. The trees mixed together without anything like order. The undergrowth was patchy and erratic. Even the shape of the organic roof was uneven and could have been considered ugly in places. This space was a miracle, but not the sort of miracle an artist would create.

To Twylan's surprise, they weren't the only ones in the cave. Waiting for them as they emerged from the tunnel were several witches and wizards, including Carol Winters and Nathaniel Oakmantle.

"Are they all Tolderai?" Kix asked.

"I think so," Twylan replied. "And there are a lot of them."

"All the Tolderai?"

She shrugged. "I have no idea. Ms. Fields doesn't like to talk about how big the tribe is, in case someone can use that information against them."

Heather Fields gestured for the Tolderai and the Underfoot Brigade to gather around her, forming a loose circle.

"By now, you'll all be wondering why you're here," she said.

"Damn right." An older Tolderai man glared around, then scratched his chest, which made a crinkling sound. "I could be out there, looking after my wood. You know they're trying to build another of those spy towers in it?"

"Telephone masts aren't spy towers, Mackam."

"Oh yeah? How do you think they do all those inter-cepts of people's messages, huh?"

"Look, that doesn't matter right now."

"Not to you maybe, but—"

"Not. Now." Heather sighed, then started again. "You're here because we're going to rearrange this cave."

That caused some murmurs among the Tolderai.

"Why?" Mackam asked. "It's all perfectly good. Every-thing's growing well."

"Because I learned a lesson here the other day." Heather nodded at Twylan and Kix, who shifted closer to each other, defensive and uncertain. "People will always want to assert order over chaos.

"That's part of why we've lost so many forests on the surface and why, when they grow back, it's just neat lines of trees, not the dense, tangled nature that the world needs. Humanity will always try to assert order, whether it's an industrial sort of order or an artistic sort of order. They can't resist meddling."

The Tolderai nodded and murmured their weary agree-ment. Down the centuries, their tribe had seen countless forests wiped out or weakened, and while they had fought to keep them alive, they hadn't always succeeded.

"For now, we're planting under the ground because it's safe. Humans can't find what we're doing here, and that means they can't interfere. But if we want to restore the world's lungs, then sooner or later, we have to go back to growing on the surface. So what if, instead of fighting to stop humans from forcing order onto our forests, we gave them that order ourselves?"

"You want us to neuter the forests?" Mackam growled. "To become as bad as them?"

He pointed at the ceiling, toward the world of men and machines above, and spat on the ground in disgust.

"No, not to neuter the forests, to shape them. To find a way of making them more pleasing to people while keeping all of their value.

"Imagine if we could make a forest that was as rich with life and variety as any we've ever known, but that met humanity's standards for beauty? One that wasn't just the messy reality of a forest, but the ideal of it, like they see in their picture books and their doctored photographs? Maybe then, enough of them would think that the forests were worth preserving.

"And if we did that, we could shift it the other way as well. We could persuade people to let more nature into their parks and gardens because it would be under their control. Because it would meet their ideals of what looks right."

Mackam snorted. "Impossible. You've seen what humans are like."

"No, I think we can do it," Carol Winters said in her gentle, soothing tone. "I've planted gardens that were far denser than most but that the humans around me called beautiful. And I've studied the aesthetic elements. I think we really can make the needs of people and nature meet."

"Hm." Mackam looked unconvinced. "So how are we supposed to work this miracle?"

"By practicing down here first, and by working with

people who understand aesthetics." Heather gestured at the Underfoot Brigade. "Carol has been teaching art and design to these young people, who have grown up in the shadow of human civilization. They're our key to grasping what looks good to humanity, and we're their key to understanding ecosystems.

"We'll work together, in these caves. You teach them how plants combine to make a healthy whole, and they'll help you make those combinations look more pleasing. If it works, we might just make something that can change the world. And if not..." She shrugged. "If not, you've taught a bunch of kids how to look after plants, so it's still a win."

"I don't want to be a teacher," Mackam growled.

"Do you want to be chief?" Heather squared up to him.

Mackam's hand tightened around the hilt of his knife, but he shook his head. "What are your orders?"

Heather split them up into teams, putting each Tolderai with a student or two. Twylan and Kix, reeling in delight at the potential of the new plan, tensed in fear when they discovered they were with Mackam.

"Little girlies." His eyes narrowed as he looked at them. "What do you understand of the world, eh?"

"Not much," Twylan said, though with her life on the streets, she knew a lot more than most girls her age. "Can you teach us?"

Mackam made a face, but he didn't say no. Instead, he led them to a corner of the forest and started pointing at plants, rapidly reeling off information about what each one was, what it needed to flourish, how it fitted with the others. He talked and talked and talked like he was trying to bury the Underfoots beneath a mulch of words.

"So this would go equally well under either tree?" Twylan said when he finally ground to a halt.

Mackam looked at her, then at the plant she had singled out and the two trees she was pointing to.

"Yes, what of it?" he said.

"Well, it would look better under this one."

"Ah, but the other bush needs to be there."

"Not if we move it here." Kix pointed at a space beneath another tree. "And its flowers would look very dramatic emerging from these thorns."

"Hm." Mackam stroked his chin. "Not a terrible choice, but you've ignored the soil quality."

"Oh no, have we?" Behind Mackam's back, Twylan winked at Kix, who had listened to the same soil lecture from Nathaniel as she had. "Please tell us more."

A little more gently this time, Mackam started talking. It wasn't only a repeat of what they knew but included new things about how different plants rotted, their impact on drainage and acidity, the way that this encouraged or discouraged the trees from spreading. By the end, the girls were less certain about their ideas.

"Could it work if we did something with moss?" Kix asked.

"What sort of moss?"

"I don't know different mosses," she admitted. "One with a light color would look best, but only if it works for the soil, of course."

"A light color, eh?" Mackam tapped a finger against his knife handle as his face shifted in thought. "I might have a few ideas…"

Heather walked past, roaming around the wood,

listening in on conversations. Even when she'd come up with this scheme, she'd had doubts about it. She had them still. But the two groups were working together, the forest was changing, and she had to admit, what she had seen did look good. Maybe this really could work, a perfect combination of form and function.

CHAPTER FORTY-TWO

VX turned away from her painting, ready to ask Double-Rezz's opinion. Except, Double-Rezz wasn't there. He hadn't turned up when they were supposed to meet an hour before dawn, hadn't brought the hangers-on who she'd gotten used to having around to encourage her and carry her materials. She was back to working alone, and while she'd always thought she liked that, it turned out she was wrong. She liked the company.

Perching on the top of her stepladder, she shook the can of white paint, then added one final flourish to the creature's eyes. With that touch, the magic came together, as she had known it would. The dinosaur, vast and predatory, loomed off the wall.

Oh yes. This was it. The past few days, she'd done small, hurried pieces, working on her own and not returning to see how anyone responded to them. The magic had been there, in the most literal sense, but the spark of inspiration hadn't. They'd been rehearsals, not pieces in their own right but part of the build-up to this.

The dinosaur dragging itself out of a deep well of oil was the perfect encapsulation of everything she had tried to say with her recent work about humanity and the environment and the predatory way people behaved. Placing it here, so close to the La Brea Tar Pits, let it evoke the prehistoric connections the district was known for, as well as that tarry aesthetic. It would bring out the sense of something thick, clinging, and destructive for anyone viewing the oil.

It would be a shortcut to make them think about death and destruction, about an unlivable environment. The piece was situational. It was street art as it should be.

It was the perfect piece to go fully public, to cast off the lies that kept magicals in the dark, to let the world see that there was magic and that it could create visions of power and beauty. No more subtlety, no more limiting her work's magic to self-defense. This was going to leap out at people in the most literal way.

She climbed down off the ladder and took a few steps back. The dinosaur reared up and shook its head. Painted jaws gaped wide, revealing teeth made of banknotes and diamonds. This wasn't a subtle world. The whole thing was huge and grand, meant to stand out at a distance, and she needed that distance to see it all.

She grabbed her ladder and her bag full of paints, then walked off down the street. Once she was far enough away to get a proper view, she turned, ready to observe her creation's movements in all their menacing majesty.

The dinosaur stood still. VX tipped her head to one side and frowned. The whole thing seemed flatter than it was supposed to be. Slowly, a terrible realization came over her. The magic had gone.

She stalked angrily back toward the painting. She didn't have time to do it all again, but perhaps some retouching could bring it back to life. Let some magic flow into the fine detailing and revive the spells that had fallen inert.

As she came within thirty feet, the magic rushed back in. The dinosaur reared up, waved its forelegs, and bared its teeth. The oil ran, thick and dark and dreadful, off the wall and into the street. The beast's shadow fell across her and light gleamed from its teeth.

VX stepped back. The magic vanished, and the dinosaur went flat. She stepped forward. It sprang forth again, imbued with the power she had poured through her paint.

"What the…"

"So you're VX," a gruff voice said.

VX spun and glared at the figure standing in an alley mouth. He was a dwarf dressed in black biker leathers with a neatly trimmed beard. He looked made for this sort of skulking.

"You. What did you do to my painting?"

"Not me. I'm a big admirer of your work. I want to see it flourish."

"But you know, don't you? I can see it by your smug grin."

"Some people might take offense at that." The dwarf stuck a cigar between his lips and lit it with a chunky silver lighter. The flame from the lighter reflected in his dark eyes. "I'm a lawyer, not an Internet celebrity. I don't gain anything by wallowing in outrage."

VX walked slowly toward him. He wasn't like the other

admirers of her work. Those wannabe Banksy clones had turned up with Double-Rezz, full of excitement and jabbering away about their big dreams, then tried to rip off her style because they didn't understand the difference between spellcraft and design. He was calm, composed, almost indifferent.

"You're not an artist, are you?" she said.

"Not in the way you mean. I've dabbled in more mechanical crafts, but mostly I appreciate the things people create. Something like this..." He gestured at the dinosaur, which had gone still again. "The message isn't one I'm keen on, but the skill, the effort, the ingenuity, I admire that. I don't like to see it disrupted."

"I know lawyers get paid by the hour, so this bullshit is probably habit, but I'm not paying, so cut to the chase."

The dwarf tapped his cigar, and a sprinkling of ash drifted into the gutter.

"You know this has been happening for days, right?" he asked. "Magical art becoming mundane."

"Really?"

"You haven't listened to the other artists talk?"

"Why would I?"

He almost laughed. "Success has turned you into a diva, huh?"

"You want me to set him on you?" VX pointed at the dinosaur.

"You're welcome to try, but that monster will turn back into paint the moment you're thirty feet away. So will anything else you create. There's an enchantment over the whole city for this sort of work."

"What? That's crazy. That's stupid. That's censorship!"

"That's certainly one way to look at it."

"And the power involved is staggering. All that, just to mess with creativity?"

"Some people are always ruining others' fun. That's the way of the world."

"Who did this?"

"Who's always messing with your art, sucking the magic out of it?"

"The Silver Griffins?"

"Exactly." He took a long drag on his cigar, watching her with an evaluating gaze. "You should be proud of yourself. You pushed them to this. You created work so bold and powerful that they had to stamp down on every magical artist in the city to keep you from doing what you do."

"That's not fair. Not to me or the others. Art should be free!"

The dwarf shrugged. "What can you do? You're one artist, and they're the Silver Griffins."

"No. That's not how this works." The magic flowed through VX, carried by the rising tide of her anger. She lifted into the air, and a wind billowed around her. The cans rattled. "Art is power. Art is life. Art calls the mighty to account. Art can bring a government to its knees."

"Right now, art is in chains, so far as magic is concerned."

"Then I'm going to cast those chains off." VX's backpack burst open, and the paint cans shot out. They spun through the air around her, orbiting her body like planets around the bright heart of a sun. The ladder lay abandoned at her feet. "I'm going to bring down the Silver Griffins."

Her power, rage, and art lifted her above the street and through the sky above L.A. With her spray cans circling her, she hurtled toward the Griffith Observatory.

Back in the street, Gruffbar looked at the dinosaur.

"What do you reckon?" he asked. "Do you think she can win?" The dinosaur stood unmoving, nothing but mundane paint on inert concrete. "No, I don't know either, but any time the Griffins are busy, that's a win for the rest of my clients."

His cigar clamped between his lips, Gruffbar headed off into the dawn.

It was quiet outside the Griffith Observatory, too early in the morning for anyone to have arrived for work yet, and far too early for any visitors. VX landed in a swirl of spray cans in front of the main entrance. Her eyes glowed with magic, and her heart raced with anger.

She waved her hand. Red, orange, and yellow cans danced through the air in front of the door, painting a vision of fire. As VX's magic flowed through the paint, the flames became real, a searing inferno that buckled and melted the door. Glass and metal sagged, collapsed, and spattered hissing on the ground. VX floated above it through the open doorway, ash and smoke flowing around her.

A security guard ran across the hall, waving his arms in alarm.

"Hey, you can't be in here!" he shouted. "And what the hell did you do to the doors?"

The magical flames still warmed VX's back as she sent another can into action. Paintings of ropes turned to real ropes on the floor, then wrapped themselves around the guard, who cried out in alarm. He toppled while struggling, knocked his head on the tiles, and fell unconscious.

"I don't blame you," VX said. "You probably don't even know, do you? That's part of the tragedy, how much ordinary people miss out on. That's going to end. But how do I find them? They're not going to have signs up saying 'secret magical base this way.'"

She painted a compass, one that pointed toward magic instead of magnetic north, then plucked it off the wall. Its needle rotated, then led her down a gallery, past unlit exhibitions about space and the planets floating through it, to a blank stretch of wall. Behind her, the fire turned back to paint, but she didn't need it anymore.

"A magical door?" VX shrugged, running her hand over the featureless wall. "I can work with that."

A can of gray paint floated forward, sprayed a picture of a lock onto the door and a key next to it. VX picked up the key, stuck it into the lock, and turned it. The door swung open.

"Art unlocks the world for us," she said. "It frees the mind and the heart."

Through the door was a reception room, like this was an ordinary office, not the heart of an oppressive monster crushing the city's spirit. A receptionist looked up at her from the cheap paperback thriller he had been reading, then frowned.

"Are you here to meet someone?" he asked. "It's only the night shift on duty now, and most of them are out answering calls. Whatever it's about, you might have a long wait."

"Am I here to meet someone?" VX asked. "I suppose I am, in a way." Her cans spread out around the room and started painting on the walls. "But mostly I'm here to create something, to tear down the old and bring in the new."

"Hey, you can't do that!" The receptionist slammed his book down on the reception desk and pointed at the floating cans. "That's vandalism. Stop it at once."

"Stop?" A bird with fire for a beak and claws like razors flew off the wall and landed on VX's shoulder. She had barely known she had that image in her head, but here it was, ready to do her bidding. She was flowing over with the wonders of art. How much more she would create once she had shattered the works of the censors. "I've barely started."

Too late, she spotted the receptionist's hand sliding under the desk, reaching for a hidden button. A red light flashed, and an alarm wailed.

"Give up now," the receptionist said. "They'll all be coming now."

"Good." VX sent the bird flying at him claws-first. "I love an audience."

CHAPTER FORTY-THREE

Lucy bolted upright in bed. Her phone was blaring at her with a high-pitched wail that she'd only ever heard before in emergency drills. Next to it on the nightstand, her wand was flashing. She leapt out of bed and grabbed her pants.

"What's happening?" Charlie rolled over and looked around in bewilderment.

"Emergency at work," Lucy said. She tapped her phone screen, switching off the alarm, and carried on hurriedly getting dressed. "I've got to go."

"Right now?"

"They wouldn't have sent out the alert otherwise."

Charlie sat up and rubbed his eyes. "Can I help?"

"You stay here and deal with the kids when they wake up." A sound from the next room made her realize how redundant "when they wake up" had been. No one in the house could have slept through that alarm. Even Buddy was yapping away, wanting to know what the strange noise was.

She stuck her wand in her pocket and ran out of the

room. She was pulling on her sneakers when a portal appeared next to her in the hallway, and Jackie stepped out.

"Come on," Jackie said. "No time to drive."

"Did the transport team—"

"This one's my doing. Figured it was worth the risk to get there quick."

She waved her wand and the portal shifted, then they leapt through.

They arrived hanging in the air at their desks in the Silver Griffins' main office. Lucy fell a foot onto her keyboard, which made an ominous crunch, but better to break the technology than her bones. She and Jackie rolled down onto the floor, wands raised, looking around.

"That was almost spot on," Lucy said. "You're better at portals than me."

"Would have gotten messy if I'd gone too far down instead of up."

"Better practice before next time then."

"I'm hoping that alarm doesn't have a next time."

Chaos reigned in the Silver Griffins' L.A. headquarters. The intruder had flung desks and chairs everywhere, over-turned filing cabinets, and shattered glass walls. Torn papers and broken computers littered the floor. There were charred patches on the walls.

There were also pictures—images of fires, monsters, and angry-looking warriors holding swords and axes. All of them had been spray-painted in a style that Lucy recognized, blockish and cartoony but full of life.

"Looks like VX," she said.

"Great, now how do we stop them?"

"Follow that sound."

They ran out of the main office, along a corridor, and down a set of stairs, following the screeches of monsters and *thuds* of violence. They passed more scorch marks, injured Griffins lying slumped on the floor, and battered places in the walls, floor, and ceiling.

They also passed paintings on every available surface, images of plants and animals, storms and roaring seas, even people. The floor in front of the ocean was soaked, and the area in front of a wildfire was charred. The paintings themselves had reverted to simple pictures. In front of a pair of spray-paint ogres, everything was pounded and cracked.

"The thirty-foot bubble," Lucy said. "It means that only the paintings around VX come to life. She must be painting new picture spells everywhere she goes so there's always something working for her."

They dashed down another corridor to the entrance of the Special Equipment and Weapons lab. VX had painted a giant with a stone club on the wall, and the reinforced door was smashed open. From inside came screeches, flaps, and growls.

Lucy and Jackie dashed inside. Down the firing range, they finally saw VX. The gnome was floating in the air, paint cans spinning around her, constantly decorating the walls, floor, and ceiling. Those decorations came to life the moment she completed them, creating an army that filled the space for thirty feet around her. There were lions, tigers, a dinosaur, eagles crying as they swooped in tight circles through the air. Fire flickered near the edge of the circle, consuming some half-melted piece of experimental equipment.

Jenkins lay on the ground in front of VX, bound in chains. Their cartoonishness didn't make the chains any less solid, and though he wriggled and writhed, he couldn't break free from them. The dinosaur had placed a foot on his chest and slowly extended its claws while Jenkins cried out in pain.

"You killed the magic." VX's face twisted in rage. "I can smell it on you, smell it on this place. Undo what you did, now."

"I can't," Jenkins said. "It wasn't me, and even if it was, that ritual took the power of dozens of people. One of us can't undo it on our own."

"Excuses. You did this, you can undo it, and if you don't—"

"Stop!" Lucy strode down the room, wand raised. "Get off him."

VX looked around. "Or what? You've already taken my art from me. You think there's anything you can do that would be worse than that?" Tears of anger ran down her cheeks. "I was making things of beauty and you monsters destroyed them."

"They were giving away the magical world," Jackie said. "You know that's not allowed."

"The humans deserve to know. They deserve to see the things we have in all their glory and beauty. They deserve real art!"

"That's not your decision to make."

"And my art isn't yours to censor."

VX flung out an arm and a red spray can spun, painting flames on the air. The fire hurtled toward Jackie and Lucy, the air rippling from the blaze of its heat, then turned to paint and fell in a fine spray only feet from them.

"You're right," Lucy said. "You were making things of beauty. You still are. But there's a time and a place for magical art, and it's not out in the open."

"Art lives in the open. It dies when it's caged. Do you think it should all be locked away in galleries for those who can afford it, or who know the right people and passwords to reach the secret places? Should it only exist for those plugged into artistic circles?"

"What you're doing isn't only art. It's power. It's threatening people, putting lives in danger."

"Only the ones who deserved it."

"That's not your decision to make."

"They made the decision when they damaged my art."

"And the people here?"

"They all damaged my art when they cast that spell and sucked the magic away. They brought this on themselves, every charred and crushed and bloody moment of it."

"You can't value art over people's lives."

"Art is life. It's the thing that makes life worth living. People who drain the art from the world drain everything good out of it. I won't let them win."

"How are you going to stop us?" Jackie asked. "Your monsters will vanish the minute they move away from you."

"Then I'll move with them."

VX hurtled forward, and her painted creatures came with her. They leapt at Lucy and Jackie, fangs and claws flashing. A lion roared and bared its teeth. The dinosaur opened its jaws wide. The eagles flapped their wings as they dived in, talons extended.

"Refrigero," Lucy exclaimed, and a blast of icy magic leapt from her wand, freezing one of the lions.

"Stupefacio," Jackie shouted, and the dinosaur stumbled, shook its head. "Stupefacio, stupefacio, stupefacio!"

The dinosaur sank to its knees, then slumped to the ground, stunned into unconsciousness. There was an almighty *thud* as it hit the floor.

The paint cans were still flying around. They drew spiked vines on the ground, which writhed up to wrap themselves around the two witches. As Lucy and Jackie cut themselves free with magically summoned blades, chains descended around them, then cages. They were trapped, unable to back away as the creatures closed in, claws raised.

"Fine, you've got us trapped," Lucy said, "but your creatures can't finish us off either, not with these bars in the way. While we're here, others will be coming. They'll stop you. There's no winning here. Just give in."

As if to make her point, more wizards and witches appeared through the door of the testing range. Applegate was in the lead, wearing a dressing gown and fluffy slippers. Others followed, some half-dressed, some in their pajamas, all disheveled except for Kelly, whose makeup was somehow perfect even when rushed out of bed in the middle of the night.

"Step back from my agents," Applegate commanded, raising his wand.

"You step back," VX said, her voice rising with tension and uncertainty. "Step back, or I'll kill them."

Silver and gray spray cans darted through the air, painting a pair of knives that hovered between the cage bars, inches from Lucy's and Jackie's faces.

"You don't have to do this," Lucy said. "You could keep making art. Just give up the magical side of it."

"The magic is the art, art magic. You can't pull them apart. They're together." VX tapped her chest. "In here. I am the art. My magic is the art. Together, we're too strong for you to stop." A wild glee spread across her face. "Yes, that's it. I can become the art. Then you'll never stop me."

The spray cans pulled in to form a tighter ring around VX. They sprayed, and the paint hung in the air, magic suspending it in place. An image emerged, a picture of a gnome, but ten times larger than in reality. As the cans danced back and forth, the details appeared. The mask, the hood, the ladder. VX was painting herself.

With the artist distracted, Lucy dispelled a section of the cage around her and stepped out between the remaining bars. Cautiously, she crept toward the whirl of flying paint.

The original VX was disappearing, concealed within her portrait. The reality of flesh vanished behind the imaginary version. Where the diminutive figure of the gnome artist had been, there was instead the towering edifice of her art, a thing of bold strokes and blocky colors, of the sharp contrasts and the fuzzy edges that came with a line of spray paint. As the figure neared completion, the cans flew out, becoming larger, cartoon images of themselves, spraying themselves into a new sort of existence. The painting tipped its head back and laughed.

"See?" the giant VX said. "I am the art, and art always

wins. Censorship is futile. The world will see what I can make."

"Then the world won't see the real you," Lucy said.

"This is the real me."

"No, this is only a picture. The real you has vanished between the brush strokes. We're all so much more than the things we create, but you've reduced yourself to a single dimension. There's nothing left but the spell."

"You lie, or perhaps you lack vision. Art is eternal, life fleeting. In this form, I can live forever. In this shape, I can take my art wherever I want, and the whole world will want to know."

"We'll see." Lucy waved her wand and let all the power she had flow through her. "Renuo."

The magic rose like a tide, flooding every corner of Lucy's body, rushing up her legs, through her belly and her chest, out along her arms. It became a negation, a thing to cancel what VX had done, magic to wipe away the picture. It was the strongest counterspell she had ever cast, and it nearly wasn't enough.

For a long moment, the vast cartoon gnome stood strong, towering over her. It reached out with one hand and grabbed hold of Lucy, lifting her like it was King Kong and she was the innocent the ape had fallen for, squeezing the breath out of her so that she gasped and her arms trembled.

Then there was a shaking in the air, a gust like wind down the room, and the paint flew back onto the wall, spattering in great globs upon the concrete, returning to two dimensions. Lucy dropped unceremoniously onto the concrete floor of the testing range, one knee slamming painfully hard against the surface.

A thirty-foot mural of VX looked down upon the Special Equipment and Weapons firing range. She held a spray can in her hand, and there was a twinkle in her eye, a look of inspiration. It was a work that any artist would have been proud of, a self-portrait on an epic scale.

There was no sign of the real gnome.

"Sorry." Lucy limped forward to lay a hand on the painting. "It looks like you were right. You were the art. Long may you remain that way."

CHAPTER FORTY-FOUR

"Dinosaur!" Eddie exclaimed, his arms spread wide as he gazed up at the mural.

"That's right, sweetheart," Lucy said. "It is a dinosaur. Do you know what sort?"

Eddie studied the picture carefully. He had to tip his head back to take it in, this vast figure looming over them, bold and cartoonish yet somehow menacing, with one of its legs trapped in a pool of thick black oil.

He shook his head. "Just dinosaur."

Lucy laughed. "I guess the artist was more concerned with the big picture than with the details, huh?"

"Big picture." Eddie nodded.

He took off his backpack and started rummaging around inside, rustling a bundle of papers.

"What are you doing, sweetheart?" Lucy asked.

Eddie pulled out one of his pictures and showed it to her.

"Dinosaur," he said.

"You're right. It does look a lot like that dinosaur."

"For you." He held it up for the dinosaur to see, then laid it on the ground at its feet, a small tribute to a larger talent.

"You know that dinosaur isn't alive, right?" Lucy asked. "I mean, he can't see your picture."

Eddie looked at her like she had said something stupid, then shook his head. "Still a dinosaur."

He zipped up his backpack and wriggled it back onto his shoulders, then looked up at the dinosaur again. There was the beginning of a shimmer in the air.

"Eddie," Lucy said in a low, warning tone. "You know the rules. No transforming in public."

The shimmering stopped, and Eddie looked up at her with wide, innocent eyes.

"Wasn't gonna change," he said.

Lucy laughed. "Of course not."

The others appeared around the corner, carrying ice cream cones. Charlie handed one to Lucy, and Dylan gave one to Eddie. Ashley only carried one, her other hand full of robot strings.

Charlie looked up at the mural and raised his eyebrows.

"That's quite a sight," he said. "I'm amazed someone hasn't painted over it. Like maybe someone from an oil company."

"Technically, that would be vandalism, just like the original painting," Lucy said. "And big companies are far warier about that than street artists. Besides, it's proved pretty popular. A local group has set up to make plans to preserve it."

"Very cool. It's nice to see so much art appreciation going on."

"Well, they have had some encouragement."

Lucy waved the map that they'd bought from one of the tourist-oriented shops. It showed the locations of all the best paintings by VX around the city and gave a little background about the works and their appearance. It didn't say anything about magic, of course, though Lucy doubted that was a matter of ignorance. She had it on good authority that Penley was behind these maps and that they were helping to fund his gallery. It was one of the reasons she had been happy to buy it, even though she had seen, and even de-spelled, half of these paintings already.

"What about the magic?" Charlie asked. "Isn't there a risk that this thing will come alive again one day?"

"The Silver Griffins have removed all the magic," Lucy said. "We're pretty sure we got it from all the other paintings too. Now people can enjoy them in safety, without a tiger leaping out to tell them off for dropping litter."

"Seems kind of ironic."

"How's that?"

"Well, half the reason these things are so famous is the wild stories about them, the rumors that slipped out despite all your hard work. That's why people want to see them, but they can only see them because you folks undid the wild side. It's like going on safari, only to find that the animals are in cages."

"I prefer to think of it as a safari where the lion can't bite your head off."

"I'm a lion." Eddie held his hands up like claws. This time, he didn't start to change.

"My favorite lion," Lucy said.

She took Eddie's hand, and they walked on down the

street, following the map to the next location. Lucy noticed other pieces of graffiti art on their way past, some good, some bad, many indifferent. Hopefully one day the not-so-good artists would develop into great ones, and those great ones would refrain from summoning magical paint monsters. In the meantime, the whole city was her art gallery, and while she might not be blown away by every work that was on display, they were all a reminder of how wonderful and creative people could be.

"Mom, can we go draw in the park again this afternoon?" Dylan asked.

"Sure, sweetheart," Lucy said. "What's inspired this?"

"I've been working on my comic, the one I was doing at school."

"I thought you finished that homework."

"I did, but it was a lot of fun. I want to carry on."

"Your teachers will be pleased."

"Maybe. I might not show them. They're kind of busy helping Sofia with hers because it's really good."

"I'm sure yours is good too."

"I guess. The main thing is that I'm enjoying it."

"You know, sometimes you're more mature than half the adults I meet."

"Hm." Dylan considered that for a moment while he ate his ice cream. "I guess that's probably a good thing, depending on the adults."

They stopped for lunch at Vista Hermosa Natural Park, enjoying one of the areas of calming nature amid the bustle of the city. As had been happening so often lately, the sketch pads came out alongside the sandwiches. Even

Charlie had a pencil in hand, though he didn't seem to be drawing the scene around them.

"What is that?" Lucy asked, peering at his notes and runes. "Working on a new piece of magical software?"

"Considering the ingredients for our car paint. With the new system, we can make more cars greener more easily. We might even be able to do it to mundane people's cars, make them magically green without them knowing."

"Careful, this is starting to sound like rogue magic. I don't want to end up arresting my husband."

Charlie laughed. "It's all right. I'll hold back from the giant animated dinosaurs. What about you? After your triumph at the PTA, do you want to take your art to a wider audience?"

Lucy shook her head. "It's a hobby. I like that I can do it well, but I already have a job, one that makes a big difference."

"You don't want to be made immortal by your art, to leave a legacy like VX?"

"I already have a legacy." Lucy looked at her children as they sipped lemonade and made art in the sunshine. "It's the best legacy a mum could have."

Lucy, the Heron Family and the Silver Griffin's story doesn't end here. Follow their adventures in MOM'S GOT THIS!

Everyday Bread Recipe

Sure, quarantine is over, and life is slowly getting onto something new. I mean, maybe baking bread is so 2020, but sometimes getting your hands in a little dough and kneading it, tucking it someplace warm and waiting for it to rise – is just what the day called for.

Back in the day, we had a tricky oven that wasn't good for rising dough, so I found sunny spots by a window in the summer or over an air vent if it was winter. Somehow it always worked out and lent a bit of magic to the whole thing.

That's what we need right now. A sense of magic that good things are happening. Let's start with a basic bread recipe and see what happens from there.

Ingredients:

- 5 c. bread flour (bread flour has more protein

than all-purpose flour and will add strength and
help the bread to rise higher)
- 1 T sugar
- 2 ¼ t instant yeast
- 2 ½ t table salt or 3 ½ t kosher salt (bigger flakes)
- 1 2/3 cup warm water

Mix all the ingredients in a bowl starting with only 4 ½
cups of the bread flour. Mix with a sturdy spoon until it's
resembling a rough-looking ball of dough. Sprinkle of the
remaining flour onto a clean surface and roll the dough
ball out of the bowl and onto the surface. Knead with the
heel of your palm away from you, turning the dough in
small measures, rolling over a quarter to a third as you
turn for about five minutes.

Lightly oil the inside of the same bowl and put the
lovely looking dough ball back inside. Cover the bowl with
plastic wrap and find a warm spot for it to rise for 1 ½ to 2
hours.

Take the dough and place back on the floured surface
and gently flatten, cutting the ball in half. Shape each ball
into a flat, elongated oval. With the first oval, fold over in
thirds till it looks like a puffy brick. Do the same with the
second oval.

Place seam-side down on a baking sheet lined with
parchment paper and generously sprinkled with cornmeal
to prevent sticking. Cover again with plastic wrap and find
that warm place again so the bread can rise for another 45
minutes. Once it's risen again and you can easily leave a
fingerprint, it's ready to bake. Cut three shallow lines

across the top of each loaf to help them rise evenly while they bake.

Preheat the oven to 450 degrees Fahrenheit. Place a pan of boiling water on the bottom rack (for steam to get a crunchy crust). Bake for 20 to 25 minutes until golden brown and tapping on the top sounds kind of hollow. Let cool on a rack before cutting and enjoy!

Get sneak peeks, exclusive giveaways, behind the scenes content, and more. PLUS you'll be notified of special **one day only fan pricing** on new releases.

Sign up today to get free stories.

Visit: https://marthacarr.com/read-free-stories/

AUTHOR NOTES - MARTHA CARR
JULY 6, 2021

I used to think that being able to do everything myself was a positive attribute. Simpler, faster and I got exactly what I wanted in the first place. Well... sorta.

I grew up in a quiet, yet chaotic household where it was definitely better to figure things out for myself and just move along. It mistakenly taught me that we learn best through observation. It was at least safer.

What I wasn't getting was that observation is a limited view of things. Kind of like looking at someone's Instagram pics and assuming their life is one big glamorous, expensive fantasy. Normally that picture was the best part of their day and the rest looked pretty much like yours and mine.

It's a tiny peek of a very large, multi-colored, fascinating universe with a million moving parts. To truly get the best out of what the world has to offer takes connections to others and lots of questions and even more listening. But... if you're like me and you've been relying on just yourself for so long you don't even notice, you may not know what you're missing.

It's hard to imagine what you don't know about. Instead, what I've learned to do is accept that there's cool stuff out there to explore – much like a ten year old on a Saturday morning might approach the new day – and head out with the idea that this would be more fun with others.

By the way, complete transparency – this took a lot of therapy to get me there and I can still sometimes catch myself trying to do more than I need to, all by myself.

However, I'm a lot better at asking for help *just because* and listening to the creative answers.

What I've learned is that I don't know what people are thinking. Most people are happy to help. If the first few people can't add anything useful, someone will be able to – keep going. (In other words, I don't give up just because gather info isn't easy. That's called contempt ahead of information. Always knowing why something won't work even though not a single step has been taken and no info has been gathered. Think about that one the next time you're about to utter the words, "The reason why that won't work..." and maybe not say them. It's actually not helpful and there's a good chance, not true. Another thing I learned.)

Here's the other big thing I got from it. When I can be vulnerable and ask for help, and then even accept it, I create community for myself. There's less wear and tear on me and my world grows in wonderous ways that I can't describe till they're happening and would have missed out on if I had just done it myself. It turns out, just me is not more efficient and not better. And they won't put on my tombstone, "She did it all, she had no help." More adventures to follow.

Thank you for both reading this book and these author notes in the back.

I'm totally riffing off Martha's author notes.

There is no way I could have grown LMBPN without support from others.

In the beginning it was me, and then it was not.

There is a gentleman who was in the Australian Navy on a submarine (I'm not sure if I can share his name) and then Stephen Russell (author S. R. Russell) who both helped edit one book and then managed the growing horde of readers who wanted to help as I put fingers to keyboard for the next book.

Come to think of it, we don't even consider the many people who built the tools we use in the process of writing solo.

Regardless, I am saying all that to explain that I had a fair amount of "I did it" need earlier in my life and career. Most of this desire (I suspect—no therapy) from a need to figure out a way to prove I am special.

Instead of just allowing myself to believe it to be true.

I am not built for stardom.

Since writing *The Kurtherian Gambit* and starting the group 20Booksto50k®, I have encountered moments where I am treated to a small taste of stardom.

It didn't take very long for me to realize I don't like it. I'm not saying the first few times weren't a high (they were) but I would immediately seek to engage the person and prove I'm not special.

Which is ironic, since that was what I thought I wanted my whole life: to have others show me by their actions that I was special. When it happened, I didn't enjoy it at all.

In a week, I will be traveling to speak at my first convention in a year and a half. At this event (Realm Makers) I hope to share that becoming Indie as a distribution option allows authors the choice when releasing their stories.

I have low-level anxiety about going.

Why? Well, I know that I am not known very well outside of 20BooksTo50k® and I feel like I will have to give a bit of my background. Basically, I will have to prove myself.

I guess that is part of the friction. I am there to help, and the best I can do is give my story of success, share the information, and accept that some will benefit and many will not.

It's not up to me what others decide to do with the information I share. I can force no one to accept that what worked for me might work for them. My excitement about being an indie publisher is NOT the path everyone would enjoy, and therefore I am sharing information to help them choose not to become an indie as much as helping others choose to publish themselves.

Whichever decision is right for them is the right decision.

I just need to accept that truth and walk into the future.

Ad Aeternitatem,

Michael Anderle

Solve a murder, save her mother, and stop the apocalypse?

What would you do when elves ask you to investigate a prince's murder and you didn't even know elves, or magic, was real?

Meet Leira Berens, Austin homicide detective who's good at what she does – track down the bad guys and lock them away.

Which is why the elves want her to solve this murder – fast. It's not just about tracking down the killer and bringing them to justice. It's about saving the world!

If you're looking for a heroine who prefers fighting to flirting, check out The Leira Chronicles today!

AVAILABLE ON AMAZON AND IN KINDLE UNLIMITED!

BOOKS BY MICHAEL ANDERLE

Sign up for the **LMBPN** email list to be notified of new releases and special deals!

https://lmbpn.com/email/

For a complete list of books by Michael Anderle, please visit:

www.lmbpn.com/ma-books/

CONNECT WITH THE AUTHORS

Martha Carr Social

Website: http://www.marthacarr.com

Facebook: https://www.facebook.com/
groups/MarthaCarrFans/

Michael Anderle Social

Website: http://lmbpn.com

Email List: http://lmbpn.com/email/

Social Media:

https://www.facebook.com/LMBPNPublishing

https://twitter.com/MichaelAnderle

https://www.instagram.com/lmbpn_publishing/

https://www.bookbub.com/authors/michael-anderle